REWIRE

Also by Marc Pye

Lollipop

REWIRE

Marc Pye

SCEPTRE

Grateful acknowledgement is made for permission to reprint
excerpts from the following copyrighted material:

Grateful acknowledgement is made to the Provost and Scholars of
King's College, Cambridge and the Society of Authors as the Literary
Representatives of the E.M. Forster Estate to reprint an excerpt from
Two Cheers For Democracy by E.M. Forster.

'A Crabbit Old Woman' from *An Ageing Population*. Anon.
Copyright © 1978 by Hodder and Stoughton in association
with Open University Press. Reprinted by permission.

First published in Great Britain in 2001 by Hodder and Stoughton
A division of Hodder Headline
A Sceptre Book

A CIP catalogue record for this title
is available from the British Library

ISBN 0 340 76610 7

Typeset by Hewer Text Ltd, Edinburgh
Printed and bound in Great Britain by
Clays Ltd, St Ives plc

Hodder and Stoughton
A division of Hodder Headline
338 Euston Road
London NW1 3BH

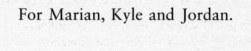

For Marian, Kyle and Jordan.

'I hate the idea of causes, and if I had to choose between betraying my country and betraying my friend, I hope I should have the guts to betray my country.'

E. M. Forster

REWIRE

Nathan woke up with the noise coming from the hall. He knew it was Angie bouncing off the walls as she came up the stairs. He looked at the alarm clock: 6.13 a.m. He'd set it for six thirty and she was only just home from work. Her shift finished at two.

He heard the key scraping on the outside of the door as she tried to get it in the lock. '*Fuck it*.' She banged on the door.

Nathan pulled the covers over his head, hoping she'd go away: he didn't want to look at her stupid, drunken, haggard face ever again.

'*Naaaaathaaaaan! Open up!*' He swung his legs out of bed, grabbed the bedclothes in anger and tried to calm down. It wasn't easy – he'd had enough of this: it was time to make a stand.

His friends, and especially his parents, had all warned him not to marry her. He thought it was because of the race thing – him having a white mum and a black dad and them not wanting him to have to face the same prejudice that they had. It was nothing to do with prejudice, more like gut feeling. Angie was a barmaid at the South London club, Juice, where Nathan and his mates went. A smile led to a chat, a chat led to some flirting, the flirting led to a night out, and the night out ended with him back at her place for the best sex he'd ever had. She was awesome. She reminded him of that model in her forties, Jilly Johnstone – gorgeous. Long blonde hair and an all-over tan.

She wasn't the least bit inhibited and was willing to try anything. She badgered him to tell her what his fantasies were, and had no qualms about acting them out for him. She'd tie him to the bed and have him begging. She'd put music on and dance about in front of him, massaging herself with baby oil till she glistened all over. She'd tell him what she was going to do to him. How she was in control. She'd kneel over him and lick him from his head to his toes. She'd stand over him, caressing herself. He'd struggle against the ties, belts or whatever else she'd found to tie him up with. Finally she'd lower herself slowly on to him, putting him out of his misery. He'd be lucky if he could last a minute.

Nathan looked down at his boxers. He still got a semi thinking about shagging her, then quickly realised he probably wasn't the only one around here.

'*Nayyyythaaaaannnn!!*'

'Fuck.' He got up, pulled on his tracksuit bottoms and opened the front door. She stood leaning against the doorframe. What a fucking mess. Jilly Johnstone? More like Lily Savage after a fight. She turned and tried to focus on him. He stepped back, allowing her to walk into the room unaided.

'Hiya, daaaarrlin.' She stumbled in, rebounding off the couch as she headed for the bedroom. He could smell the reek of stale drink and the unmistakable hint of Paco Rabanne on her. He considered asking her when she'd started wearing aftershave but decided against it. He closed the door and followed her into the bedroom, looking down at her sitting on the edge of the bed, taking off her jacket.

'Before ya ask I've been to Tina's. I had half a bottle of Scotch an fell asleep on her couch.'

'Leave your tights there, did you?' he asked, staring at her bare legs, then at the tights sticking out of her bag.

She looked at her legs and hid a wry smile. 'Yeah, must ave done.'

He took a deep breath, trying to compose himself. 'Do you think I'm fucking stupid, Ange?'

'I don't remember saying that, darlin. Did I say you were stupid?' she retorted, patronisingly.

'You don't have to – you treat me like a cunt.' He walked over, pulled the tights from her bag and tossed them in her face.

She turned her head away. 'What?' she asked, as innocently as she could. 'I took them off when I went to her bog – couldn't be bothered putting them back on again.'

'Yeah, right,' said Nathan, pulling the collar of her

blouse away from her neck and confirming his suspicions. Two lovebites. 'Are you gonna tell me Tina's got a dog as well? If she has it's got a fucking great taste in aftershave! Must have been all over you!'

She looked up at him, knowing she'd been well and truly caught. She was too confused to think her way out of this one now. It wasn't her fault men found her attractive. She could feel them staring at her arse as she walked about behind the bar. They'd look down her blouse as she stood pouring a pint. She liked the attention – the compliments. It was worth spending an hour getting ready for work if it meant you felt good about yourself when you got there. Fuck knows the last time Nathan paid her a compliment. He was becoming a boring bastard – didn't want to go out, always complained about money, didn't want to take Ecstasy, said it *shaved your brain*. Silly bastard. He'd even stopped smoking dope, saying it was costing too much. He was a fucking miser, only interested in his work.

Well, it didn't stop her taking the occasional E. She'd had two tonight and felt fucking wonderful. Big Stevie, the bouncer, had called her into the cloakroom at the beginning of the night and handed her one – said he'd taken them off a bloke at the door. She'd smiled mischievously at him. She liked Stevie – said if he grew a beard he'd look just like Wesley Snipes, but a lot handsomer.

Stevie'd held out his palm with the E on it. She tried to

take it, but he closed his hand and slowly reached the other inside her bra, looking her in the eye as he stroked his forefinger across her nipple. He stepped back and looked her up and down. 'There's plenty more where this came from,' he said, and handed over the E.

Angie took it off him, put her hand between his legs and squeezed his balls. 'And there's plenty more of *this*, darlin,' she said, thrusting her cleavage up towards his face and laughing at him.

'*Faaakkkin hell!*' He laughed, looking about to see if anyone was watching, pretending to be shocked.

At the end of the night the staff all stayed behind for a drink as usual. She'd caught his eye as she got up to go to the ladies'. Stevie followed her in and closed the cubicle door behind them. 'I think we've got some unfinished business,' he said, grabbing her waist, spinning her round and kissing her. She kissed him back, then tilted her head away from him and looked at his face. He meant business. She wasn't going to argue. 'What's that then?' She smiled, knowing full well.

'This.' He spun her round and bent her over the cistern. She didn't protest as he tugged her tights and knickers down to her knees and put a hand between the cheeks of her arse. She felt his palm move down to cup her pussy. He moved his index finger round in a slow, deliberate circle. She arched her back. Here was a guy who didn't need a map.

'You're a peach – do you know that?' he said, moving

two fingers slowly up and down, getting her wetter and wetter. She exhaled deeply as he slipped his index finger deep into her pussy and moved it around. She took a deep breath and pushed herself away from the cistern back on to his long, probing finger. If this was his finger-fuck who knows what his cock was like? She reached behind her for her skirt and hoisted it over her hips, looking back at him with a come-on smile and wiggling her arse at him. She felt his finger pull out and heard him undoing his belt, unzipping his trousers . . .

'Are you fucking listening to me or what?'

Nathan was standing over her, expecting an answer. She didn't have one. What was the question again?

'Oh, I fucking give up.' He walked round the bed and sat on the other side with his back to her, his head in his hands. She got up and followed him to stand in front of him. He glanced up at her dishevelled frame, standing there, trying to focus on him. In two years she'd be forty. She looked fifty. He was only twenty-five. How the fuck had he ever managed to tie himself to such a horrible bitch? If only he'd known how things were going to turn out he'd never have suggested they get married. He thought back to the day he'd asked her. They'd spent the day lying in bed with a bottle of red wine, rolling spliffs. It was his day off. The whole day they'd shagged, got stoned, drunk wine and shagged even more. He'd thought he was in love. He was stoned out of his mind. He mentioned marriage. Why not? – they were good together. Angie didn't have to be asked twice. She hugged and kissed him with tears in her eyes and said he was the best thing that had ever happened to her. After all the bastards she'd been out with, how did she ever get so lucky? She'd spent the next hour on the phone to her old mum, crying and laughing and talking about bridesmaids, wedding-cakes and honeymoons. Nathan had sat up in bed, skinning himself another joint, wondering what the fuck he'd done. It was too late to go back now.

From that moment on it was like a rollercoaster ride, straight to the church. Do not pass Go. Do not collect £200. You may kiss the bride.

Angie sat on the bed next to him, trying to look him in the eyes. She put her arm round him and rubbed his back. 'I didn't shag him, Nathan . . . honest. It was just a kiss, that's all.'

'Oh, fuck off, will you?' he said, standing up. 'I can't do this any more, Ange, I've had it.'

'What do you mean, you've *had it*?'

'I'm leaving. I'm off. I'm not putting up with it any more.'

'*You*'re not putting up wiv it?' she said, standing up to face him. 'What do you fink I have to put up wiv? You're at work all day, and when you get in you don't even look at me. We have our dinner in front of the telly, then I have to get ready for work and I'm out all night.'

'Well, it's obviously not working out, then, is it?' He

walked over to the window and looked out into the
street at the milkman doing his rounds. He glanced
across the horizon to the South Bank. The four mena-
cing chimneys of Battersea power station cut through
the morning mist like an upside-down oil rig. There was
talk of turning it into a circus. That was all he needed, a
fucking circus on his doorstep. There was enough
madness in his life.

'You're a bastard, Nathan – a *bastard*!' She pushed
him in the back and sat down on the bed, turning on the
waterworks. 'I got married to you because I loved you,
and you want to run away and leave me the minute
things start going wrong.' She sobbed. 'Well, fuck off,
then! Go on – fuck off! You'll be sorry.'

He stared out of the window. 'Oh, I will, will I? And
how do you work that one out?' he said, coldly.

'Don't concern yourself wiv it, darlin – you just take
care of number one. That's what you're good at!' She
wiped her eyes on her sleeve and looked at the black
mascara on her white blouse, wondering if it would
come out in the wash.

'You're talking bollocks.' He continued to stare outside, watching a milk boy jump on the back of the float.

'Yeah? Well, my *life*'s bollocks, Nathan, a big pile of
bollocks.' She kicked off her shoes. 'I'll be thirty-nine
next month and I'm still working behind the bar in a
fucking disco! I knew you'd do this to me.'

'What the fuck are you talking about?' He turned

away from the window to see her lolling about on the bed, trying to sit up straight. He diverted his gaze, casting his eyes instead over her perfume collection on the dressing-table. He mentally totted up the cost: over three hundred quid. It still wasn't enough to cover up the smell of bullshit.

She looked up at him, menacingly. Her eyes were black from the running mascara. She looked like Alice Cooper in a blonde wig. 'I made you promise me before we got married that you wouldn't leave me.'

'So?' he said.

'And I told you that if I thought for *one minute* you were going to leave me because I was too old I'd kill myself. I don't want people pitying me.'

He smiled sarcastically and pointed a finger at her. 'Save your fucking threats, Ange, because this isn't about you being over the hill. This is about you slagging around – again. I've played this fucking game for far too long. I'm out of here!' He stormed off to the bathroom and slammed the door. The draught caught the dreamcatcher above the bed, making the chimes tinkle. *Dreamcatcher*. He snorted at the irony: his life was a nightmare.

What a fucking way to start the day. He looked at his reflection in the mirror as he took a piss – his dick had shrunk in anger. He looked almost white – the colour had completely drained out of him. He could hear her sobbing in the bedroom. Breaking her heart. Fuck her, he thought. If he was going to have any quality of life he'd have to leave her. She was as mad as a hatter. Manic, unstable. He was sick of treading on eggshells around her, wondering what kind of mood she was going to be in today. If Angie's happy then *Nathan*'s happy, if Angie's sad then *Nathan*'s sad. Well, he wasn't going to depend on her for his happiness any more. This was it – goodnight, Vienna. He'd move in with his mum till he could find a flat. She wouldn't mind. His mate Karl could help him decorate it. He'd be able to come and go as he pleased. Get a good night's kip without waking up every hour wondering where that stupid wife of his was – if she was all right or if some cunt had grabbed her on the way home and raped her because she was either too pissed or too lazy to get a taxi home. Well, fuck her; she could be someone else's responsibility from now on. Let some other poor bastard take care of her, because it sure as fuck wasn't going to be him.

He listened as the sobbing died down in the bedroom. Good, she was probably in bed. Just as long as she wasn't still there when he got back from work. He turned on the shower and stepped out of his tracksuit bottoms, thinking it might be an idea to go to the chippy tonight for his tea, then head off to the pub for a couple of hours. That way he could avoid her. She'd have to leave for work by nine. He could pack his stuff and be out of the door in an hour.

He stepped into the shower and sighed deeply as the

water ran down his face and body. He thought he heard a bang come from the bedroom so he turned off the water and listened intently. Nothing. The silly cow was probably stomping about in a mood. He turned the water back on again and squirted a big glob of blue shower gel on to his palm. Serves her right, the dirty bitch. Now he knew where he'd got that thrush from, last month. You don't just get thrush off your missus. Angie had told him that women get it all the time. Fuck knows what he'd catch if he stayed around here much longer. And she wondered why he didn't want to shag her any more! 'As ye sow so ye shall reap,' his dad always said.

Keighley walked through the Leven woods on her way to work. She loved taking this short cut to and from work, especially at this time in the morning. It was quiet, peaceful. A twig snapped under her foot and she watched a rabbit freeze in its tracks, then look back at her before scurrying off through the trees. She ruffled the fringe of her Peter Pan-styled short blonde hair, pulled the strap of her black leather bag over her shoulder and put her hands into the pockets of her denim jacket. She glanced up at a flapping sound above her and saw a magpie flying from a tree. She smiled to herself – Lianne would have crossed herself or walked round in a circle three times or something. Very super-stitious that girl. A single magpie was supposed to be bad luck. It was okay if there were two of them, cancelled each other out, she supposed. *Three* was worse than having *one*. She couldn't remember what it was supposed to mean, but knew that three unnerved Lianne. She was into omens, signs, all that stuff. If something bad ever happened at work Lianne always said it was **A SIGN**. Just bad luck, thought Keighley, nothing you can do about it. Lianne said there were ways you could protect yourself. She had a book on spells that she'd picked up in a bookshop somewhere. She really believed in all that rubbish.

The poor girl was confused. Her head was in the clouds all the time. Keighley knew what Lianne really wanted out of life: a career in the public eye, show-business, modelling, a singer, something like that. Just some attention, really, someone to love her. She knew Lianne secretly resented being a nurse and if someone came along tomorrow and offered her a job presenting a TV show or singing in a girl band she'd drop nursing like a hot potato and be off without a backward glance.

Lianne was right about one thing, though: Josh wasn't the man for Keighley. She knew it, too, deep down but thought, Better the devil you know. She couldn't just break it off: he'd talk her back into it. She knew she wasn't as happy as she could be. It was as though they'd been going through the motions for so long it had become second nature and they'd be together for eternity. She wondered if she was just going along with his plans, allowing him to make all the decisions for them. Surely she wasn't letting someone else take charge of her life for her? Not again? She thought about the way he had changed lately, becoming increasingly unapproachable, flying off the handle for the slightest thing. She knew he was worried about work, but that wasn't an excuse. She was always making excuses for him. Sometimes she couldn't help feeling sorry for him – the jobs weren't coming in as fast as they used to. It showed on his face. When he first arrived in Glen Leven he couldn't keep up with the demand and spoke about having his own electrical firm if it continued, hiring people to do the work while he sat back and reaped the rewards. It didn't take people long to catch on to the fact that he was overcharging them and using bullying tactics to get work. One young bloke had decided to try to fix his fuse box himself to save money and gave himself a shock. When Josh got wind of this he laughed at the bloke in the pub and told him to let the professionals deal with it in future.

Keighley grasped hold of a large tree root and hauled herself up the small incline. She stood on a patch of grass, dusting the dry earth off her hands. She hitched her bag over her shoulder again and continued across the grass, along a small log bridge that spanned a trickling stream. The sunlight shone through gaps between the dense trees, glinting off a couple of wet rocks to dance inches above the river. She breathed deeply in the clear morning air and trudged along the dry muddy path on the other side of the bridge. Then she saw it. A young deer, grazing up ahead in the glen. You hardly ever saw them at this time of year: they were always too quick for you. They only came down into the glen in the winter for food.

She stopped in her tracks and watched as it sniffed at the buttercups, then turned and looked across at her. She expected it to run off now that it had seen her but it stood its ground and seemed to be weighing her up, deciding if she was a danger or not. She moved forward slowly and sat down gingerly on a tree stump.

The deer spotted a clump of grass a few yards away from her, trotted over to it and began to munch, turning its back to her. She listened to it chewing, glad that it could trust her. She glanced at her watch – she'd better get a move on if she was to be in work on time. She changed her mind: she'd wait until the deer moved on. She didn't want to scare it, not now that she'd gained its confidence. A couple more minutes' relaxing wouldn't hurt. Besides, once she got in to work she'd be lucky if she had a minute to herself all day.

She thought about the day she'd started at Craigellachie House, how glad she was to be doing something worthwhile. She knew her dad must have heard about her job by now, but he hadn't been in touch since he left the village. Couldn't be bothered to congratulate her. She knew why: he would have thought a job in nursing was beneath her.

Her, a surgeon? Imagine it. She laughed at the thought of herself in an operating theatre in a life-or-death situation, people wiping her brow, passing her scalpels and hanging on her every command. When the patient was out of danger she'd swan off, leaving a minion to sew them back up.

No chance.

She'd heard her dad talking about operations to her mum over the breakfast table. He'd describe the mechanics of a heart transplant he'd recently performed as though he'd just done an oil change on an Escort.

She could understand her parents having such high hopes for their kids, but he was over the top. He had it all worked out: she'd succeed at school, go on to college, then uni, get a degree in medicine then go on to be a surgeon. It would take a few years but it'd be worth it in the long run. It all seemed *so straightforward, so pre-planned*. He had her whole life mapped out for her and she couldn't argue with him. Wouldn't dare, more like. It was *her* life yet she never had a say in it. Maybe it had been a blessing in disguise that her mum had been diagnosed with Alzheimer's.

He hadn't planned that, had he? Couldn't fix it – sort it out like it was a dodgy ticker. Keighley had never seen him so helpless before. The man who played God was reduced to a mere mortal. What a comedown that must have been. He'd sit there night after night in his study, drinking brandy and poring over medical books. Keighley would put her mum to bed, then come downstairs to see if he was all right. He'd be flaked out over his desk, snoring. She'd take the glass out of his hand and wake him up gently, glancing at the papers and books he'd been reading. The subject was always the same: Alzheimer's. He'd have notes written on a pad, cross-referencing different papers with numerous case histories and treatments. She knew what he was planning: he was going to use a cocktail of drugs on her poor old mum that had never been tried before. Or a radical new treatment he'd dreamed up – electrotherapy with a difference, designed to stimulate the part of her brain that was withering and dying. She'd never fully understood what he was reading – how could she? She was only fifteen and still at school. But she knew he was the kind of man to try a dozen or more treatments before he'd concede defeat. She'd wait till he was asleep, rip the notes out of the pad and bin them. It was bad enough having to watch her mum changing before her eyes without him using her as a guinea pig.

She knew it must have been difficult for him, seeing the woman he loved recoil from him in fear and call him an impostor. She said he *looked* like her husband but she knew, sure as hell, that he wasn't.

It wasn't long before he started staying later and later at work, hardly coming home at all, leaving Keighley to look after her mum. Once he went a full week without seeing either of them. Keighley could remember it as though it were yesterday. Her mum kept asking where he was. Keighley could only reply, 'At work Mum,' knowing full well that he was out with that bitch from Oncology. She'd seen them together a couple of times, laughing and joking, not a care in the world, as though he was *quite right* to see someone else – his wife was almost a vegetable, after all. Live and let live. Some days Keighley would sit across from the hospital, watching them return from lunch, holding hands like a couple of teenagers. She would stare right at him, willing him to turn round and see her so that he'd have to offer her an explanation . . . That was a joke – he'd explain *nothing*. He was God, after all. God in his job, God in his house. You don't ask God what the hell he thinks he's playing at. He'd say, 'I'm God, I can do what I like, now piss off and leave me alone, I'm far too busy to be explaining myself to the likes of you!'

She did get one explanation – the day he moved in with Janice. That was her name. Now she wasn't an oncologist with tied-back blonde hair . . . she was a *person* and he loved her. They were going to live together. *Janice* – who was only twenty-three, just eight years older than Keighley – was stealing Keighley's dad away from her.

Keighley had stood in his study, staring at her shoes, the tears streaming down her face and dripping on to them. She looked up at him but he avoided her eyes. She asked what she and her mum were going to do without him. They needed him here. He said it was a shame, but that's the way things go sometimes . . . She stared at the back of his head, wishing a tumour on him. He was a bastard – she hated him. She'd been robbed of her mother by a disease that was slowly replacing her adult brain with that of a child, and now *this*, her own father, the man who should be taking care of them both, was leaving to live the good life with another woman whom, he said, *he loved*. If he loved anyone it should have been them, especially at a time like this, not some woman from work. Before he left he said he hoped Keighley would keep up her studies and make him proud. That was a good one. The family he was once so proud of had become an embarrassment to him. She'd smiled sadly to herself and shaken her head, but he never even noticed. If only he knew that she'd had to forget uni. She'd been offered a place and had tried to talk to him about what she should do – stay at home and nurse her mum or get a carer to look after her? But he was always too busy. In the end she'd had to let the uni know she wouldn't be going. She'd decided to stay at home and nurse her mum. That's what family was for. *Real* family.

And that was the last she had seen of him. Five years and one Christmas card with an Edinburgh postmark and no return address. He hadn't even come to the funeral – left Keighley to deal with it herself. She knew it was a bad thing she was feeling but she didn't care if he was alive or dead any more. He deserved it.

After her mum died she decided to get her life back on

track and continue her studies. She was all set to reapply to uni and start where she'd left off before reality set in: all this time he'd been brainwashing her into thinking that this was what she really wanted to do with her life. She sat and thought about it. It wasn't what she wanted at all. She didn't have a clue what she wanted. Her relatives had often remarked about the patience she had had with her mum when she was ill, how she was a natural and should follow a career in 'a caring profession'. She considered training for the Macmillan nurses but realised that nursing people in their homes till they died would just bring back all she had gone through with her mum, so she decided against it. She wondered what kind of saint could do a job like that. Those people must have hearts bigger than Scotland.

She decided to enrol as a nurse, and slowly drifted into geriatrics. She sat her exams, and before she knew it she was an RMN, a registered mental nurse. Taking the plunge and applying for a position in a private hospital had been worth it. Craigellachie House was on her doorstep and she liked it here in Glen Leven. The people were friendly and she had no desire to move away.

Things had turned out well, considering all the heart-ache she'd had with her family. She had her health, her job, and her boyfriend . . . She got up off the log and brushed a couple of leaves off the back of her clean blue uniform trousers. She sighed to herself. The less she thought about him the better.

*　　*　　*

Josh drove the van along the loch-side. He reached into the glove compartment, took out a Clannad tape and put it in the player. Looking across at the calm loch, he remembered why he stayed here. It was beautiful, tranquil – a million miles away from Glasgow. Well, forty-two miles to be precise, but there wasn't a *Big Issue* seller in sight. You could leave your car unlocked all night, and he couldn't even remember when he'd last seen a smack-head.

Glen Leven had its downside, though. Boring as fuck in the winter. The place took on a bleak, grey look. It was a hell of a place to live if you suffered from depression.

He took a deep breath as the haunting music came from the speakers. What was that track called again? It was his favourite. He knew it was the one the Scottish Tourist Board used to try to get the English to come and spend their money here. He could do without that lot coming up with their Beefeater restaurants and craft shops, turning the place into some shortbread-tin tourist attraction. Josh was doing all right for himself and that was the way he wanted to keep it. The only electrician in a ten-mile radius. Nice one.

Old Donnie McBain had been the local spark before him. A good old bloke but completely away with the budgies. Used to do jobs for a half and a beer. Mad. Dead now but. Half and a beer? thought Josh. Fuck that – the going rate *plus* half for these fuckers round here.

They were good for it. Crofters were like that – pleading poverty for years, then dying and leaving fifty grand to their fucking sheepdog. Silly old bastards. He'd caught on to them a long time ago.

Josh had arrived at just the right time. He'd been made redundant by the firm he worked for in Glasgow and had just signed on with an electrical agency. He'd managed to get a month's work out of them before things went quiet again. When he'd asked his gaffer what was going on, he'd told Josh he'd have to wait a couple of weeks before they could use him again, there were boys in line for the jobs before him, so he'd decided to use some of his redundancy money and go on a wee camping break. He packed his tent and a crate of Miller into the van, and decided to follow the west coast to see where it took him. Glen Leven appeared out of the mist so he stopped and put up his tent for the night. He stuck around long enough to meet Donnie and a few of the old boys in the local pub, and ended up comparing notes with Donnie over a few drams.

The more Grouse Donnie swallowed the more Josh realised that the old boy was like a monkey in charge of a Ferrari. This place could be a gold mine. None of the crofts had been rewired since the seventies. There were barns needing power, and some required three-phase supplies to enable them to use automatic milking machinery.

Josh was just about to ask him if he fancied going into

partnership when it dawned on him that, apart from his contacts, the guy would be useless – a liability. He bit his tongue and continued to listen. Donnie couldn't be arsed with work any more – he was past retirement age and could barely remember how to put a plug on a Hoover. The odd job here and there kept him in beer but he no longer had the drive to chase the money.

The following morning Josh got up early, left his tent and took a hike up to the village to get some bacon, eggs, tattie scones and a pint of milk. He breezed into the local shop and delved into the fridge. A couple of old women were sniffling to the shopkeeper about old Donnie dying during the night. Josh heard them and turned round with surprise. 'The auld electrician boay? Ah wis only talkin tae hum laist night,' he said.

One of the women nodded. 'He was telt tae stay aff the whisky. Bit a typical man – wouldnae listen . . . heart-attack.'

Poor old basta, thought Josh, then remembered that he'd poured the best part of a bottle of Grouse down the old cunt's scrawny neck to get the low-down on the business around here.

So now Glen Leven needed a spark – there was a gap in the market. Old Donnie was barely cold before Josh had jumped into his van, driven to Glasgow, arrived back with his tools and put an ad in the paper.

Callous, some of them called it. *Fucking genius*, more like. You don't get a business opportunity like that every day, he thought. Big Alan and some of the other boys at the Glasgow agency wanted to know where Josh was going, what he was going to do, but he told them he needed some time out – he was fed up working for a pish wage. He said he was going to give London a try. Big Alan said he'd come with him. He was like that, the dozy cunt. You couldn't even go for a shite without him wanting to tag along. Fucking stalker. 'Gies a ring, eh?' said Alan, when Josh was leaving.

'Aye, right,' said Josh. 'So ah fuckin will,' he muttered to himself, as he went out of the door. He didn't want Alan or any of the others up here shooting his golden goose.

Occasionally Josh needed a hand, though, when things started getting on top of him, but there were enough numpties in this place who were short of a few bob and only too willing to get electrocuted for twenty quid for a day's labour. Moose and Gavin Ritchie were two such local yokels. They were in their mid-thirties and had only been as far as Blackpool in their quest for experiences of life outside the glen. After a wee bit of persuasion, though, they worked like a pair of bastards. Josh always got his money's worth out of them by gentle intimidation – making them feel inadequate whenever they asked if they could stop for a break. He'd go on about how he had had to work like a dog for these Glasgow firms and anyone who didn't come up to scratch was out on their arse. They soon got the message that working for Josh wasn't easy, but the patter was good. They were like sponges, soaking up his vast wealth of experience from *the big city*. Most of it he made up – like the time he was involved in a 'hit' on a guy who'd beaten up his pal's wife. 'Basta deserved tae be shot,' mused Josh. They'd nodded in agreement as they drank their tea.

Moose was like a whippet, buck teeth and no arse in his jeans. He'd always have the shakes from the night before and be puking out of the back of the van on the way to the job. Poor bastard had ulcers with the drink and could only eat at night after a couple of pints of Guinness had anaesthetised his stomach. Once the feeling had started to come back into his skinny wee frame he turned into a good laugh with a bizarre sense of humour. He made Josh laugh with some of his antics, and Josh had a bit of a soft spot for him. He wished the wee cunt would eat sometimes – even if he forced himself.

Gavin Ritchie was a big gobshite. 'Captain Trivia', Moose called him. He knew bits and pieces about everything but fuck-all about life. Gavin had a view on every subject under the sun – cheese, sunbeds, the Great Wall of China, women's stockings, battery life, food additives, bulimia, mobile-phone tariffs, hypothermia, why pubic hair was curly. You name it, he'd read about it and had developed 'The Gospel According to Gavin'. But it was easy enough for Josh to change Gavin's opinion with a little intelligent persuasion and the threat of a smack in the gob if he didn't stop going on and on all the time, trying to prove his point. Gavin was a big bloke but no match for Josh, who, at six feet two and no stranger to steroids, could still fly off the handle if the wrong thing were said. So Gavin always backed down, and Josh lorded it over him and Moose. And why not? He provided their living, their entertainment . . . and, more importantly, their education.

Josh was starting to feel queasy. He wound down the window of the van. God, it was like a sauna in here. He looked at the heater – it was turned down. He turned off the tape as he tried to figure out what was wrong with him. He could feel a vibration in his chest and stomach. He looked at the speedo – 65 m.p.h. That was it – fucking wheel balance was out again. He'd been driving this van home pished so many times that he knew he must have knocked the wheels out of alignment by hitting the kerb.

He accelerated to seventy and checked the steering-wheel for vibration. Nothing. He dropped his speed slowly, right down to thirty-five. Still nothing. Strange, it couldn't be the balance. Then he realised it wasn't the van that was shaking – it was *him*.

He could feel pressure on his chest. *Heart-attack*. Fuck, he was only twenty-five. He started to get *the fear* as he glanced in the mirror. Christ, he looked like a ghost! His stomach was in knots, like someone was reaching in, grabbing handfuls of intestines and twisting

25

them. *A stroke* . . . It had to be a stroke. He could feel pins and needles, not just in his arms but up and down his entire body. He pulled the van into the loch-side, grabbed his mobile and swung open the door of the van.

Right. 999. He looked at the signal bar on the phone – *fuck-all*. He's about to have a stroke and he can't even get a signal? *Bastard!*

The future's shite.

He threw the phone on the passenger seat and jumped out of the van. He tried to straighten up but his stomach was in spasm. He breathed deeply and tried to compose himself. 'Strokes an heart-attacks are caused by lack ay oxygen,' Gavin had once told him. 'Ye have to get the oxygen flowin through yir lungs again.' It was worth a try, he thought, as he bent over with his hands on his knees, trying to breathe. He'd be glad to see the big bastard now actually – take any advice he had. It was then he felt it – Mount Vesuvius . . . A burning sensation in the pit of his stomach. It was heading downwards. It could only mean one thing. He waddled swiftly across to the ditch at the side of the road and unbuttoned his jeans. He just managed to get them round his ankles and squat down when Vesuvius erupted. He breathed a sigh of relief as various expressions came to mind – 'Gandhi's revenge' and 'shitting through the eye of a needle' to name just two.

Fucking heart-attack. It must have been a dodgy pint at the Ptarmigan last night. He'd have a word with wee Brendan later. He'd put enough money over that bar since arriving here. The least the wee cunt could do was make sure the pipes were cleaned once in a blue moon.

Josh farted and another batch of brown water jettisoned from his arse with a *parp!*. He sniggered and looked about, wondering what people would think if they saw him crouched in the grass. Fuck them. He was just glad he was okay. Or was he? He'd always had a cast-iron stomach – could eat anything. And he'd eaten nothing out of the ordinary last night, just drunk his usual quota of lager. He vowed to stick to bottles in future; they were safer. Although he had heard once about some Glasgow boy getting that rat-catchers' disease from drinking lager out of the bottle in a Glasgow pub. It turned out that the rats were climbing all over the crates in the cellar and pissing on them.

He'd been in the Ptarmigan last night with Moose and Gavin when Keighley had turned up with her pal Lianne and one of the loonies from the hospital. Stuart, they called him. Keighley came over to Josh and gave him a peck on the cheek. Lianne went off to the ladies' and Stuart stood looking at the fruit-machine.

'Whit's he dein here?' asked Josh, looking at Stuart.

'Who, Stuart?' Keighley said.

'Aye . . . *Stuart* . . . Whit huv Ah telt ye aboot bringin a spaz in here?'

Keighley looked at him and shook her head. 'An whit have Ah told you about callin the patients spazzes? They're mentally ill.'

'Oh, soarry, Ah meant loonies', He looked at Moose and Gavin. They laughed and turned away from Keighley.

'They're no different from yir mates,' she said, eyeing the pair of laughing hyenas at the bar. She dropped her bag at her feet and took off her denim jacket. He glanced at the blue checked tunic and navy trousers of her nurse's uniform as she hung her jacket over a nearby chair. He thought back to last night when he had made her wear the tunic in bed and wondered if *he* was the one who was mentally ill. 'Whit ye drinkin?' he asked.

She gave him a look as if to say, 'That's better.' 'Ah'll huv a Hooch, Lianne'll huv a hof ay cider and Stuart'll huv . . .'

'Aw, fuck sakes!' said Josh.

'What?'

'He's no stayin is he?'

'For a wee while, aye . . . Git him a pint ay lager.'

'He kin huv a *hof* pint . . . *shandy*.'

'No, he kin huv ay *pint ay lager*.'

Josh stared at her for a moment. She gave him a wry smile and went back to Stuart. Josh turned to wee Brendan, the barman. 'Brendan, gonnae gies a Hooch, a hof ay cider . . .'

'Sweet or dry?' asked Brendan, pulling a Hooch from the fridge.

'It's fir Lianne. Better mek it dry – tae match hur fanny, eh?' Moose and Gavin howled with laughter. Lianne came out of the ladies', rubbing her scalp with her fingers and flicking away a couple of long hairs that had been pulled out by the hairband she'd been wearing for work. She leaned forward and tossed back her long brown mane. She glanced over to where the laughter was coming from. Josh gave her a sarky smile. She drew him a look – there was no love lost between them.

'Whit else,' asked Brendan.

'Er, a pint ay lager fir the spaz . . . Prozak-top, eh?' Moose and Gavin looked at him, puzzled. 'Ach, ah'll explain later,' he said.

So that was how he'd spent his night, with Keighley, Moose, Gavin, Keighley's so-called pal – the one who thought she was a fucking model and wouldn't even look at the road he was on, and a loony patient who kept on picking up Josh's pint and drinking from it all night. Twice Josh told him to keep it while he fumed quietly and went to the bar to get another. Then that bitch Lianne stuck Josh in it, asking, did he think Stuart was a leper, or have some incurable disease. He was mentally ill – he didn't have Aids. Even if he did, Josh couldn't catch it from a glass – ignorant bastard. She said Josh was 'acting like a wee schoolgirl, refusing to drink from the same glass'. Josh ignored her and went to the toilet. When he came back he thought the whole thing had been forgotten. He picked up his pint and finished it. Lianne took great pleasure in informing him that they'd swapped his lager with Stuart's when he was in the toilet, so any disease that Stuart had, *he* now had. Mental illness included.

Lianne sat there looking smug, so pleased with herself for getting one up on him. That fucking spastic Stuart sat there with his big scarred forehead and his stupid high-pitched laugh until Josh gave him a look that made him realise if he didn't shut the fuck up Josh would take his big scarred head off his shoulders. He soon got the message – couldn't be that much of a loony, then. Josh glared over at Moose and Gavin. They looked back at him as if to say, 'We tried to warn ye.' Keighley stopped laughing and put her hand on his leg, telling him that Lianne had been trying to teach him a lesson to stop him being prejudiced. There was nothing wrong with Stuart, so Josh had nothing to worry about.

Aye, that mist huv bin it, thought Josh, as he reached for a clump of grass to wipe his arse. He spotted nettles in it and threw it away. Holding his jeans about his knees, he shuffled over to the van to get the *Daily Record* off the passenger seat. '*Nothin tae worry aboot.* Aye, try tellin that tae me noo, ya fuckin bitch!' He grabbed the newspaper and waddled back over to the ditch to give his arse a wipe. He'd picked up something from that loony's saliva, he was sure of it. Those cunts sat there in the nut-house, dribbling all day – half of that lager he'd drunk was probably Stuart's drool. He shuddered, wondering what virus was taking hold of him. Whatever it was it could probably live okay in a loony but was causing fucking havoc with his system.

He tore a page out of the *Record* and vowed to see a

doctor for a blood test as soon as he could. He was going to have a word with that bird of his as well when he got home. That was out of order, winding him up like that. Totally disrespectful – making him look a right cunt in front of his mates. He'd have to start laying down the law again.

Nathan stepped out of the shower and reached for the towel, listening for noise from the bedroom. All calm. Good. He rubbed his hair thinking that if he was quiet enough getting ready for work she wouldn't wake up. He wrapped the towel round his waist and opened the bathroom door, wincing as the chimes on the dream-catcher tinkled again above the bed. He crept through the bedroom, glancing at her matted blonde hair flowing across the pillow. Then something caught his eye. A paracetamol bottle. A couple of tablets lay on the floor. He picked up the bottle. It was empty. He remembered taking two tablets on Sunday morning to try to get rid of the bastard of a hangover. The bottle had been almost full then, he was sure of it. He pulled the covers off Angie's face. She was staring straight ahead, blinking occasionally, tears running down her cheeks.

'Ange?' He indicated the empty bottle in his hand. 'How many of these have you took?'

She looked up at him slowly but said nothing.

He started to panic. 'Ange, speak to me – how many?'

'Enough.'

'Oh, fuck . . . You stupid cow!' He dragged her to her feet then saw that she was only wearing her knickers. He wasn't dressed much better either, with only a towel wrapped round him. 'Fuck, fuck, *fuuuuck*!' He sat her on the bed and pulled open the wardrobe door, grabbed a pair of her jeans and threw them on to the bed beside her. She sat on the edge, staring at the floor, tears streaming down her face. He threw one of her T-shirts on to the bed, then grabbed a pair of his jeans and an old sweatshirt, and pulled them on. He shuffled into his trainers, as he hobbled into the kitchen to grab his car keys and mobile off the table.

When he came back in she was lying down again.

'Oh no you don't!' He grabbed her arms and pulled her back up. He threw the T-shirt over her head and pulled out her long hair through the neck hole. Her eyes opened. He could feel her staring at him, but he didn't want to look at her stupid face. She'd really done it this time.

'I can't live without you, Nathan,' she said. He glanced at her. She was searching his face for an answer. Behind her eyes he glimpsed – he could almost swear it – a child. There was a little girl inside this mad bitch.

'You don't have to,' he said as he put her legs into her jeans.

'You're leaving me,' she said, and burst into tears.

'I'm not.' *Fuck*, this wasn't going as planned. Five minutes ago he was all set to pack his bags and now here he was acting like it was all a big mistake.

'You hate me – I'm old, I'm ugly—'

'You're not.'

'You think I talk bollocks, Nathan.'

'No, I don't.' He hauled her to her feet and pulled up her jeans, then laid her down on the bed and fastened them at the waist.

'I told you if you ever left me I'd kill myself, didn't I?' she said, as though this was his fault. He pulled on her trainers. 'Well, I'm not talking bollocks now, am I?' she sneered at him.

'Come on.' He pulled her on to her feet and led her to the door. He gave the flat a quick glance before he closed it behind them. He was trapped, destined to stay with Angie for the rest of his days. She could do whatever she liked, shag whom she pleased, and if he had anything to say about it she'd reach for the bottle of pills and it would be all his fault that she died. He'd have to live with it for the rest of his life. People would point at him in the street, saying, 'That's the bloke poor Angie committed suicide over. The bastard didn't love her – he was shagging about behind her back. When she found out it was all too much for her so she topped herself. Stay away from him, girls – he's a right bastard.'

Karl sat at the kitchen table, eating cornflakes. He put the spoon in the bowl and scratched his chin. He'd forgotten to shave again. Fuck it. It wasn't as if he was going anywhere till the weekend. Come to think of it, there'd be no chance of a few beers with Nathan and the boys this week, especially with the way money had been lately. He looked at the newspaper and tried to take his mind off his problems – there was always someone else worse off than you were. He cast his eyes over page eight of the *Sun*. 'Vanessa Feltz loses weight and the whole fucking world grinds to a halt,' he said.

'Language in front of the girls, please.' His wife, Liz, placed the teapot in front of him. He lowered the paper and realised his six-year-old daughter Lucy was sitting opposite, studying him, a mass of blonde curls with a tiny face in the middle of it. She was eating half a slice of toast covered in jam, a sticky line of which ran from both corners of her mouth and up her cheeks.

'Sorry, Loose,' he said.

'Dad said a swearie word, Mum.' Lucy looked up at Liz. A blob of jam fell off the toast and on to the white-tiled floor.

'I know he did. He's very naughty.' Liz took a cloth from the drainer and wiped up the jam. 'He's worse than a football hooligan, isn't he?'

'Mmm-hmm.' Lucy nodded and tried to guide the floppy toast into her mouth. She climbed down from the chair and went into the living room.

'Well, it's no bloody wonder, is it? I mean, look at this – it'd make the bleedin Pope swear.' Karl waved the paper at Liz. 'Rubbish.'

'Then why do you get it?'

'For the tits.' He grinned.

'You're the tit for buying it.' She flicked a tea-cloth at his arm. He dodged out of the way.

'That's quite funny, that – for this time in the morning. Ever thought of doing stand-up?' he asked, sarcastically.

'Da-ad.' He turned round to see Jade, Lucy's twin, swinging on the doorframe with one hand while holding a broken video-cassette in front of him with the other. Another mass of blonde curls – a carbon copy of her sister. To an outsider they'd be identifiable only by the different-coloured hairbands they were wearing this morning, but Liz and Karl could spot the differences a mile off. They were like chalk and cheese.

'What's up, darlin?' he asked, hardly noticing the broken cassette.

'My *Postman Pat* video's broken. The video ate it again.'

'Oh, for f—' He took the cassette and examined the tape, aware that Liz was eyeing him because of his near slip-up on the language front. 'What happened?' he asked.

'I just pressed rewind on the choke-a-mole and it broke my tape.'

Liz smiled as she switched on the kettle. *Choke-a-mole* was what Jade had called the remote control since she was two years old. For Liz, it had long since conjured up images of a mole being throttled and now they all called it the choke-a-mole, just as they all called the Hoover the *hooboo*, thanks to Lucy.

Karl gazed at the tape. Chewed to bits – beyond repair. 'What have I told you about pressing rewind while the tape's playing? You know the video chews them up. You have to press stop first, *then* rewind. How many times do I have to tell you?'

'It's not her fault,' said Liz, scooping a teaspoon of coffee into a cup and pouring in boiling water. 'It's that bloody video – when are you going to get it sorted out?'

Karl ignored her. 'Well?' he asked Lucy.

'I forgot . . . Daddy, fix it for me.'

'I can't fix that – it's had it.'

'But it's my favourite.'

'Then you should have thought about that before you stuck it in the video.'

'Oh, that's logical, isn't it?' said Liz, sitting down at the table with her coffee. 'What else is she supposed to watch it on?'

'All I'm saying is, just be careful with the video till I get it fixed. You know it's temperamental.' Jade glared at him, then turned on her heel and stormed off to the living room. He called after her, 'I'll try and fix it when I get home from work, all right, darlin? You can help me, eh?' He waited for an answer. He knew he'd have a bloody long wait. He looked at Liz. She gave him a look that said, 'You deserved that.' He hated it when one of them wasn't talking to him. It was worse when the three of them ganged up together and sent him to Coventry for the slightest thing. Bloody women. He held his hands out, palms up. 'What have I done now?'

'You know how she feels about *Postman Pat*.'

'Well, I think we could all do with a break. Some days I can't get that fucking song out of my head.'

'And Daddy of the Year goes to Karl Weston, for the sixth year in a row.' She sipped her coffee and eyed him disdainfully.

'Yeah, yeah,' he said, taking her point. 'I'll make it up to her.'

'Just buy her a new one.' Liz placed her coffee down on the table.

'Thirteen fucking quid? You've got to be joking.' He picked up the cassette and glanced at it. 'I'll fix it with Sellotape – she won't notice the difference.'

'She'll notice there's bits missing.'

'She won't.'

'She will – it'll be jumping from one bit to another. It's up to you, but you know she'll make your life hell if you don't get her another. You know what she's like when she's in a mood.'

'Oh, all right . . . The cash register's going, is it?' He threw down the tape on the table.

'What's that supposed to mean?'

'From the minute I get up it's "I need this, we have to buy one of these, this has run out, that bill's due." Some days I feel like I'm going under – I'm lucky if I can break even with what that shower of bastards are paying on this job.'

'Then leave them.'

'It's not that simple, is it? They're an agency, aren't they? They get the jobs and send us lot to them. If I don't work for them it'll be for some other bunch of fuckers just like them.' He glanced at his watch and gulped down the last of his tea. 'I'd better be going – I'll be late for Nathan.' He stood up.

'Listen, before you go,' said Liz, 'I'm going to need some money – the girls need shoes.'

'What?' He couldn't believe what he was hearing. Had she been listening to a word he'd said?

Liz shrugged her shoulders. 'Well, I thought since you were in a mood . . .'

'Is Lucy still dragging her feet?' he asked.

'No, she's stopped doing that.'

'But they got shoes last month . . . didn't they?'

'They did, but now they've grown out of them.'

'Already? So, how much is that going to cost?

'About thirty pounds each.'

'Sixty quid for shoes and another thirteen for a *Postman Pat* video and I haven't even left the house yet . . . Is there anything else?'

'Well, since you ask, the gas bill's due.'

'Oh, for fuck sake.'

'Well, you started it.'

The phone rang. They stood looking at each other.

'I'm not going to answer that – it'll probably cost me a tenner.' Karl lifted his denim jacket off a hook in the kitchen cupboard and started putting it on.

'You make it sound like it's all my fault,' said Liz.

'Look, I don't mean it like that . . . Sometimes I just feel like I'm going under, you know? I'm doing all the hours I can. I hardly get to see you or the girls. God's sake, Liz, we can't even afford to go out for a night.'

'I don't mind. You know me, I like staying in.'

'Yeah, but it would be nice to have the choice, wouldn't it? A holiday once in a while instead of work, work, work all the time?'

'Dad.' Karl turned round. Jade was back, swinging on the doorframe, 'Nathan says don't bother picking him up for work . . . he'll see you later.' She swung back round the door, out of sight.

'Well, look on the bright side,' said Liz, 'at least Jade's speaking to you again.'

Josh pulled up the van in the grounds of Craigellachie House. He got out and looked up at the windows. A female patient gazed down intently at him. He tried to outstare her, like a cat, but she just looked right through him. He gave up and walked to the front door, pressed the intercom and looked about the grounds. He didn't know how Keighley could work here. The money was rubbish. She had to deal with all kinds – cunts shitting their beds every day. If he worked here he'd rub their fucking noses in it . . .

'Hello?' An English voice came from the intercom. Colin, the community manager, a right miserable bastard when it came to money.

'Colin, it's Josh.'

Bzzzzzz. The door lock released. Josh pushed it open and went inside. He walked up the main corridor, breathing in the smell of pish and bleach mixed with the stench of what he could only imagine was old men's trousers. Some nights Keighley came home smelling like that. He hated the thought of her being in bed with him, touching him after wiping someone's wrinkled old arse.

He passed by a bloke in a tank top who was mopping the floor. Josh gave him a half-smile before realising that the guy didn't work here, he was a patient. The man glanced back then diverted his eyes to the wet floor. He turned his back to Josh as he mopped, hunching his shoulders as though he expected a whack across the back of the head.

Josh ignored him and knocked on the door of Colin's office.

'Come in,' said Colin, from inside. Josh opened the door and walked in casually. That was the way to do it with these bastards – walk about casual, as if you don't really want to be here, as though you're doing them a favour in doing a job for them. The more they felt they were inconveniencing you the more they were likely to pay. Stupid cunts fell for it every time.

Colin sat behind his desk in a battered old leather armchair. He looked up from a folder, smiled broadly and indicated a seat. 'Have a seat, Josh, I'll not be a tick.'

Josh nodded without smiling back. He sat down and looked at the diplomas on the wall. Colin frowned and shook his head from side to side as he read the report. His black hair was Brylcreemed back, hiding an obvious bald spot, although he was no more than forty. His specs were perched on the end of his nose, much lower than his angle of vision as he scanned the pages.

Josh cleared his throat and sighed deeply. Colin took the hint and looked up. If Josh hadn't known better he'd have been sure the bastard was playing him at his own game. Colin put down the report. 'Sorry about that,' he said. 'Bloody legislation . . . I'd like to see them run this place on a shoestring budget.' Josh smirked. He *was* playing him at his own game – pretending to be skint. He had a good mind to add another grand on to the quote for Colin's fucking cheek.

'So,' said Colin, 'you've got a price for me, then?'

Josh nodded: the nod of inconvenience. The here-it-comes – take-it-or-leave-it nod. The I've-got-better-things-to-do-with-my-time-than-sit-here-giving-you-free-quotes nod. He sat up in his chair then leaned back to make himself more comfortable. 'Twenty grand should cover it . . . but Ah'll dae it fir eighteen.' He looked Colin straight in the eyes. Colin opened his mouth as if to speak, then thought better of it. Josh studied his expression. He looked as though he was mulling it over, going for it, thinking about how he'd get the money together. 'Ah'll need hof up front fir materials,' added Josh.

Colin clasped his hands together and sat back in his chair. 'Eighteen thousand pounds?' he asked, clarifying the sum.

'Aye,' said Josh, as seriously as he could without breaking into a fit of the giggles.

'To rewire this hospital?'

'Aye,' said Josh. What was wrong with this cunt? Did he have a hearing problem?

'You're not serious?'

Josh sighed inwardly. Here we fucking go. Another tight-fisted bastard wanting a job done on the cheap. 'I'm sorry, but that's as cheap as ah kin dae it. Ah only agreed tae drop mah price tae the bare minimum cos Keighley asked me tae. Dae you know the goin rate?'

'I'm afraid I don't, but I assume it's nowhere near what you're charging.'

Josh gave him a sarky smile. Very funny. 'Over hof the money's goin oan materials. Ye need yir whole conduit system replacin, cause that stuff ye've goat is illegal,' he said, pointing to the nearest wall. 'Naebody uses metal anymair. Ah'll huv tae rip the whole loat oot. Then yir talking Gyproc, plasterers, brickies, you name it, the rest ay the money'll huv tae go oan payin these guys.'

'I still think it's far too much.'

'Aye, well, ye obviously didnae know how big a job it wid be!'

Colin breathed in deeply, then sighed slowly through his nose. He looked down at his desk and shook his head, as though he'd just done a mental sum and realised that the bright red sports car he'd had his eye on for some time just wasn't for him. He'd never be able to afford it as long as he lived. 'I'll, er . . . have to leave it,' he said, standing up: meeting over. The ball was in Josh's court. Josh sighed and stared at the floor. He nodded as though agreeing to the new terms. 'Awright, Ah kin cut back on some ay the labour, dae the plasterin masel . . . It'll tek a wee bit longer but . . . let's say fifteen . . . fifteen an a hof.' He looked up, expecting Colin to smile and shake his hand, but Colin looked back at him, impassive, before walking across to the door and opening it. There's a fucking hint for you, thought Josh.

'Sorry,' said Colin, almost apologetically. Josh stood up. Last chance. Time to put the frighteners on him. 'Whit ye gonnae dae? Wait till someone gets electrocuted?' He looked accusingly at Colin, who nodded and smiled knowingly, aware of the tactics. He was a psychiatrist, after all. He knew a sad attempt at emotional blackmail when he saw one.

'Bye, Josh . . . and thanks.'

'Well, if you can get it done cheaper you let me know, eh?'

Josh walked out of the office. He turned to give Colin a piece of his mind for wasting his time but Colin had already closed the door on him. Josh clenched his fist. He'd overpriced himself again but they usually went for it. They had to – there was no one else for miles. He walked back along the corridor, mentally kicking himself. He knew the job was only worth about seven and a half grand, tops. He could do it for five if he really wanted to. He'd wait until later on today to give the specky cunt time to cool down then casually phone him, saying he'd managed to *acquire* a load of materials and could do the job, as a favour, for four grand – can't say fairer than that. He'd go for it then, all right.

He glanced at the metal mop bucket by the door then looked about for the loony. Nowhere to be seen. Probably jacking off in a cupboard somewhere. Josh gave the bucket a kick. It tipped over, clattered against the wall and soapy water washed across the tiles. He grinned to himself and walked out.

Colin sat down at his desk and ran his finger across the mouse pad on his laptop. A double click on Internet Explorer and it dialled the server. **Doo dit dit doot dit boop bip beep dit doot**. He sat back in his chair and reached for his glasses cloth, took off his spectacles and gave them a quick polish as his laptop whirred away in front of him, dialling and connecting. He put them back on and watched the screen *locating server, verifying user* *name and password*. He snorted to himself. The arrogance of the man. Who does he think he is? Does he think the council are going to hand out money left, right and centre to cowboys like him? The *Lineone* homepage came up. He was right. He knew he'd seen it somewhere before. *Find a business. (Plumber, Courier)* in *(Manchester, Sheffield)*. He typed *Electrical* into the box and clicked *Go*.

Nathan sat in the hospital corridor, looking down at his trainers. He glanced at his watch, hoping Karl would cover for him until he got to the job. A young Chinese girl wearing a white doctor's coat over a red dress came out of a ward and walked up to him. 'Mr Weller?'

'Yeah?'

'Hi, I'm Dr Cheung.'

'Oh, hi . . . Is my wife going to be okay?'

The doctor nodded and sat down beside him. 'You did the right thing in bringing her straight here. The tablets were still whole.'

'What does that mean?

'The paracetamol didn't have much time to get into her system.'

Nathan studied her face as she spoke to him. She wore a look of pity. Maybe she'd spotted that Angie was a nutter and felt sorry for him for having to live with her. Then he wondered if she wore dresses like that to work every day. It seemed more suited to a night out than walking around a ward.

'Has she done this kind of thing before?' she asked.

Nathan nodded. 'Tried to slit her wrists once after we had a blazing row . . . Sometimes I'm scared to get into an argument with her in case she does it again.'

The doctor nodded sympathetically. 'Does she suffer from depression?'

He thought for a second. Sometimes she was a right moody cow. 'It's hard to say. One minute she's laughing and joking, the next she's sitting there sulking . . . I don't know.'

'Is she on any medication?'

'No, not that I know of.'

'Well, we'd like to keep her in overnight for observation, just in case.'

'In case of what?' he asked, concerned.

'Damage to her liver. People who take an overdose of paracetamol usually end up here getting their stomachs pumped . . . But if it's gone into their system it can result in liver damage, which in some cases can be fatal.'

'The stupid cow.' He looked up. 'Sorry.'

'It's all right,' said the doctor. 'I don't think you've much to worry about . . . But if we let her out, do you think it's likely she'll do it again?' She tilted her head at him.

What? Was he expected to predict the future? 'I couldn't say. I can't watch her all the time – I've got to go to work.'

'Is there no one else who can look after her for the time being?'

'Only her mum, but Ange'd kill me if I told her what she'd done. Her mum thinks there's nothing wrong with her. She doesn't know the half of it.'

The doctor nodded understandingly. 'You think she's a danger to herself.'

Nathan considered it for a moment. 'Yeah, I do.'

She looked up the corridor, biting her bottom lip as she thought. She gave a slight shrug. 'We could always get a psychiatrist to section her. If you think she's likely to do it again.'

'You mean lock her up?' The doctor gave him a half-smile that said she knew it was medieval but it was the best thing to do. 'She'd kill me,' he said.

The doctor stood up. 'It's up to you. I'll let you think about it.' She started to walk away then stopped and turned. 'Why don't you get some rest, Mr Weller? Come back in the morning, hey?' She smiled and walked off up the corridor.

'Whit ye goat there, Stuart? Mair photies ay the moon?' Keighley stood at the bottom of Stuart's bed, holding his medication. He nodded and looked down at the pictures strewn across his duvet: black and white ten-by-eights showing almost identical shots of the moon in all its glory, the only difference between them being the time and date in the bottom right-hand corner. Keighley walked round the bed and pointed to the dates, trying to show an interest. 'Whit's this here?'

'The time Ah took them . . . This wan was at ten o'clock.' He picked it up and handed it to her, then pointed to another. 'This wan was at eight minutes past.'

'Oh,' she said. It was important to make the patients feel as if they were doing something worthwhile. Stuart had started going to the local photography shop once a week as part of his rehabilitation. Keighley had met the owner a couple of times and enquired how Stuart was getting on. The owner told her there wasn't a thing he could teach him – he knew it all. What he couldn't understand was why he didn't take photos of anything but the moon. Keighley explained that he would . . . all in good time.

'Time exposure.'

Keighley put the print back on the bed. 'Whit?'

'That's how Ah tek them. Open shutter. Ye need a tripod, though – ye cannae hoad yir camera, ye'll git camera shake. Disnae matter how still ye hoad it, ye still get camera shake.'

'Ah'll bear that in mind, Stuart. Here.' She handed him his tablets and a small plastic cup. He put them in his mouth and knocked them back with the water. Keighley watched as he took them. You had to make sure they didn't spit them out. She knew Stuart always took his, though. He never gave her any trouble.

Suddenly his face froze and he slid further along the bed, recoiling from the door in terror.

'Stuart? Whit is it? Whit's wrang?'

He placed his cheek against the wall, as though he was trying to press his head through to the other side to escape whatever horror he'd seen.

'Stuart?'

'*Nnnnuuuuuuhhhhhhhhhhh*.' He turned his face away from her and gave a high-pitched squeal. Behind her Keighley heard a snigger. She turned to see Billy, one of the patients, wearing a big grin and a toy policeman's hat. The elastic was cutting into the layers of fat around his chin and his manic smile was fixed like a gargoyle's. Keighley marched over to him and pulled off the hat, snapping the elastic.

'Ow!' Billy put his hand to his cheek.

'Whit huv ah telt you? Noo, oot!' She pushed him into the corridor, tore the plastic hat in two and tossed it out after him. She shut the door and turned back round to Stuart.

'It's awright, he's away.'

Stuart sat shaking on the edge of the bed. She went over and sat next to him. She'd seen people with a fear or distrust of the police before but never anything like this. Billy always made it worse. He could be a right wee bastard when he wanted. Always winding Stuart up.

'Shhh . . . it's okay.' She pulled his big head on to her shoulder and stroked his hair. His breath was shaky, like a child winding down from a good sob.

'Ah've goat an idea,' she said. 'Let's huv a wee song,

eh? That aywis cheers ye up, disn't it?' She bowed her head so that her pale green eyes made contact with his. He looked away and started to rock backwards and forwards on the edge of the bed. Always a sign of distress, she thought. If I get my hands on that bloody Billy I'll . . . 'Tell you whit,' she said, 'you tell me whit song an ah'll sing it fir ye.'

'Sinatra . . . please,' he mumbled.

'Right. Sinatra it is, then.' She put her arm round him and held his shoulder, swaying from side to side to change his forward rocking motion as she sang 'Fly Me To The Moon'.

After a minute or so she felt him relax. She bent her head down and looked him in the eyes again. He glanced at her, his face breaking into a smile. She kissed his forehead.

Works every time. She smirked to herself as they rocked from side to side on the bed.

'You're going to have to divorce her.' Karl screwed the back box into the wall.

'Oh, just like that?' Nathan sat on a cable drum in the middle of the derelict toyshop.

'Why not? It's not as if you don't have grounds, is it? Mental cruelty for starters.' A screw fell from Karl's hand. He bent to pick it up.

Nathan looked up at the bare grey Gyproc walls and tried to imagine Angie's face if he ever had the guts to tell her he was divorcing her. He didn't want to think about it. 'It would kill her,' he said.

Karl put the screw through the hole in the back box and twisted it into the Rawlplug. 'That's not your problem.'

'Oh, that's fucking easy for you to say – what if it was Liz?'

'If my Liz was carrying on like that I'd be off like a shot, mate, no messing about.'

'Yeah, yeah.'

Karl pointed the screwdriver at him, as though emphasising his point. 'I would, and I'd take the girls wiv me. I wouldn't have them round no nutter.' He saw Nathan's dejected look and remembered he was talking about a mate's wife. 'No offence.' Nathan nodded. Karl tightened the screws then bent down and picked up the front of the box. 'Look, mate, you can't live your life like this, wondering if she's gonna top herself or not. She might be your wife but she's not your fucking responsibility. You're not a psychiatrist, are you?' Nathan shook his head. 'Well, then,' said Karl, 'leave her . . . before it's too late.'

'It's not as simple as that.'

Karl screwed the live wire into the back of the socket. 'Yes, it is. You pack a bag and go. You can stay wiv us for a while if you like – Liz won't mind.'

'I'll think about it.' Nathan jumped up as he heard the shuffling sound of the foreman's boots coming through

the back of the shop. He picked up a couple of screwdrivers and put them in his toolbox as Barry Ellis came
in.

'How's it going, lads?' Ellis took off his hard hat and
scratched his head. He looked about the room as though
expecting to see a total transformation from yesterday.

'Fine,' said Nathan, trying to look busy.

Karl indicated the socket holes in the Gyproc with his
screwdriver. 'Two more of these and we're done in
here,' he said.

'Good,' said Ellis. 'What have you got on after this?'

'Nothing,' said Karl.

Nathan picked up another back box from the floor
and walked over to Karl with it. 'We were hoping *you*
could tell *us*.'

Ellis looked at them as though making a decision. He
stuck his head round the door to see if anyone was
about. Satisfied that the coast was clear he walked
closer, as if to inspect the work. 'I might have *something*,' he said shiftily. He pulled out a job sheet and
looked at it for a second then handed it to Nathan, who
scanned it. Karl screwed the neutral wire into the socket,
watching them both.

'Rewire on a hospital?' asked Nathan. 'Where is it?'

'Place called Glen Leven . . . in Scotland.'

'Fucking *Scotland*?' Karl butted in. 'Bit far, innit? And
how long's that likely to take?'

Ellis shrugged his shoulders. 'Well, that's up to you,

isn't it? The quicker you get it done, the quicker you get home.'

'Here, let me see that.' Karl took the job sheet from Nathan and studied it. His brow furrowed.

'Who's on it?' asked Nathan.

'No one yet.' Ellis looked about the room at the walls and ceilings. 'I was hoping to send just you two – that's if you're up for it.'

'This is a five-man job!' said Karl, waving the sheet at him.

Ellis glanced across to the door, hoping no one had heard him. 'I know that. I can send five of you, if you like, but after you've paid your commission you'll end up wiv buttons. If you two do it between you, you'll end up wiv a lot more, won't you?' Nathan nodded in agreement. It made sense. He looked at Karl for a decision. Karl handed the job sheet back to Ellis.

'But fucking *Jock Land*? I've got a wife and kids, you know. I don't want to be stuck up there wiv me kids down here.'

Ellis folded the sheet and put it into his pocket. 'Fine, I'll give it to someone else.'

'Wait a minute,' said Nathan, 'he didn't say he didn't want it.'

Ellis stopped and turned round. 'Well?' He looked at Karl.

'Let me think about it,' said Karl. 'When do you need to know by?'

'Four o'clock,' said Ellis, 'I can't afford to hang about on this one.' He opened the door. 'You know where I'll be if you want me,' he said, and left.

Nathan glanced across at Karl. He could see him staring at the floor, trying to figure it out. The money would come in handy, but it would kill Karl to be away from his girls. Nathan though, would have the perfect opportunity to distance himself from mad Angie. Telling her, 'I've got to go to Scotland for a while,' wasn't half as bad as 'I want a divorce.'

'What do you think?' asked Nathan.

Karl looked up from the floor. 'I fucking hate Jocks,' he said.

'You've never said that before. Why? What's wrong wiv them?'

'They're all inbred, aren't they? Thick as two short planks.' He threaded the cable through the back box.

Nathan laughed. 'You're racist, mate.'

'I am fucking not!' said Karl, dignified. 'Colour doesn't bother me – you know that.'

'This isn't about colour, it's about race.' Nathan picked up the cable drum and rolled it to the corner of the room.

'A fucking backward one, if you ask me,' Karl muttered. He carried on screwing the wire in.

'How do you work that out?'

'I just know, don't I? Mate of mine worked up there for a while – couldn't wait to get home again. Said the nosh was fucking disgusting. Everyone was called Mac-fucking this and Mac-fucking-that – they were all related to each other.'

'He was having a laugh,' sniggered Nathan.

'He wasn't. They're all fucking mental up there.'

'How many Scots are living in London?' said Nathan. 'I've never heard you complain before.'

'Yeah, because they're all as quiet as mice till there's a fucking match on, or the rugby or something. Then they all come out the woodwork shouting "Scotland The Brave" in your face. I'd be fucking brave if I had hundreds of my mates wiv me . . . fucking inbreeds.'

Nathan laughed at Karl's theory.

'They are – straight up,' said Karl. 'Congenital madness, I think it's called. All those little villages they've got up there. Nothing to do at night but shag your aunties. Place is worse than fucking Somerset.'

Nathan was still laughing at his friend's audacity.

'You think I'm joking, don't you?' said Karl.

Nathan closed the lid of his toolbox. 'What a load of bollocks. It's like saying all black guys have got big dicks.'

'You ave.' Karl screwed the earth wire into the back of the socket.

Nathan rolled his eyes, as if he'd be wasting his time answering him.

Karl glanced at him. 'Bigger than mine anyway,' he said, as though confirming his theory.

'A fucking flea's got a bigger one than you, mate. I don't know how you piss without tweezers . . . So, what about this job? Are we going or what?'

'I'm not stopping you.' Karl screwed the neutral wire into the socket.

'I know that . . . but are *you* going?'

Karl stopped working and thought about it for a second. He sighed. 'I don't think I've got much choice, have I? I just don't like the idea of leaving Liz and the kids.'

'They'll be all right,' said Nathan.

'Yeah, suppose so. Besides, it'd be daft to knock it back, wouldn't it?'

'You not scared they'll shag you and eat you?' asked Nathan.

'Fuck off,' said Karl. 'Go on, go and tell him we'll do it.'

Nathan grinned and walked out of the door. He was going to enjoy this.

Josh came out of the shop eating an ice-cream while he dialled the number of Craigellachie House on his mobile. He squinted in the sunlight as he leaned on the bonnet of his van, admiring the green splendour of Ben Leven as it loomed above him. You don't get sights like this in Glasgow, he thought.

'Craigellachie House Psychiatric Hospital,' came Colin's voice.

'Colin, this is yir lucky day.' Josh licked his ice-cream.

'Ah . . . *Josh*,' came the less-than-enthusiastic reply.

Josh pulled the mobile from his ear and sneered at the mouthpiece. The smarmy bastard was in danger of ruining what would otherwise be a beautiful day. He put the phone back to his ear and fixed his face in a fake smile. 'Aye . . . see, whit we were talking aboot earlier?'

'I really don't think there's much left to say, Josh. As far as I'm concerned the matter's—'

'Could ye jist gies a minute before ye stert bumpin yir gums?' Josh interrupted. He took a deep breath to steady his nerves. He knew how easily he could lose it: his big mouth had cost him a few jobs in the past. Sometimes you had to take a wee bit of shite from people, but if you screwed the nut you could always find a way to get your pound of flesh out of the bastards once you were actually on the job. 'Ah've managed tae git mah hons oan a load ay conduit an cable. A mate ay mine's changin hus business an wants me tae clear oot hus garage fir um.'

'Really . . . So what does that have to do with me?'

Josh bit his lip. He felt like telling him he'd be right round to ram the conduit up his arse. 'Well, whit it means is ah kin dae that joab a hell ay a loat cheaper noo – ah've saved ye the cost ay materials.'

'Thanks, Josh, but like I said before, I'm not interested.'

'Bit ye don't underston – yir gettin it done fir next tae nothin, ya daft—'

'Sorry, I've already got someone else for the job,' Colin interrupted.

Josh was puzzled. He turned away from the van, looked up at Ben Leven and scratched the back of his head. Someone could have just told him that earth had just been invaded by Martians and he wouldn't have been more surprised. *How? What? Where? Someone else? Who?* He was just about to ask when . . .

'I'll have to go. Thanks, anyway . . . Bye.' *Bzzzzzzzzzzt*. The line went dead. Josh looked at his hand. His ice-cream was dripping down his wrist. He flung it away, turned and kicked the nearest tyre on his van. This wasn't on. It wasn't on at all.

Keighley placed a loaf of bread on the table in front of Josh.

'An English company . . . Who?' he asked.

She put a plate of haddock in batter with chips on the table and shrugged. 'Don't know. Whit dis it matter?' She sat down at the table with a plate of salad and sprinkled salt over the lettuce.

Josh pulled his plate towards him and squirted tomato ketchup over his fish. 'It matters tae *me* . . . Ye must know *somehun*?'

Keighley eyed him as he ate a forkful of chips. It didn't do to rile him when he was like this. She knew how he felt about his work. He thought he had the right to every electrical contract around here. This time his own stupid greed had done him out of a job, but there was no way she could tell him that. Sympathise, that was the best option. 'Don't let it git tae ye,' she told him, cutting a ripe cherry tomato in half and digging her fork into it.

'That's easy fir you tae say,' he said, spitting flakes of batter on to the table.

She looked at him. He was like a bulldog trying to eat its dinner while being distracted by a hungry pup hovering near its bowl.

'Ah nearly hud that joab!' he said. 'That basta's gien it tae these English cunts just tae save hissel a few quid. Is it any wonder Scotland's in the fuckin state it's in?'

'This you gittin political?' she asked, with a wry grin, chewing nonchalantly.

'It widnae be that if some snooty English cow came up here an snatched yir joab fae underneath yir nose, wid it?' He pointed his knife at her. A small piece of sauce-covered fish fell on to the white lace tablecloth. She sighed inwardly. There was no use trying to keep things nice when you lived with a slob. Fourteen pounds she'd paid for that tablecloth – the stain would never come out. She thought about pulling him up but decided against it. She knew what to expect – 'Sauce? Fuckin sauce, is it? Here's me worryin aboot mah livin an yir oan aboot *sauce*? I'll gie ye sauce!' Then he'd empty the whole bottle over the table and storm out to the pub. Sometimes it was best just to keep quiet.

She often wondered why the hell she stayed with him.

Lianne always said she got a bad vibe off Josh. Keighley knew exactly what Lianne was on about: Josh wasn't averse to raising his hands and there was no hiding it from Lianne.

Keighley thought back to when she started going out with him. She'd always felt safe in his company, protected. She'd been out with guys before who had stood by in a pub and let her fear for her life when trouble broke out, but there was no way that would ever happen with Josh. If anyone even looked at her the wrong way they'd have him to answer to. Sure he'd hit her, but in the cold light of day she could see it from his point of view: she did have a bit of a mouth on her, especially when she'd been drinking, and it didn't do to give him cheek, make him look stupid in front of his friends. She supposed most guys would feel the same way. Disrespected.

He was always remorseful after he'd hit her – especially the time he gave her a black eye. He'd cried when he saw the state she was in, and swore that he'd cut his hand off before he'd lift it to her again. The following week he'd dragged her out of the pub by the hair for flirting with a bloke who was on holiday. Looking back she could see his point. It had definitely been her fault. She'd brought that one on herself by being drunk and not bothering to tell the guy she was seeing someone. She only did it for a laugh – to see how far it would go before she waved ta-ta and left the guy standing at the bar with his mouth open. It had never got that far: the last thing she'd expected was for Josh to finish the job early, walk into the bar and stand behind her, listening in. She'd wondered why half the people in the place were drawing her looks. Thinking back, it was a shame for that poor wee guy. There had been no need for Josh to punch him around the bar like that – it hadn't been his fault. It had completely ruined his holiday. He'd gone home the next day.

Things were better now, though, as she'd learned to read the signs. Sometimes he had a faraway look in his eyes. A mad glare, like he was reliving an old argument, only this time coming out best. Once she caught him talking to himself in the bathroom mirror. His mouth was twitching away, like Humphrey Bogart's. She stood outside, watching him through the crack in the door. She thought he was trying out an impression so she stayed there, listening. He was mumbling away, pointing to himself in the mirror, pretending to turn away, then look back as if someone had just called him an arsehole. She swore she heard him say, 'You talkin to me?' Like de Niro in *Taxi Driver*. She stood with her back to the wall and put her hand over her mouth to stifle a snigger. He was away with the mixer this time, she thought. She peered again through the crack in the door and caught the look in his eyes reflected in the mirror. This time it was the look that said he meant business. A look that reminded her not to get lippy if she knew what was good for her. She watched as the light from the spotlights he'd fitted above the bathroom mirror shone off his short-cropped dome. She flinched as he lunged at the mirror like he was going to stick his forehead through it. He stopped inches away from it, sneering at his reflection as if to say, 'Who's laughing now?' A shiver went through her as she realised that she worked with patients who were nowhere near as bad as him. She crept back to the bedroom, thinking it best not to mention what she'd seen. We all have our mad moments, she thought . . . but then again, they're usually nothing like his.

'Well?' He stared at her in anticipation, clenching his knife and fork in his fists, one at either side of his plate, as though he was in some sort of pie-eating competition. What was he waiting for? 'Ready, steady, go – eat, yer mad basta'?

'Ah don't know.' She dug her fork into a couple of slices of cucumber.

'Whit? Ye don't know whit ah'm oan aboot or ye don't know whit ye'd dae if some English bitch came an nicked yir joab?' he asked.

'It widnae happen,' she said, nonchalantly. Her mind was elsewhere. She was wondering if she could allow herself a slice of bread, then reminded herself of how fattening it was. The calorie content was totting up in her brain as if it was a calculator.

'Don't you kid yirsel.' He shovelled half a chip butty into his mouth. She often wondered how the hell he could still speak when his mouth was almost constantly full. 'These cunts jist need tae see an opportunity an they git themselves up here, suss the place oot then bring up aw their pals,' he said, mopping up ketchup from his plate with the remainder of the bread. 'Before ye know it they're runnin the shoap, an we end up the ones workin fir *them*. Ah've seen it happenin in Glesga. It's like the white man in Africa aw over again.'

Her stomach rumbled. She cut the slice of low-fat cheese and speared it. She put it into her mouth, watching him slap the remaining half of the fish on to a slice of bread and dip it in the sauce. 'Aye, well, we'll see how long the cunts laist, eh?' he said, raising his eyebrows at her, then shoving the bread and fish into his mouth. 'Hmm?' he grunted. She sighed inwardly knowing with Josh around, when these English boys arrived they'd wish they never had.

'You're doing it on purpose.'

'I'm not.' Nathan watched as the lights changed to green. He put the car into first gear and drove away from the hospital. He could feel Angie staring at him from the passenger seat. He kept his eyes fixed on the road.

'It's because I took those tablets, isn't it?' she said.

'It's got nothing to do with that. It's just the timing of it, that's all. How do you think I feel at having to leave you when you're like this?'

'It didn't stop you yesterday – you were all set to walk out on me then,' she accused him. He glanced across at her. She was as white as a sheet. Her hair was matted and had lost its shine. God, she looked old. 'That was just talk,' he said. 'I was angry – I didn't mean anything by it.' He indicated left and took the corner. The car swung round it and Angie swayed to the right, bumping into him. She wasn't wearing a seatbelt again but he decided not to bother telling her to put it on. He was sick of telling her. If she wanted to end up going through the fucking windscreen it was her lookout.

'Very convenient, though, isn't it?' she asked.

'What?'

'You going away.'

'Look, it's money. I could sit on my arse waiting for the next job, or I take this one and be quids in.'

'You'll meet someone else.' She looked away from him, out of the window at some people standing outside a shop. He felt his hackles rising, but tried not to react. It was the same shit all the time, he thought. He might as well go out and get fucked because she always accused him of it anyway.

'I will not meet someone else,' he said, as though he was saying it for the thousandth time. 'I am going there to work.' He stared ahead through the windscreen. The bastard in the Fiat Punto had been arsing about for far too long – what lane was he in? He glanced at Angie, then looked at the speedo – 20 m.p.h. Silly old cunt, what was this bloke in the Punto playing at? Was he lost or something?

'Out of sight out of mind,' she said. He looked across at her again, and realised that the old git in the car in front had nothing to do with his mood. Out of mind? he thought. He sincerely hoped so. She'd been taking up space in his head for far too long.

A spray of soapy water jetted from the bonnet and bounced off the windscreen of the rusty dark blue Escort van to hover momentarily, like mist, above the M73 before it evaporated into the hot afternoon sun. Karl switched off the wipers: a good car wash was the only thing that was going to remove the dried fly wings and blood.

'Glen Leven. Sounds like one of those cheap whiskies, doesn't it?' he said, indicating the road sign they'd just passed.

'You what?' asked Nathan.

'Like that cheap whisky Macca gets – fiver a bottle? "Highland Glen, Tartan Cunt, *Glen Leven*." '

Nathan shook his head.

'You never tried it, then?' asking Karl, glancing at him.

'Nah, don't really drink spirits, do I?'

'Don't fuckin blame you, mate. I tried the stuff once – bit strapped for cash, usual . . . Had a cunt of a week – nuffin went right. I thought, Fuck it, I'm gonna get out my skull. Liz was away wiv the girls at her mum's or somefin, so I gets a bottle of this stuff Macca hijacks from the back of a lorry or whatever, and a bottle of Coke from the Greek's . . . Good video – can't remember what it was now . . . I sits meself down to watch the film an I conk out. When I wake up the telly's hissin away an the bottle's empty. I can't feel me teeth and I'm dehydratin, so I gets a drink of water an staggers to the bathroom to brush me teeth. I looks in the mirror and, fuck me, I fink I've got smallpox or chickenpox or *some sort* of pox. Me face is beetroot an I've come out in a mass of zits like a spotty teenager. Took the best part of a week for them to die down.'

'You sure it was the whisky?' asked Nathan, distracted by the splendour of a field of grazing Highland cattle.

'Course it was. I've never been like that before. Fuck knows what was in that stuff – antifreeze probably. The cunt got it from France, didn't he?'

'What's France got to do wiv anything?' asked Nathan, turning back to face him.

'Well, they put it in their wine, don't they? They've been doin it for years, the French – dirty bastards.' Karl glanced in the rear-view mirror as a red Freelander came up behind him and flashed its lights. He indicated left and moved into the inside lane. 'We only cottoned on to it a few years back. Preserves the stuff or somefink,' he said. The guy in the Freelander glanced across at them through designer shades, chewing gum and passing a sarky comment to his missus, which made her turn to look at the rust on the van. A small blond boy with curls like Shirley Temple sat in the back, drinking from a bottle of juice. A young baby was tilted almost horizontal in the car seat beside him. Karl glanced at the kid with the curls and was sure the little boy looked back at him and the van with contempt. The Freelander whizzed past in the outside lane and disappeared into the distance. Obviously a native of these parts. 'Fuck knows what it does to your guts,' said Karl. 'My arse was ragged for a week.'

'I really didn't really need to know that,' mused Nathan.

'Like a blood orange,' said Karl.

Nathan winced. The man had no sense of decorum and prided himself on telling it like it was.

'Lily, will ye stoap that?' Lianne stood at the bottom of Lily's bed, shaking her head at the old woman as she rummaged through her bedside unit.

'Ah need tae fun mah necklace,' said Lily, pulling out the top drawer. It clattered to the ground and the contents spilled on to the floor. Lily tore them apart in search of the necklace.

Lianne sighed. Here we go again. It was the same business every couple of days and she was getting sick to the back teeth of it. These old bastards were all the same: somebody gives them something, like a toy from Burger King, and they act all sentimental over it, as though it was the Golden Fleece or something. This necklace Lily banged on about every few days had never existed, only in her mind. Lianne stood and watched as the old woman threw underwear over her shoulder in her quest for the Fleece.

'Where is it? Somebody's stolen it!' said Lily.

Lianne hoped that if any of *her* pals ever saw her displaying signs of dementia they'd shoot her. This silly old bat was supposed to have been a writer when she was younger, poetry and all that. Looking at her now, she'd be lucky if she could write her name.

Compassion was top priority in this job, but it was hard when you had to deal with twenty rejects of society who *looked* like human beings but vomited, shat themselves, made unearthly noises and generally behaved like animals. Lianne knew the score – she had it sussed. If one of the bigwigs from head office came to the hospital, she made sure that the patients looked happy enough. They were always fed, clean and in their routine. Sometimes she wondered if she was suited to all this. She was twenty-two, had a bod that was made for sin, not cleaning up shite, and hair that could put Jennifer Aniston's to shame any day, when it wasn't pulled back for work into an unflattering ponytail. Lianne had the looks, but she definitely lacked the patience.

'He gave it tae me. I put it here, so's ah widnae lose it,' said Lily, panicking as she scanned the contents of her top drawer.

The imaginary boyfriend, thought Lianne. 'Lily,' she said, humouring her, 'Ah think ah know where it is. Ye gave me it laist night afore ye went tae sleep. Ah put it in mah loacker . . . You git yirsel back tae bed an ah'll git it fir ye.'

Lily looked at her contemplatively.

Lianne suspected she'd been half sussed, but the medication was due to kick in soon. Besides, she wanted a quiet night. She pulled back Lily's sheet. 'You git yirsel in there an ah'll go and git it,' she said. Lily thought for a second, then threw a skinny, wrinkled leg on to the bed and hauled herself on to the mattress.

Lianne watched her climb into bed like a child who'd just been promised a bag of sweets if she was a good girl and stopped messing about. It was the same psychology; only the age was different. Lianne thanked God that old age was in another lifetime for her, if at all. She was young, she had her looks. She couldn't imagine being thirty. Thirty years old? She'd die off. She saw women of that age in the clubs, trying to look young, laughing and joking with the young guys, enjoying the attention. It was worse when they were forty, mutton dressed as lamb, their husbands at home, watching the weans while their women looked about desperately for anyone who would pay them the slightest bit of attention under dim ultraviolet lights that could make Quasimodo look good. After the DJ had played the last song the white fluorescent lights would come back on and the guys soon sobered up. Bugger that, thought Lianne. Old age can git tae fuck.

Nathan and Karl got out of the van and stretched. Karl looked up at Craigellachie House: he was sure he'd seen this place before in a Hammer horror film. A smiling woman waved at him from an upstairs window, as if he was a lost relative. He waved back, expecting her to be one of the nurses or a cleaner, then realised, as his eye fell on a lower-floor window which a Down's syndrome man was licking, that all was not as he had expected.

'Don't worry, they're quite harmless,' said Keighley, walking up the corridor. Nathan and Karl followed close behind her, looking about suspiciously as though the patients were going to jump out of the shadows at them. Eyes were fixed on the new arrivals from either side of the corridor. Fresh meat, thought Karl. Keighley was the closest thing they had in here to Buffy the Vampire Slayer.

Scotland, and their first dealings with the natives. Surrounded by fucking nutters. They wouldn't stand a chance if this lot kicked off. Karl had a vision of throwing the nurse to them and running like fuck. Nathan smiled at a guy with red hair and overgrown sideburns that made him look like a ginger werewolf. He had a small brown ball in his hand, which he tossed in the air and caught as he stood watching them. Karl swore to himself to have a word with that bastard Ellis – he had a lot of explaining to do. *Hospital?* It was a funny farm, for Christ's sake!

'Maist ay the patients ye see huv bin rehabilitated an assessed as well enough tae go back an live in the community,' said Keighley. Karl snorted derisively. Keighley ignored him.

'Because ay the lack ay Social Service funds there's nae council money tae care fae them ootside,' she said. 'It's actually coastin the council mair tae keep them *inside*.' Nathan shook his head at the twisted logic.

Keighley continued along the corridor, noticing the way Karl was looking at the patients. Nathan saw that she was on to him and tried to make an effort on their behalf. He smiled broadly at a man in his fifties who had his back pressed firmly against the wall. He wore a denim jacket with the collar turned up and his hair was jet black, cut in a DA like a rock-and-roller from a fifties film. 'Awright, mate?' enquired Nathan, nodding at the Rockabilly Rebel as they passed by. The guy smiled back suspiciously, then looked away, pressing his back harder against the wall. Give up, thought Nathan.

'That's Rob,' said Keighley. 'Thinks he's Elvis Presley . . . *sometimes* . . . In times of stress. It's how he deals with it.'

'Elvis is alive and well and living in Scotland then, is he?' asked Karl, with more than an ounce of cynicism.

Keighley stopped in her tracks and turned to face him.

She'd had enough of his smartarse comments. Karl stopped too, knowing he'd hit a nerve. Nathan stood behind him, looking nonchalantly about the corridor – this wasn't his argument.

'Rob comes here oan a voluntary basis,' said Keighley. 'He can live quite happily in the community wi his family.' She stared at Karl, awaiting his words of wisdom. An *electrician* versus her professional diagnosis. No contest.

'He's got a family?' asked Karl. 'So what's he doing coming in here then?'

'He *chooses* tae come here. It helps his development.' She furrowed her brow and stared at him in a way that said *he* was the odd one out today in this establishment.

'What? You sayin there's people out there who aren't one hundred per cent sane and we're walkin about among them?' Karl asked.

'Well,' said Keighley, with a wry grin at Nathan, 'you should know. Yir the wans livin in London, aren't ye?' She turned on her heel, walked up the corridor and went round the corner. Karl flicked a 'What's her problem?' look at Nathan, who smiled back at him: *Touché.*

Karl hurried up the corridor after Keighley: he didn't particularly like her but she was the only person who could provide a bit of safety from whatever was lurking here. Nathan watched him scurry after her and laughed to himself as he followed them.

*   *   *

Karl stood with his hands in his pockets, looking about the ward at the patients who carried on as though he wasn't there or as if they couldn't see him and Nathan. He sighed deeply as he checked out the metal cable trunking that housed God knew what delights. He scratched his neck and listened to his four-day-growth bristle. The sooner he got checked in to the guesthouse and had a shit, shower and shave the better. He felt as though he'd been cooking one all the way from London. He looked about at the patients, then at Nathan, who raised his eyebrows at him.

Keighley grabbed a metal trolley that was standing near the door and pushed it out of the way into the corner of the room. One man sat on his bed, gazing at them and holding his camera as though his life depended on it. Nathan watched him polish it with his sleeve. He nodded at him, wondering what the bloke's story was. The man gave him a half-smile as he wiped his camera again.

'There's aboot twenty nurses between the five wards,' said Keighley. She indicated across the room. 'Eddie ower there is usually oan the same shift as me an Lianne.' They looked over to where a large, gangly male nurse sat playing cards with three patients. He smiled and waved.

'How ye doin?' Keighley asked him.

Eddie indicated an almost empty cigarette packet, then the pile of cigarettes sitting in front of a young, overweight patient with dark greasy hair and jowls that wobbled when his head spun round with a smile. 'He's thrashin me,' he said.

Keighley laughed. 'Serves ye right – you taught hum the gemme.'

Karl was puzzled. 'Wait a minute . . . are you sayin there's only one bloke and you two women on this ward?'

'Aye,' she replied.

'But what happens if one of them kicks off . . . you know, gets violent?'

'We press an alarm bell,' she said, indicating a red button on the wall. Karl noticed two other buttons, strategically placed. 'We soon git help. Anyway, ah don't think ye've much tae worry aboot,' she said. 'We don't huv axe murderers, necrophiliacs or serial killers at Craigellachie House. Carstairs usually gets *them*. We jist git the borin wans – manic depressives, the senile . . . the *casualties ay society*.'

'Casualties of society? Is that what you call them?' Karl looked at her as if she was the one who was mentally ill for buying into that particular regime. 'London's full of people who are *casualties of society*. You can't walk round a corner where I live without bumping into a nutter. They don't get free bed and board,' he said, then saw that his choice of words hadn't been particularly apt in his present surroundings.

'Well, since yir goin tae be here fir a while it might be

best if ye try an git tae know wan or two ay them . . .
They won't bite ye,' Keighley replied, then indicated a
shaven-headed young man perched on the edge of his
bed, who watched them like a dog chained up in a
backyard into which they'd just jumped the fence. 'Then
again, Jonty might. He thinks he's a Border terrier.'

'You're joking?' said Nathan, glancing between Jonty
and Keighley. 'What kind of treatment does he get?'

'Well,' said Keighley, glancing at her watch, then at
the clock on the wall, 'it's mainly discipline – keepin
hum aff the furniture an that. Ah mean, jist look at hum
noo. He knows he's no allowed up on that bed. Nae
bone fir him tonight.' She smiled wryly at Nathan, who
caught on to her humour and sniggered quietly, then
tried to stifle it. Karl looked at her sarcastically as if to
say, 'Very funny. *Nurse humour*, is it?' She gave him a
cheeky smile that told him to lighten up. Karl realised he
was the odd one out here and would get on a hell of a lot
better if he made an effort. The last thing he needed was
to upset a nurse with an attitude who might go to her
boss, who would get on to Ellis and have them taken off
the job before they'd even started. Fuck that, he thought.
Not after all the driving they'd done to get up here.

He watched the bloke with the camera take out a box
from his bedside unit and open it to reveal a bunch of ten-
by-eight black and white photos, which he started to lay
on his bed. A photo enthusiast, thought Karl. Something
they had in common. A year ago he'd started a portrait-

photography course but had had to give up because of work pressures. He'd wanted to be able to take pictures of his two angelic, beautiful girls that would do them justice. He'd bought a Minolta SLR from an Irish bloke he once worked with: Franny Sheehan. Three weeks into the job and Franny's missus had run off with a bank manager. Franny had decided there was nothing left for him in London so he sold off all his stuff to raise the fare to Ireland. The camera came boxed with the manual, the lot. Franny had hardly used it. A steal at fifty quid. Karl swotted up on the manual, then ran a couple of films through it and grasped that the camera could think for itself. It gave him a cracking picture every time he left it on 'P' for program. He couldn't go wrong with it.

He walked over to the camera man's bed. 'What you got there, mate?' he asked, looking down at the almost identical black-and-white photos of the moon that were strewn about the bed. The man looked down at the floor, avoiding Karl's gaze. Karl glanced at the camera. A Nikon F2. Not bad. He'd learned a bit about cameras and their value since he'd had his Minolta.

'That's Stuart', said Keighley to Nathan. 'He only ever takes photies ay the moon. It's a wee bit ay an obsession wi hum actually. He's moon daft.' Nathan wondered how she could deliver information like this and make it sound as if she really had an interest in these people. Maybe she did.

'We've bin tryin tae encourage hum tae tek photies ay

other things, but ah don't really think he's ready fir that yet.'

'Hey, that's really good, that.' Karl eyed the detail of the moon's craters on one photo. Stuart nodded and handed him another that had been taken half an hour later. 'What kind of lens do you use for that, then?' asked Karl, looking for a difference between the two prints. Stuart was starting to come out of his shell. Lenses, film speeds, aperture, reciprocity failure: you ask it, he'd answer. 'Eight hunnert mil mirror lens. Needs tae be on a tripod, though, cause ay the camera shake. Ah took that wan oan a four hunnert speed – twenty-second exposure at F8,' he said, touching the edge of the photo in Karl's right hand with his forefinger. Karl gave him a knowing smile: the speed of this guy's actions and his slow relaxed speech must mean he was doped up to the gills with elephant pills or the like.

Billy put his head round the door and saw Stuart talking to the new visitors. He'd have to put a stop to this.

Keighley indicated the ward to Nathan. 'This is where the main works tae be carried oot. There's also the other four wards, corridors, offices, staffroom, front of the buildin and the security system, bit ah'll let ye see fir yirselves. Yis kin huv a look aboot an ah'll tell mah boss yir here?' She raised her eyebrows. Nathan grinned and nodded: they'd be fine. She gave him a good-humoured smile and walked off. Nathan couldn't help checking out her arse as she went through the door and turned left up the corridor. He wondered what it was like under that uniform. It was fit, that was for sure.

He noticed one of the patients creeping round the door and into the ward with a mischievous smile on his face and a Sellotape-repaired police hat on his head. Nathan watched him as he walked slowly along the ward, glancing at Stuart who was sitting on his bed, handing Karl his photos.

Nathan's attention was then drawn to a guy at the far end of the room as he picked up a glass bottle of juice from on his bedside cabinet to pour his friend a drink. He shared a joke with the man as he added iced water from a jug. They were just like a couple of mates in a pub, having a laugh and a drink. Nathan watched the bloke in the police hat as he slid under the guy's bed. The two men glanced down at him, then evidently decided to ignore him and carry on their conversation. Nathan watched in disbelief as the fat bogus copper struggled to pull himself along on his belly. He'd seen some strange things in his time . . . He thought about drawing Karl's attention to the guy in the police hat approaching him, but he'd find out soon enough.

Billy's fat face popped up two beds behind them. He sniggered, then bobbed back down and slid across the polished floor like a commando to end up underneath the bed next to Stuart's.

Stuart handed another ten-by-eight to Karl, who had by now lost interest.

'Nee-naw, nee-naw!' shouted Billy, leaping out from behind the bed. Stuart jumped up and dropped the box of photos on the floor. He tried to pick them up but Billy giggled and jumped on his bed. Stuart took a step back, as though fearful for his life. Karl backed off too, not knowing what the hell was going on here. Where the fuck was that nurse to control these cunts?

'It's the polis!' Billy shouted, pointing at Karl.

'I am not!' said Karl, slightly indignant.

'I telt ye they were comin fir ye!' said Billy, gleefully. He bounced up and down on the bed, laughing like a small boy. Stuart went white and turned to Karl. Karl wondered whether he should explain this false accusation, if it was worth trying. Stuart shuffled backwards and forwards, looking past him, trying to get round him like a cornered rat. Karl stepped back, allowing him to dart past and bound across the ward.

'Nee-naw, nee-naw. Yir *lifted*, pal, yir comin wi us!' Billy shouted after him. Stuart put his hands over his ears, knocking Nathan to one side as he lurched through the door.

'Chopped ham with pork, corned beef, something to make a butty wiv in the mornings for the job. We're here to make some money, mate, not be out eating out at cafés every day,' said Karl, as they walked along the high street. 'We need a loaf and some marge as well.'

'You'd be lucky to find a café round here,' said

Nathan. 'Anyway, what do you mean marge, you skin-flint bastard? I can't eat that shit, I want butter.' He looked about for anything that resembled a supermarket. Harry McPherson, kilt-maker, Anne McBride, woollen shop, a post office, a butcher, a quaint Scottish pub with an unpronounceable name. Where the fuck was Tesco's?

'Hey, start as you mean to go on,' said Karl. 'All that butter shit clogs up your arteries – it's not good for you. You'll be thanking me by the time we've finished here for showing you the light.'

'Just show me where the guesthouse is and that'll do me. A quick shower and we can be out on the town.'

'I think we're *in* the fuckin town, mate.' Karl stopped in the middle of the pavement and looked about. 'Ere, what's the local football team around here – Hibernian, is it?'

'Nah, it's Glasgow Rangers, innit? Celtic and that,' said Nathan.

'*Chel-sea!*' boomed Karl, clapping his hands above his head.

Two old women slowed down as they approached. Nathan smiled at them, but they glanced at him and Karl fearfully then crossed the road to avoid them, clutching their handbags to their sides.

'We're right oot ay the potted meat yir man likes . . . Soarry aboot that,' said Davie Mackie, the Aberdonian butcher to his regular customer, Mrs Campbell. She wrinkled her face as though a sour fart had just drifted over the counter and perched itself under her nose. She studied the selection of meat, looking as though she'd be here for the day. Davie sighed and tilted up his pork-pie hat to scratch his red scalp, which matched his big red face, that was peppered with broken veins. He glanced at the clock on the wall: five twenty-five. Only another five minutes and he could shut up shop. A nice juicy steak for tea, then off to the Ptarmigan for a few wee drams and a bit of lively crack. Just what he needed after being stuck behind the counter all day, trying to be nice to folk while hiding the fact that his body creaked and ached and his head continued to thump. Hardly surprising after the bottle of Grant's he'd put away last night. Never again. Christ, he was gagging for a pint. At his time of life there wasn't much else to look forward to apart from retirement.

Ding. The door opened, and he jumped. He'd been getting increasingly jittery as the day wore on, with the alcohol dispersing from his body.

Two strangers walked in. Never seen these two before, he thought, and never seen a darkie at all in Glen Leven. Saw a couple in Glasgow once. He looked up at the clock again, five twenty-six, then at Mrs Campbell, then back at the two young men standing behind her. What were they doing coming in at this time of night? The white one calmly pulled out a packet of chewing-gum and handed a piece to the darkie feller. They stood with their backs to the wall and chewed, looking about the shop.

'Yes, gentlemen, whit can ah dae fir ye?'

'You're all right, mate, we're in no hurry,' said the darkie, exposing a row of pearly whites at him. London accent.

Davie looked back at them, an uncertain smile fixed across his face. He'd heard stories about thieves who spent a bit of time casing businesses to get an idea of the takings. They watched you for a few days, worked out when the quietest part of the day was, and when the time was right they grabbed the till. Davie's chest tightened as he remembered what a good day it had been. It was always the same at the weekend: people wanted a nice bit of meat for their Sunday dinner. Only one thing for it, best to call their bluff, he thought, try to get them out of the way.

'Er, it's nae bother, boys. Fit ye after?' he asked, the smile still etched on his face.

'Just you serve the lady here, we don't mind waiting.' The white guy smiled and pointed at Mrs Campbell, who turned and smiled back at them. The dizzy cow! Did she not know what their game was? Davie thought about excusing himself for a minute to go through the back and phone the police, just to be on the safe side, but these boys probably knew what they were doing. They'd soon catch on to him, maybe take his hand off with a cleaver! Londoners were like that when it came down to robbing small businesses, shops and the like. He should know – it was in the *News of the World* every week. He'd have to play it by ear. 'Dis yir man no like a bit ay potted heid fir his piece?' he asked Mrs Campbell. She wrinkled her nose even more and shook her head.

Karl nudged Nathan. 'Did he just say they've potted someone's head? I told you they had some strange eatin habits, didn't I?'

Davie glanced at them, his big red face going white. He felt a trickle of sweat run down his back. Fuck, if he got out of here alive he'd need a dram or two to steady his nerves. He looked back at Mrs Campbell anxiously, then at the clock on the wall: five twenty-seven.

'Ere,' said Karl, nudging Nathan again, 'if he tries to sell me a pork sword or a mutton dagger I'm out of here, mate!' He creased up laughing, and Nathan did likewise.

Mrs Campbell straightened up from the counter. 'Ah'll leave it,' she said to Davie, and walked out.

Nathan and Karl stopped laughing and tried to be serious as they stepped up to the counter to eye the meat. 'Nice ham shank,' said Karl, pointing at the display, then moving his hand in a wanking motion for Nathan's benefit. 'Oh, look, they sell beef curtains!' He pointed at a side of beef as though his day was now complete. Nathan held his stomach and creased himself laughing. Karl tried to keep a straight face and looked at the shop-keeper. Nathan got his breath back and wiped his eyes.

'So, er . . . fit can ah get yis boays?' asked Davie nervously.

'Do you sell wasps?' asked Karl, as seriously as he could.

Davie looked puzzled. 'W-wasps?' he asked. 'No. I'm afraid we dinnae.'

'You sure, mate?' Karl squinted in the warm summer sun as it shone through the front of the shop. 'You've got two in the window.'

Nathan burst into hysterics again and walked across to the door, howling with laughter. He leaned against the jamb to catch his breath.

'I'm only havin a laugh, mate – couldn't resist it,' said Karl, before turning to look at his friend, who was bent double with laughter. Davie tried to smile at the joke, but couldn't. So this was their act. They take the piss out of you, belittle you, laugh and joke at your expense. It was how they got their fun. Then they'd rob you and run to their car, laughing about how shit scared they'd made you feel. The darkie boy had straightened up and was leaning against the door, obviously guarding it. His accomplice stood in front of the counter, acting daft. Any minute now they'd pull out shotguns. Only one thing for it. 'Look, boys,' said Davie, nervously, 'Ah dinnae huv a loat ay money in the shop, ken? We're jist a small butcher's here . . .' He looked at their faces. They'd stopped laughing. The darkie was looking at him as if he wasn't sure he'd heard him right. The look on his accomplice's face was angry.

84

'What did you say?' asked the white guy tightly.

'Ah sais if it's money yir after ah've no goat a lot, ken? This is jist a wee shoap, we dinnae dae much business.'

Nathan snorted and shook his head in disgust. He stepped back from the door and opened it, ready to walk out. Karl moved closer to the high glass counter and pushed his head over it. Davie took a step backwards.

'I don't know who you fink I am, mate, but I'm not fucking *Ken*. And I didn't want your money. I wanted some chopped pork.'

Davie looked at him, puzzled, then at the black guy, whose disappointed expression seemed to confirm what his pal had said. 'Well, why did ye no say?' said Davie, and heaved a sigh of relief. 'How much? A quarter, half a poon?'

'Arsehole,' said Karl, and followed Nathan out of the shop. Davie watched the door swing shut behind them. He looked down at his trembling hands. He was going to have to knock the whisky on the head after all. It was making him far too jittery.

Karl sat back in an armchair in the staffroom, munching a packet of crisps and reading the news in the *Leven Journal*. He'd been slagging off the paper about its news content – 'Crofter Loses Sheep'. 'Twenty poonds reward!' he said, in a mock-Scottish accent. He stopped messing about when Keighley came in. He managed a small smile at her then glanced up at Nathan, who was eyeing her from the ladder as he pulled the new cable through the hole for the light fitting. Probably trying to get a look down her uniform, thought Karl. That dirty bastard was after her. He always smiled a bit too long whenever he saw her. Karl could read him like a book.

He reached across to the table next to his chair for his sandwich box and opened it to reveal a floppy, dog-eared sandwich, which he lifted out. He glanced at Nathan again. His friend's mind obviously wasn't on the job – he was still staring at Keighley. Karl considered saying something to him about the state of the sandwich before remembering that he'd made them *himself* this morning. They'd decided to take separate lunch breaks, half an hour each. That way at least one of them was still working and bringing Karl a step further to his goal of 'getting the fuck out of this place as soon as possible'.

The guesthouse was okay – he had no complaints there. It was clean and tidy, the shower was functional – a high-powered one, just what you needed after a hard day's graft. The landlady, Mrs Grant, had pointed it out to them when she gave them the grand tour. Karl got the impression that the shower was the centrepiece of the guesthouse: she demonstrated it as though it was a top-of-the-range Nicam TV with surround sound and a DVD player sitting on top of it. A million miles away from the hissing portable that sat on the dressing-table in their room and lost reception every time you went near it.

'Feel free tae use the shower whenever you want,' said Mrs Grant. 'It's no like *Risin Damp* here, ye know. Ah'll no be turning the water aff after sivin o'clock.' Nathan laughed at the old woman's quaint sense of humour. Karl smiled politely at her well-rehearsed landlady joke, wondering if he was the millionth person to whom she'd told it.

'The name's *Mrs Grant*, no *Rigsby*,' she said to Karl, nudging his arm. He smiled again and looked back at the shower unit. He noticed it had started to come free of its mounting. Fucking cowboy, whoever fitted it, he thought. He reminded himself to give it the once-over before he took his first shower. He was too young to die.

'It coast a wee bit but it was worth it. Aw mah customers comment oan whit a good shower it is,' she said, and shuffled away along the landing. Karl followed her, carrying his holdall. She stopped outside a room and reached into her cardigan pocket for the key. 'This is yir room,' she said.

'Do you mind me asking, how much did you pay for it?' Nathan was mesmerised by the unit hanging precariously on the wall.

She gave him a quizzical look. 'The shower,' he added, indicating the bathroom as he walked towards her.

'Oh.' She screwed up her face and looked at the ceiling for the answer. 'Ah think it wis nearly three hunnert pounds . . . Aye, three hunnert.' She nodded to herself, as though confirming the figure, unlocked the bedroom door and pushed it open.

'Three hundred?' asked Nathan, looking at Karl. Karl shrugged his shoulders: there was one born every minute. They followed Mrs Grant into the room. She put the key on the bedside unit, walked over to the window and pulled open the curtains. The warm sunlight lit up the silver design on the flowery wallpaper. Karl winced at the décor.

Nathan stood in the doorway. 'That's a bit expensive, if you don't mind me sayin,' he remarked. Mrs Grant had gone over to the two single beds that stood side by side and was turning the covers down. 'Ah know, dear, but there wisnae much else ah could dae. Until you boays came he wis the only electrician roon here . . . To tell ye the truth he's a wee bitty expensive.'

Nathan strolled into the room and put down his bag. 'We could have done that for half the price, couldn't we, Karl?' He sat down on the bed.

'Hmm,' agreed Karl, non-committal, gazing at Ben Leven through the window.

'Well, if there's any jobs that need doing while we're here, you just tell us, eh? We won't charge you a penny,' said Nathan, trying not to react to Karl who was standing behind Mrs Grant, shaking his head and mouthing 'Fuck off.'

'That's very kind ay ye,' she said, 'Ahll bear that in mind . . . Come tae think ay it, mah washin-machine's no bin too—'

'What's that mountain called?' Karl interrupted. Mrs Grant forgot about her washing-machine and ducked her head beneath Karl's arm as if there was more than one mountain out there and she wanted to see which one he was talking about. Karl studied her silver-grey hair. She reminded him of his nan. He could smell her flowery perfume: violets if he wasn't mistaken – the same as his nan used to wear. Her whole house had smelt of it.

'That's Ben Leven,' Mrs Grant said. 'It's lovely in the winter when it's covered in snow. Sometimes ah've known old Ben tae huv snow on hum in *May*.' Nathan smiled politely – until Karl turned away from the window and mouthed, '*Old Ben?*' at him. Nathan smirked and bit his lip.

'So, are ye East-Enders, then?'

Karl took another bite of his corned-beef and plough-man's pickle sandwich. 'Sorry, what?'

Keighley filled the kettle and plugged it in. 'Ye know, East-Enders – "lav a duck, apples an pears," aw that?' Nathan wobbled on the ladder as he giggled at her terrible Cockney accent. She felt glad she was amusing at least one of them. Karl gave her a look that said she wasn't right in the head.

'*Rickeeee!*' She laughed, and took four mugs out of a cupboard.

'More like *Saaf-Enders*, darlin,' said Karl, grabbing a handful of cheese and onion crisps, and stuffing them between the slices of bread to give his sandwich a bit of taste.

'Ah've never bin tae London,' she said, giving the dusty mugs a quick rinse under the hot tap.

'Haven't you?' said Nathan. 'You should go . . . You'd like it.' He hauled on the cable in the ceiling. It freed itself and spilled out of the hole to fall across the ladder. A shower of white plaster dust followed it, covering Nathan's face and hair. He blinked.

'Maybe ah will,' said Keighley, and got out a jar of coffee. 'Ah've goat some holidays comin up.'

'Well, if you're coming down the Smoke you let me know. I'll show you the sights.'

'Thanks.' Keighley turned her back to him and made the coffee.

There was no way she'd ever get down to London, and she knew this guy was teasing her, but she was enjoying it – it wasn't doing anyone any harm. Besides, it had been a while since anyone had paid her any attention.

'Lianne? It's Josh. Gonnae let us in?' *Bzzzttttt*. The front door of Craigellachie House opened. Josh pushed it wide and walked in to see the back of Lianne's uniform as she strode up the corridor. As he watched her he thought that the occasional pleasantry wouldn't go amiss. No chance, he thought. Lianne wouldn't give him the steam off her pish. She was walking briskly, nose in the air, not missing a step. Josh thought he could have been anyone – she hadn't even checked that it was him – but if he'd mentioned it she would have come back with a smart comment like, 'Ah knew it wis you, ah could smell ye.' Cheeky cow.

He wouldn't say no, though. She was as fit as fuck, but she knew it. That was the trouble with birds like that. Over the years he'd found that if you treated them like shite they soon came round. They were too used to having guys all over them. The minute he started acting like he wasn't bothered the bird got a complex and was soon trying to get him to pay her some attention. It had worked for Josh with birds in the past, but he knew he'd have a fucking long wait before anything like that happened with Lianne. Best just to keep treating her like shite, he thought. It was a two-way street.

He glanced back at the van parked outside – Southend Electrical. He'd considered letting down their tyres but decided that one of the loonies who stared constantly out of the windows would probably grass him up to Lianne, who would then grass him up to Colin. There was plenty of time for revenge.

He let the door close and trudged up the corridor. His Reebok trainers squeaked on the tiled floor, as though he had hamsters tied to the soles. He sneered as he passed Colin's office: he was probably in there now counting his money, the fucking tightwad. He hoped the English cunts blew the whole place up – when Keighley was on her day off, of course. *Then* the specky bastard would be sorry he hadn't given Josh the job.

The door to the storeroom was ajar. He moved closer to take a look. A tiny offcut of plastic conduit had got stuck, wedging it open. He looked about – the coast was clear. He opened the door, walked in and turned on the light. He glanced about at the mops, the polish and the huge orange buffer that was propped up against the wall. Tiny red, blue and green cuttings of cable were scattered across the floor. They'd been working in here but hadn't even bothered to close the door properly when they'd finished, he thought. He looked up at the new fluorescent light fitting, then the white plastic conduit which they'd replaced the old metal stuff with. He snorted, noticing that the conduit ran all the way down the wall to the original light switch, which was made of metal. Fucking scrimpers. At least *he* would have renewed that. What was the point of replacing the metal conduit then leaving one of those stupid danger-ous switches? He considered grassing them up, but Colin would put it down to sour grapes or something. Fucking shrinks, they analysed everything. They even had his bird thinking the same way.

He looked about at the quality of the work. Someone should catch on to what these shoddy cunts were like. Then it hit him – *! Fucking ingenious!*

He pulled out an insulated screwdriver and a small torch from his combat trousers pocket. He peered round the door to check that the corridor was still empty, then switched off the light, turned on the torch and put the handle in his mouth. He shone the beam on the light switch. 'Noo, then,' he said, and unscrewed the metal casing around the switch. He disconnected the live and earth wires, sniggering as he swapped them over and screwed them back tightly into the wrong connectors. He pictured the loony from the other day coming in here for his mop bucket, turning on the light and getting a shock, then Keighley coming home from work and telling him all about it. He'd sit there innocently, eating his tea, tutting at the thought of one of those poor patients getting a shock. Then he'd mention nonchalantly that it wasn't too late: if Keighley wanted to let Colin know he was still available they could tell those Cockney wankers to fuck off and he could come in and do a proper job. He screwed the cover back into place, and sidled out into the corridor.

'Guy the Gorilla's here,' said Lianne, closing the door of the staffroom and flouncing over to the worktop to get her coffee. She glanced across at Keighley, standing beside Nathan, offering him a biscuit. Keighley gave her a look.

'Whit?' Lianne sipped her coffee. She always referred to Josh by names like that. Keighley had never seemed bothered about it before. She watched them from across the top of her cup. Nathan was looking suspiciously from her to Keighley as he munched a Hobnob. Lianne glanced down at Karl, who was reading a paper. Mr Charisma, she thought sarcastically. Although, come to think of it, he did have a certain way about him. Mean and moody. Married, though. It was stamped on his forehead.

'Where is he?' asked Keighley, putting down her mug.

'He's oan his way up.' Lianne grinned, and plonked herself next to Karl on the old worn two-seater couch.

Keighley sighed and left the room. Karl glanced up from his paper. Lianne gave him a cheeky grin and he looked at her for a second, then flicked his paper and continued to read.

'Who's Guy the Gorilla?' asked Nathan.

'Hur boyfriend,' said Lianne.

'Oh,' said Nathan, flatly.

She could have sworn his face dropped. She smirked to herself as she drank her coffee. This was going to be fun.

Josh sat on the edge of the bed, putting on his Cat boots. The sound of Keighley singing in the shower drifted into the room above the hiss of the water. What was that song she was singing? One of those old ones again probably. He was embarrassed to let anyone see their CD collection on the rare occasion that they entertained, and he was always quick to point out to people that it was *her* taste, not his. He glanced across at the CDs in the unit – *Music To Watch Girls By*. Tony Bennett. Frank Sinatra, Shirley Bassey, Nina Simone. He was sure half of them were dead. This lot were out before his old man was even born.

Keighley had a good voice, though. Everyone always said so. They were forever asking her to get up and sing in the pub. That's what had made her stand out from the crowd when he first arrived here. He remembered his second night in the village: a few of the old boys were at the bar, drinking to old Donnie McBain's memory. Josh's claim to fame was that he was the last person to have drunk with the old buzzard so the whisky was flowing in his direction all night. He'd been listening to stories about Donnie from his brother, Pat McBain, who stood at the bar next to him. A bowling bag sat on the floor by his feet. Sixty-five years old, old Donnie's wee brother. He'd been telling Josh about how he wished he'd had the chance to say goodbye to him. The last time they spoke they'd had a stupid argument about Donnie nearly losing Pat's bowls. He'd been that drunk he'd forgotten what he'd done with them. It was only tonight that Brendan the barman remembered they'd been put for safekeeping behind the bar. They'd been there all the time.

Josh had turned away from the bar, thinking. You never know the minute. It was then that he saw her: a small bird with spiky blonde hair, pert tits and a lovely smile, sitting at the back of the room with a few of her friends. He watched her laugh, but he could tell her heart wasn't in it: something else was on her mind. There was something sad about her. She looked across to the bar, stared right through him. He watched, transfixed, as she stood up and came across the room in his direction. He took a swig of his whisky as she approached the bar. 'Pat?' she said.

Pat turned round. Josh glanced at his face: his old features were etched with sadness, and his droopy eyelids were red and sore-looking after all the rubbing he'd done to them throughout the day. The amount of drink he'd had wasn't helping: it made him more emotional. Josh saw the old boy's face light up at the sight of her. She held out her arms and gave him a hug, almost squeezing the life out of him. A tear ran down her cheek and she sniffed. 'Ah'm so soarry, Pat,' she said. 'He wis a lovely auld feller . . . a real gentleman.' Was this the same bloke? thought Josh. Was she talking about the old Jakey in the pub?

'Thanks, darlin,' said Pat.

'How're ye copin?' she asked, wiping her eyes with the back of her hand.

She was gorgeous. Josh wanted her to turn round and look at him so he could smile at her – let her know that everything was going to be all right . . . Then, when she was crying on his shoulder he'd slip the hand . . .

'Ach, ye know,' said Pat. 'Wannae they things, isn't it? Happens tae us aw,' he said bravely.

'The funeral's Thursday, Mags wis sayin?' she said, reaching out to hold his hand.

Josh watched jealously, wishing *he* had just lost a relative.

'Aye . . . ah'll see ye there, eh?' said Pat.

'If there's anything ah kin dae?'

Before Pat could respond, one of the other old boys standing near him said, 'Gie us wanna yir songs, hen – liven this place up a wee bit, eh?'

She looked at Pat, who nodded. 'Well, it is supposed tae be Karaoke Night,' he said.

Keighley walked over to the small stage, in the middle of which sat a karaoke machine. The place was usually swinging at this time of the night but old Donnie's death had put a dampener on things. No one had dared to get up and sing out of respect for Pat but now he had given the okay it was different.

Josh watched in awe as Keighley stepped on to the stage and picked up the mike. She announced a one-minute silence for old Donnie McBain – a well-respected pillar of the community, he'd be sorely missed. Josh glanced about at the thoughtful faces. Had the old boy really been that popular? Maybe it was because he'd been the only spark around here and now they knew they would have to pay Josh the going rate. He felt a fart coming on and clenched the cheeks of his arse. The last thing this lot wanted to hear was a **parp!** in the middle of the silence. If anything was guaranteed to be bad for business, that was it.

Keighley had pressed play on the karaoke machine, and the haunting melody of Clannad came from the speakers. Josh had listened, spellbound, as the voice of an angel soothed his soul. He'd heard old Pat sigh beside him . . .

Ahh, thought Josh now. *That* was why he liked the song so much – it reminded him of the night when he'd fallen in love.

He heard the shower turn off but the singing was still coming from the bathroom. He tied his bootlace, stood up, walked to the window and looked down on the street below. He watched Moose bouncing along the pavement, looking lively and energetic. The couple of cans he'd had in the house before coming out would account for the spring in his step. Josh considered banging on the window to attract his attention, then changed his mind as Keighley came in wrapped in a towel, her short hair sticking up where she'd rubbed it dry. She threw a pair of clean white panties and a bra over the back of the grey leather armchair and waltzed across to the CD player. He caught a whiff of shower gel – she smelt good enough to eat. She picked up a Frank Sinatra CD and clicked open the cover. He caught a glimpse of her cleavage as she knelt on the carpet and put the disc in the player. He could swear her tits were looking smaller. Come to think of it, her shoulders were skinnier too.

'Are you losin weight?' he asked.

'Oh, ye've noticed, huv ye? Five pounds this week – whit dae ye think?' She stood up, opened the towel and displayed her lithe naked figure. He glanced at the window, aware that the blinds were open. Sinatra sprang into life and sang 'The Lady Is A Tramp', almost as a cue for Josh to do something in case the neighbours saw her.

'Whit huv ah telt ye aboot that?' he said, marching over and pulling down the blinds. A shaft of sunlight streamed through one of the narrow slits and glinted off her golden bush. She stood in front of him, awaiting his approval.

He scanned her up and down. 'Ye look fuckin gorgeous,' he said. He felt his cock stir in his jeans. She'd lost weight, all right – in fact, she looked like someone else. It wasn't as though she'd been fat before but she was prone to putting the weight on her arse. She turned round to give him the full effect. Her arse still looked the same. Mind you, there was nothing wrong with it in the first place. His cock twitched again. He moved over to her, put his arms around her waist and nuzzled her ear. His hand ran down her flat stomach and rested on the warm mound between her legs.

She smiled, pulled away his hand and turned to face him. 'Ah've jist hud a shower.'

'So huv ah.' He grabbed her and pulled her closer to him, pressing her stomach against his semi so she'd get the message. She eased herself away from him and reached for her bra. She started to put it on so that *he* would get the message. 'Ah said ah'd meet Lianne at seven. She'll be waitin fir me.' She glanced at the clock on the hi-fi: 18.50.

'Fuck Lianne – let her wait.' He came closer. Keighley grabbed her knickers and stood on one leg like a stork while she put her left leg in. 'Ah'm aywis keeping hur waitin,' she said, holding on to the armchair with one hand while putting the other leg into her knickers. He stood behind her and rested his hands on her waist. She could feel his hard-on through his jeans, digging into her back. She pulled up her knickers. He grabbed the sides and pulled them down again across her hips. She tried to turn round to face him but he held her shoulders firmly from behind and nudged her with his groin, shuffling her towards the back of the chair. He kissed the nape of her neck and pressed her against the hard leather armchair while he undid his belt with one hand and tugged her knickers down further with the other.

'Jo-osh!' she protested, 'Ah'm tryin tae git ready!'

'Come oan, it'll only tek a minute.' He held an arm round her waist to stop her getting away, then pulled her knickers down over her knees. They dropped to the floor. She tried to pick them up but he stood on them with one foot so that she would have to step out of them if she wanted to move anywhere. He put a hand on her back and pushed her gently over the high-backed seat.

'Josh, pack it in – Ah'm no in the mood!'

'Keighley, ah cannae help masel. Ah luv ye – ah want ye aw the time, darlin.' He undid his zip and tried to pull down his jeans with one hand.

She tried a different approach. She held on to the chair and tried to lever herself back on to her feet: if she could get to the bedroom she could lock herself in and get ready while she reasoned with him through the door. He pulled his jeans and boxers down, and pressed his hard dick against her lower back.

'We'll dae it later – ah promise!' she said, knowing he was past the point of no return. He ignored her and pushed himself against her. 'Ah'll huv tae huv another shower,' she said. 'Josh!'

He held her over the chair with one hand and grabbed his cock with the other. He bent his knees and wedged it between her legs, standing up again so that she was resting on it, as though she'd just slipped off a bike seat and on to the crossbar. She was scared. How could she get out of this one? 'Josh! Ah'm no even wet! Will ye stoap it?' She flailed her arms backwards and writhed from side to side, but he grabbed her by her neck and pinned her down over the chair. She could hear him breathing deeply and felt him forcing himself upwards and into her. She held her breath, waiting for the pain that was about to come. She tried to kick him but it was too late. She thought about what he had said. He *loved* her? This wasn't love.

*   *   *

Gavin was easy: he could take or leave work, but he knew Moose felt differently. If he had no work Moose would start to panic and couldn't settle until he got something. Right now, Gavin had no choice: there was nothing doing with Josh but hopefully Moose would find something elsewhere for them.

Gavin tuned in Moose's TV to a spare channel for the Dreamcast. His friend's two eldest, Michael and Derek, waited excitedly, cheering when he succeeded. Gavin smiled. The poor buggers, they never had much. He thought back to when he was ten, the same age that Michael was now. He was sure he'd had more then than Michael had now, and that was fifteen years ago. Derek was a year younger than his brother: the trainers he had on were Michael's cast-offs. Gavin remembered because he had bought them. His one and only pair of Adidas. Now Michael got shit in school from the other kids because he didn't have decent trainers, just Asda ones. They could be right cruel wee bastards, kids, when they put their minds to it. Anyone who looked different or didn't conform, anyone who stood out, was a target. Gavin reminded himself that Michael's birthday was coming up soon. He'd get him a decent pair this year. That's what uncles were for.

He wasn't their real uncle, but they'd always called him that. He liked it – it made him feel like part of the family. Moose's wife Jeanette was always nice to him, confided in him. He was a good listener, that's why.

Never judged, just listened, and tried to offer advice wherever he could. That's how he knew Michael was being bullied – Michael had told him, making him swear not to tell his ma or da. Gavin had kept his promise, but one dark night he had followed the bully, George Sweeney, and pinned him against a wall. He held a blade against the kid's throat and snarled through a rubber mask of a wizened old man that if he ever – *ever!* – heard that he was picking on any of the other kids in school he'd slit his fucking throat while he slept. George was so scared his legs gave way underneath him, and Gavin left him crying in a pool of his own piss, while he darted off back through the streets, pulling off the mask and stuffing it into his pocket with the blunt penknife. He'd felt guilty afterwards for using such shock tactics on a kid, but it had worked. A few days later he asked Michael if he was still taking crap from George Sweeney. Michael laughed and said he was as quiet as a mouse now, and in fact *George* was the one getting picked on. He couldn't figure it out. None of the kids could.

Gavin handed the boys the controls and sat on the settee next to them. Jeanette came in, carrying a small plate with a slice of cake on it and a cup of tea. She was thirty-six but still good-looking, even after three kids. Her long blonde hair hadn't lost its shine, and still looked the same as it had when she was a teenager. When he was younger he had had a crush on her. She'd always talked to him because he was sensible, and a pal of her brother Philip who'd left Glen Leven to join the army and was now making good money. Gavin sometimes wondered if he should have joined up with his pal, but it was the year before the Falklands and Gavin realised that if he didn't get his bollocks shot off in Ireland then it would be by some Argie so he had decided to stay at home. The only consolation about the Falklands was that on many a night Gavin got to comfort the crying Jeanette, who worried herself sick over her younger brother. Gavin knew he should have made his move on her then, but He'd hung around too long, as usual, and now she was Moose's woman.

Moose didn't deserve her, thought Gavin. He didn't deserve these kids either. He should have got himself a proper job, instead of ducking and diving, claiming invalidity while he was out in all weathers doing jobs for everyone, then drinking the money while the kids went short. He only escaped being grassed to the dole because he was well liked in the village. People accepted him for what he was. He was harmless. So was Gavin – that was how he, too, got away with signing on and working on the side – because he always worked with the 'gregarious Moose'.

'Here ye go, Gavin.' Jeanette handed him the plate and put the tea at his feet.

'Oh, Jeanette, ah couldnae. Ah'm full up,' he protested.

'Well, if you don't eat it, it'll go tae waste. *He* won't touch it.' She pointed upstairs towards the bathroom, from which came the sound of running water. Moose had been up there for the past half-hour. He'd said he was only going up for a shave.

'Thanks.' Gavin took the plate and perched on the edge of the settee to eat his cake as Michael and Derek selected their options on the game.

'Hey, you,' said Jeanette, tapping Derek's shoulder. He looked up at her, annoyed by the disturbance. 'Watch they big feet ay yirs oan Uncle Gavin's tea.' She pointed to the mug on the beige carpet, then went back through to the kitchen. Gavin looked down at it. Brown stains mingled with the swirling pattern, reminding Gavin of the many nights he sat on the carpet with Moose and spilt more than his fair share of beer. Gavin always went into the kitchen for a cloth, but Moose rubbed it in with his foot saying, 'A hoose is fir livin in.'

'You are a very useful engine.'

Gavin looked to the corner of the room where two-year-old Sean was playing with a *Thomas the Tank Engine* train set. He'd been amusing himself quite happily for the past half-hour, not a peep out of him. He was a good kid – they all were. Moose was a lucky bastard and didn't even know it, thought Gavin. He stuffed the last of the cake into his mouth and took a mouthful of warm milky tea. He put the mug on the table out of range of Derek's size sixes, and shuffled over on his knees to Sean.

'Whit's hus name, wee man?' asked Gavin, pointing to the red train with a mad-looking face.

'James,' said Sean.

'Is he a steam engine?' asked Gavin, lying on his side and pointing to the black funnel on James's head.

'He's a *splendid* engine,' said Sean.

Derek giggled as he frantically pressed his thumbs on and off the control pad. The sound of racing rally cars came from the TV. 'He aywis says that, don't ye, Sean? He knows aw their names, ye know.' There was a screech and a crashing sound from the TV. 'Aw shit!' said Derek, then turned round to see if Jeanette was in the room. He glanced at Michael and grinned.

'Who's this wan?' asked Gavin, holding up a green engine.

'Henry,' said Sean.

'An this wan?' He held up an evil-looking black engine.

'That's naughty Diesel. He played a trick oan Duck,' said Sean.

'Did he noo?' said Gavin, amused.

Jeanette came in from the kitchen, carrying Sean's night-time bottle. 'Right, wee man, bedtime.'

Sean jumped to his feet and hid behind Gavin, swinging on his neck and almost choking him. 'No!' he shouted.

Tina walked round to catch the imp. 'Come oan, milky bottle an bed. It's late.'

She reached out for him but he darted behind the settee. 'No – want tae play wi mah trains!'

'Ye kin play th'morra, come oan.' Jeanette walked over to the settee, but Sean climbed up on to a box of toys and toppled, like a midget gymnast, over the back of the settee, landing on Michael, who pushed him away and on to Derek.

'Aw, Sean!' Derek tried to free himself from Sean's legs, which now entwined his arms. Tina grabbed the toddler, knocking the control pad out of Derek's hands. 'Mu-um!' It was too late – **SCREECH, CRASH!** came from the TV. Thanks to Sean, Derek had lost the game.

Sean kicked out, catching Derek on the side of the head. Derek slapped his leg and Sean burst into tears. At last, an excuse to greet.

'Hey, smartarse, whit huv ah telt ye aboot hittin hum? He's only a baby!' Jeanette hoisted Sean up to her shoulder and clipped Derek around the ear.

Gavin hauled himself off the floor, stood up and stroked Sean's soft curly blond hair to calm him. Sean turned, still crying, and held out his arms for Gavin to give him a cuddle. 'De ye think he'll go up fir me?' he asked, and took him for his mother. Sean put his arms around Gavin's neck. 'He might dae,' she said. 'He's dog-tired – hasn't slept a wink aw day.'

'Probably gone past it, huven't ye, wee man?' He looked at the purple rings under Sean's eyes. 'Ah'll tek hum up an tell hum a story, eh?' he asked. She gave him a look that said, 'Give it a go,' and handed him the bottle. 'Ye kin find oot whit's keeping *hum* an aw while yir at it.' She indicated the bathroom.

As Gavin, reached the top of the stairs, the bathroom door opened and Moose came out, with a razor in his hand and shaving foam down one side of his face. Gavin noticed how frighteningly skinny he was when he didn't have a shirt on. A prisoner-of-war, alive and well and living in Glen Leven. Gavin thought that if he ever looked like that he'd hide himself away, not go flaunting it. Moose breezed out of the bathroom and tickled Sean under the arm. 'Yir no greetin, are ye?' he asked. 'Eh?' He tickled Sean, who laughed. 'Eh? Whit ye greetin fir?' Gavin struggled to keep hold of the little boy and the bottle.

'Are ye away tae yir bed, then?' asked Moose.

'Yes.' Sean cuddled into Gavin's shoulder. Gavin kissed his forehead. He loved the wee feller more than anything. The proudest day of his life was when Moose and Jeanette had asked him to be godfather.

Moose kissed his son's cheek, leaving a small blob of shaving foam. 'See ye in the morning, wee man.' He went back into the bathroom. 'Ah'll no be long,' he said to Gavin.

Gavin took Sean into his room and laid him on his bed. He wiped the foam off the child's cheek and looked about the room, which was covered in Thomas the Tank Engine posters. 'Here ye go, wee feller.' Sean took the bottle from him and Gavin watched him suck it. A wee person lying in a large single bed. He was big enough to argue with you but he was still only a baby who wouldn't go to bed without his bottle of milk.

'Budge up,' said Gavin. Sean moved nearer to the wall, and Gavin lay on the bed next to him. 'Whit story dae ye want?'

Sean took the teat out of his mouth and muttered '*Jurassic Park*,' then replaced it.

Gavin had met Jeanette in the village the other day and she had told him that Sean's latest obsession was *Jurassic Park* and that he'd been acting out scenes from the film. She'd had to stop the other two showing him the video because it was giving him nightmares. He'd been waking up in the middle of the night saying a dinosaur was in the garden, trying to get in his room. Gavin supposed a story wouldn't do him any harm, particularly if Sean was the hero. He looked at the ceiling for inspiration.

'Wan day Sean drove hus car aw the way tae Jurassic Park . . .'

The teat came out of Sean's mouth again. 'Big Jeep,' he corrected, before replacing the teat and continuing to listen for mistakes.

Gavin smiled to himself. 'Sean drove hus *big Jeep* tae Jurassic Park, an when he goat there the gates were locked and aw the dinosaurs were inside. He knocked oan the gates an a man opened them an Sean drove hus big Jeep through the gates an—'

'Welcome to Jurassic Park,' said Sean, and continued to suck.

This could go on all night, thought Gavin. 'That's right. The man said, "Welcome tae Jurassic Park, Sean."'

Moose appeared in the doorway and watched them, Gavin talking a load of bollocks about dinosaurs, and his wee boy lying beside him. He realised he hadn't had a lot of time for his kids lately, but Gavin was great with them, especially Sean. Suddenly he felt jealous, redundant, as though anyone could come along and do his job. As though Jeanette could move him out and another bloke in. The kids would soon forget him. He told himself he was being stupid. The kids loved him. Jeanette loved him. If he could just stay at home the occasional night and talk to them, find out what the boys were up to at school. He vowed to make the effort, but he knew that when it came down to it he couldn't be arsed. 'Ye ready?' he said. Gavin stopped talking and looked at Sean. He was fast asleep, the bottle hanging out of his mouth. He looked at Moose and smiled proudly.

'We'll huv tae git you tae tek um up every night,' Moose joked, then left the room.

Gavin got up and took the bottle out of Sean's mouth. He went to pull the cover over him, then remembered how hot it had been lately and left it pulled back. He bent down and kissed Sean softly on the head. 'Goodnight, Sean . . . I love ye, son.' He walked out of the room and pulled the door to.

*　　*　　*

'You stay in if you want to – I'm going fuckin stir crazy.' Nathan sat on the edge of his bed and rubbed his damp hair with the clean white towel.

Karl stood at the dressing-table mirror, splashing aftershave around his face and neck and stopping to pick at a spot on his chin. 'I'm just sayin we should watch what we spend, that's all,' said Karl. 'We came here to make money, you know, not go blowing it.'

'Money's not the only thing that'll be getting blown tonight, mate,' said Nathan, standing up and grabbing the crotch of his boxer shorts.

Karl shook his head, as if this was a really bad idea. 'It's that fuckin nurse, innit? You want to steer well clear of her, mate, she's trouble.'

Nathan pulled on his freshly ironed black jeans. 'I'm just havin a laugh.'

'Yeah? Well, *don't*. I don't want to have to scrape you off the wall after *Guy the Gorilla*'s plastered you there.' He dipped his forefinger in a jar of hair wax, wiped it on to one of his palms, then rubbed his hands together briskly. 'Look, we'll go down there and have a couple of pints, keep ourselves to ourselves,' he said, bending down and looking in the mirror. He smoothed his hands over the ends of his hair, spiking it up, then flattening it down in an age-old ritual.

'Listen to Mr Sociable there,' said Nathan, reaching for his silver-grey shirt. 'You sit in the corner all night if you want but I'm here to have a bit of fun.'

'Antagonise the locals, you mean?' Karl pulled a few strands of hair forward, then went across to the sink and rinsed his hands. 'You fink that guy's gonna sit there all nice an quiet while you flirt wiv his bird? You know what these Jocks are like – he'll take your fucking head off your shoulders.'

'Look,' said Nathan, buttoning his shirt, 'if this was a bad idea, Keighley and Lianne wouldn't have invited us. They say the place is a laugh.'

'What's it called again?' asked Karl.

'The Tommygun or somefin.'

'Sounds fuckin charmin.' Karl reached for a towel.

'They have a bit of a singsong, a laugh and that. You could fuckin do wiv a laugh, you miserable cunt,' said Nathan.

Karl dried his hands and cracked a smile. 'Yeah, all right, but I don't wanna be up there every night. I'm here to make a few quid then get home to me wife and kids. Especially now Ellis is dangling the carrot.'

Nathan sat on the bed and pulled on his socks. 'What exactly did he say when he phoned? Did he mention how much the bonus would be?'

Karl scrunched up his face. 'Just that the sooner we get the job done the more there'll be in it for us.' He paced about the room as Nathan pulled on his shoes. 'I mean I don't mind doin twelve-hour shifts, you know.'

Nathan was incredulous. Had he heard him right? 'You what?'

'Yeah,' said Karl, trying to be nonchalant. 'I'm easy
. . . days or nights, don't bother me what I do. You
could do days if you like.'

'You have got to be kidding!'

Karl could see there was no way Nathan would go for
it. 'Just a thought,' he said, holding up his hands. 'I'm
only trying to think of ways to get it finished quicker.'

'April the nineteenth, eighteen sixty-six,' said Nathan,
pointing a warning finger at Karl as he walked across to
the door. He pulled it open and took the key out of the
lock.

'You what?'

'The date slavery was abolished. And don't you
fuckin forget it.' He tossed the key at Karl and walked
out of the door.

'That's right,' said Karl, following him. 'Can't think
of anything constructive to say so you just play the race
card. Ere, I'm glad my missus aint black – I wouldn't
stand a fuckin chance.'

'Jist hoad oan a minute, ah'm fuckin burstin.' Moose
ducked behind the shop, stood up against the wall and
pulled down his fly. 'Keep an eye oot, eh?'

'Can ye no wait? We're nearly there,' said Gavin.

'When ye've goat tae go, ye've goat tae go, big man.'
Moose stared down at his dick for signs of life. 'Come
oan.'

'That's prostate trouble,' Gavin commented.

'Eh?' Moose shook his dick in an attempt to wake it up, but it slept soundly while his bladder threatened to burst.

'Yir prostate gland. Ye feel like ye want tae pish aw the time but ye cannae go. Ye should git that checked oot.'

'Ah wid if ah hud the time.' Moose put away his dick, zipped up his fly and came out from behind the shop.

'Whit dae ye mean ye've nae time?' asked Gavin, as he set off in the direction of the Ptarmigan.

'Wi work – ah'm a busy man.' Moose held his bladder and winced, remembering the last time he had a pain like that he pissed blood for a week. It cleaned up itself in the end though. He took a deep breath and tried to keep up with Gavin.

'We've nae work oan,' Gavin said. He knew Moose's trouble – scared of doctors. Moose would rather die in ignorance than have someone poke about at him.

'Ah huv,' smiled Moose. 'Slabbin joab fir auld Mrs McNeil. Wants hur driveway monoblocked an slabs oot the back an aw. Sais the garden's gittin too much for hur.'

'Ye lucky git,' said Gavin.

'Ah'll need a hon, though.' Moose glanced at him.

'Right, yir oan.'

Moose checked for traffic and crossed the road with a spring in his step. He could already taste his first pint of Guinness. Gavin followed close by.

'That's no aw. Hof an oor after ah goat that, Boabby McVey asked us tae landscape hus gerden.'

'Yir jokin?' said Gavin, remembering the size of Bobby's sprawling grounds.

'Ah'm no.' Moose grinned. 'He's awready hud a couple ay quotes, so ah sais ah'd dae it for hof the price, but no till the end ay the week wi me huvin this monoblock joab oan.'

'Ya jammy wee basta,' laughed Gavin.

'So, better dig yir lawnmower oot, then, eh?'

'Aye.' Gavin smiled as they neared the Ptarmigan. Buying those trainers for Michael would be easier than he'd thought. With a bit of luck he could shame Moose into buying Derek and Sean a pair too before he drank the lot.

Nathan and Karl walked down the main street towards the Ptarmigan. The smell of ale, cigarette smoke, aftershave and perfumes floated out of the pub to meet them. Nathan breathed in deeply, catching a faint whiff of sweat from his armpit. Fuck, he'd forgotten to put on his deodorant. An hour in this place and he'd have two huge wet patches under his arms. He slowed his pace, considered telling Karl to go in without him while he ran back to the guesthouse to get it, but he knew Karl would say, 'Fuckin forget it then. Let's just get a couple of cans and watch the film.' Balls to that. They'd done that every night since they'd been here. If he saw another Channel Five film starring Donna Mills he'd go nuts.

As he approached the door Karl slowed to allow Nathan to catch him up. They stepped into the busy pub and made their way to the bar. A few of the young guys were wearing dirty T-shirts that they'd obviously been working in all day – Nathan noticed this and lightened up about his lack of deodorant.

'Lager?' asked Karl.

'Yeah.' Nathan glanced at the men next to him, knocking back pints of what looked like bitter. The smell of wood came off them. He glanced down at their workboots, which were covered with shavings, and noticed their bags at the foot of the bar. A yellow-handled chainsaw was propped against one.

Fucking hell! Nathan turned to check out the crowd and told himself to keep an eye on these boys. If a riot broke out he'd be well out of that door before the chainsaw got picked up.

He looked about, avoiding eye-contact with the big guys, aware of the occasional glance in their direction. A bunch of forty-plus women sat in one corner, drinking cocktails and laughing. They looked as if they were celebrating something – getting out of the house, prob-ably. Then he noticed Keighley, sitting with Lianne and a bunch of others near the back of the room, which was almost an extension of the bar. She was enjoying herself, singing with Stuart and the patient who looked like

Elvis. 'Elvis' stood up and swung his hips. His top lip curled as he sang. Nathan strained to hear, but behind him a jukebox burst into life, booming out a tune from an accordion band. He watched Keighley throw back her head and clap at the outrageous antics of the Elvis impersonator. Shouldn't she be discouraging him, Nathan wondered. He watched as she ran her tongue across her top teeth, noticed how white they were. How fresh-faced she was. A blonde elf. The Elvis guy swung his arm around like a propeller and continued to sing.

Nathan heard a '*Yee-ha!*' from behind him. He turned to see a couple of guys linking arms, doing some sort of barn dance to the music on the jukebox. He turned back to Keighley, who was screaming with laughter now. Nathan glimpsed her smooth, lightly tanned stomach and pierced belly button. The white crop top she was wearing strained against her breasts, showing the outline of a sports bra. She was lovely, like Angie must have looked ten years ago, but classier . . . much, much classier . . .

'Ere you go.' Karl edged his way out of the queue at the bar and handed Nathan a pint.

'Cheers.' He took a long, satisfying swig.

Karl looked about the room and did the same. 'Fuck me.' He screwed up his face. 'What's this?' He was staring at the froth on the pint as though it harboured a lethal poison.

'The local lager, mate. Better get used to it.' Nathan

smiled as Keighley caught his eye and stood up, waving him over. He grinned at Karl and started to move towards Keighley, but Karl tapped his arm and handed him his pint. 'Ere, hold this, will you? I'm goin for a slash.' He walked off through the crowd to the gents'.

'Hiya,' said Keighley, beaming up at Nathan.

'All right? This where all the action is, then?'

'It's a wee bit quieter than usual,' she said 'There's only a few ay the boays fae the Forestry Commission in tonight. The rest huv goat shinty practice or somehun . . . Want a seat?'

'Yeah, sure.' He sat down and nodded at Stuart and Rob. 'Who's this gorgeous creature?' he asked, smiling at Lianne. She couldn't stop herself smirking at his cheek. 'Could it be . . . No, not Lianne,' he said, 'wearing makeup and smiling for a change?'

'Ye mek me sound like ah'm a right miserable basta.'

'Only havin a laugh. You look lovely, both of you. Those uniforms don't do you girls any favours, you know.'

'Tell me about it,' said Lianne

Stuart nudged Elvis, indicating the one-armed bandit, which was now free. He'd been watching two of the guys from the Forestry Commission win a fiver on it, then put at least twenty quid in it to try to win the jackpot. It was time to clean up. Stuart got up, delved into his pockets for change, and trudged across the room to the machine before anyone else got there. Elvis followed him.

Karl appeared, back from the gents', and stood near the table. He looked about the pub, then down at Lianne, sitting there, relaxed and confident. He smiled at her, and she beamed back. She looked different away from work, he thought. She was quite attractive, with her hair down, flowing over her shoulders like a silky brown mane. He'd never noticed her eyes before. They were startling. Bright. And those lips. She took a drink from a half-pint glass and licked them as she looked him up and down. Suddenly he felt naked. Christ, she was checking him out! He diverted his gaze.

'Ye huvin a seat, Karl?' Lianne asked, and indicated the one next to her. Karl turned back to her. 'Oh, yeah, right,' he said. He sat down, his eyes arrested by her drink: a half of lager with a shot glass sitting inside it.

'What's that?' he asked.

'Depth Charge,' she said. 'Glass ay lager wi a Glayva in it. It gets ye pished. Taste it, it's lovely.' She held the glass under his nose. He took it, noticing the red lipstick print on the rim. He looked into her piercing blue eyes, thinking that if he drank from the glass it would be the closest he'd ever get to kissing those full red lips. As he watched they broke into a smile. God, what was he thinking? He was sitting close. *Far too close.*

'Go oan.' She nodded at the glass. He raised the glass slowly to his lips and sipped, studying her. She wasn't threatening. She was a pussycat . . . no, *a pussy. Pussy Galore.* Kiss me, Miss Moneypenny. Oh, fuck.

He tried to read her expression. Women's faces often said one thing while their bodies said another. What was hers saying? Will you make love to me? *Yes – no problem!* He handed the glass back, nodding as though he had been pleasantly surprised. 'It's not bad, actually.'

'Told ye,' she said, raising the glass to her mouth and finishing the last drops. 'Three of them and ah'm usually strippin aff or somehun.'

'How many you had?' he asked, taking a gulp of his pint and grimacing at the difference in taste.

'Jist wan.'

'I'd better get you another then. I'll make it a pint, eh?' He pretended to get up and rush to the bar as fast as he could. She laughed. He stopped, smiled back at her and sauntered over to the bar. She was all right, Lianne, he thought . . . once you got to know her.

Old Roddy McIntyre sat at a corner table with his back to the bar. He put down his whisky and sighed. He'd heard enough. For the past couple of hours Josh and his mates had been trying to outdo each other with their crass jokes and foul-mouthed opinions. Usually it wouldn't have bothered Roddy, but there was a time and a place for everything. He looked at the expression on Isabel's flushed face. His wife wasn't used to this. They'd come in here at about six o'clock and had a nice bar meal – a curry for him and steak pie for her. They'd sat discussing their grandkids, Morvern and Ross, a funny wee pair. Then Josh had bounded in with his sidekicks, and the atmosphere in the room had changed. The noise level had increased tenfold and there had been no more conversation from Isabel. She sat quietly in the corner, trying to look as though the rowdies spouting filth at the bar, didn't bother her but after thirty-two years of marriage Roddy could read her like a book. It was time somebody said something. He stood up, smoothed down the front of his open-necked Fred Perry and glared at Josh. 'Haw, big yin, gonnae put a lid oan it?' he shouted, the authority in his voice surprising him. Josh turned round slowly. Roddy dug his hands into his pockets.

'Whit?' Josh frowned.

'Ah sais, gonnae wrap it? There's women in here.' He nodded at Isabel. 'They don't want tae huv tae listen tae language like that!'

'Don't they?' said Josh. 'Well, they kin fuckin drink somewhere else then.' He turned back to Moose and Gavin.

Roddy pulled a chair out of his way and made his way over to the bar. Some of the older blokes stopped talking and nudged each other. Roddy noticed people watching him, but it was too late to back down now. Besides, if Josh got out of hand there were enough big blokes in here to stop him before he hit Roddy . . . he hoped.

He stood behind Josh, looking up at the back of his

head. His thick neck reminded Roddy of a bull. He took a deep breath and tried a different approach: the voice of reason. 'Josh.'

Josh turned and looked down at him, impassive. Roddy recognised the look, and told himself to keep the head. This guy was like a big spoilt kid: he didn't like being told what to do.

'Look, China . . .' said Roddy, 'aw ah'm sayin is ah like comin here fir a quiet drink wi mah missus, right? Ah don't want hur tae be listenin tae aw kinds ay stuff aboot shaggin an fannies an aw that – know whit ah mean?' He smiled at Moose and Gavin for support but they didn't respond.

'Is that it?' Josh continued to stare down at him.

'Aye . . . ah'm only tryin tae git ye tae see it fae oor point ay view.' He indicated Isabel in the corner, then held his hands out innocently.

Josh leaned so close to Roddy that their faces were only inches apart. Roddy could smell his sour breath. His heart-rate quickened as Josh's eyes searched his.

'Well, now ye kin see it fae mine. Ah spend a loat ay money in this pub – ah'm in here every night. The laist thing ah need is some auld **cunt** like you telling me whit ah can an cannae say . . . *Awright?*'

Roddy realised there was no talking to him or his mates. There was only one thing for it. Back down. No one would think any less of him for that. Everyone could see he was no match for the big feller, and if Roddy was stupid enough to swing a punch it would mean suicide. He had his grandkids to think about, for God's sake.

There was only one thing Roddy could do: change pubs. There was always the Glen Tavern but this had been Roddy's local for over twenty years. Josh poked a finger into the centre of Roddy's thin chest, knocking him off balance. 'Noo, git yirsel back tae yir missus, ya scrawny wee rat ye.' Roddy turned and walked back to Isabel, who was putting on her coat.

Josh drained the remainder of his pint and slammed the glass down on the bar. 'Same again, Brendan,' he said.

Karl leaned on the bar, waiting for his change and trying to avoid the big guy's eye. If he'd do that to an old boy there was no way he wanted to cross a mad cunt like that. He looked down at the drinks in front of him. The Glayva in the Depth Charge swirled about at the top of the shot glass.

Brendan handed him his change. He put it into his pocket, picked up the drinks and walked back to the table. He put down the drinks – Lianne's Depth Charge, a pint for Nathan and a vodka and Coke for himself. He'd given up on the lager. 'Are you sure you don't want anything, Keighley?' he asked.

Keighley shook her head. 'Naw, thanks, ah'm tryin tae cut doon.' She lifted her glass of white wine. 'Wine's one ay the maist fattenin things ye kin drink, ye know.'

Karl sat down beside Lianne, who smiled at him again, making him feel uneasy. He was only having a drink with her but he felt as if he was having an affair.

'You don't need to go on a diet,' said Nathan, looking Keighley up and down.

'Ah've goat an erse like the back ay a bus!' She laughed.

'No, you ain't – you've got a lov—' Nathan stopped, aware that he'd already gone too far. He looked to Karl for help, but Karl just smirked and bit his top lip to stop himself laughing. Nathan knew what he was thinking: 'Out with it, man, there's no going back now.'

Lianne leaned forward in her chair. 'She's goat a whit?' she asked.

Nathan picked up his drink and took a mouthful of lager. 'Nuffin.' He looked over the rim of his glass, wishing the ground would swallow him up.

Keighley nudged him, almost spilling his beer. 'No, c'moan, Nathan, don't be shy – oot wi it. Ah've goat a whit?'

'A lovely arse – all right?'

They all burst into laughter.

'Happy now?' Nathan said.

'Oh, yeah – very!' spluttered Karl.

'Bastards!' said Nathan, and laughed with them.

'Ye no gonnae introduce me?' said a voice from above them. Keighley stopped laughing. Josh was standing behind Karl's chair. He couldn't have heard Nathan's comment or Nathan would have been flying across the room by now. No, she could tell by the look on Josh's face that he was trying to be smart. He had no interest in meeting these guys, only noising them up. Keighley wondered what would come out of her mouth right now if she'd taken a truth drug – *'This is supposed tae be mah boayfriend, mah lover, but he's the man who raped me before ah came oot tonight. The man who cannae tek no fir an answer. He's a bully who hits me when I don't dae as he says. Ah'd ditch him in a second if the right person came along . . .'*

'This is Josh . . . mah boyfriend,' she said to Nathan and Karl, then looked away, almost embarrassed.

Nathan stood up and proffered a hand. 'Nice to meet you, Josh. I'm Nathan, this is me mate Karl.' Josh looked him up and down, ignored the hand and Karl. Nathan withdrew his hand, sighed inwardly and sat down again. The guy must have heard what he'd said about Keighley.

'Yous are the English, aren't ye?' Josh was nodding at them as though he'd just put two and two together. Nathan noticed the contemptuous way he said it – *English* – as though it was a dirty word. He glanced at Karl and noticed his hackles were up. He hoped he'd keep his mouth shut . . . but from the expression on his face he could see there wasn't much chance of that.

'Not the *entire nation*, mate, no,' Karl replied. Moose and Gavin had appeared behind Josh, and Nathan studied Keighley and Lianne's faces to see if trouble was on the cards, but the girls were cool.

'*Ah* wis lined up tae dae that joab,' said Josh. Keighley rolled her eyes.

'What? The job on the hospital?' Karl asked.

'Aye,' said Josh, with a glance at Gavin and Moose. Gavin took a swig of his pint.

'Us an aw,' said Moose.

'Sorry about that,' said Nathan.

'No hof as soarry as ah um, pal,' said Josh. 'See, ah hud tae knock back work tae tek that joab oan. Then yous come along an underprice me.'

'Fuckin oot ay order that,' piped up Moose.

Fighting talk.

'Hold on a minute, mate,' said Nathan. 'We don't know nuffin about prices – we're just sparks, workin for an agency. They send us where the work is.'

'Is there nae work in London?' asked Josh.

'Course there is . . . but the job's here, innit?' Karl butt in.

Josh looked him in the eye. 'Mek a good livin in London, dae ye?' he asked.

'Not bad,' said Nathan. 'You?'

'Ah did . . . until yous cunts sterted comin up here an tekin oor joabs,' Josh replied. It sounded like a threat.

Karl picked up his drink. 'You should be more worried in case we nick your women, mate.'

Lianne sniggered. Josh glared at her. 'Aye, well, yir

fuckin welcome tae that one,' he said, jerking a thumb at Lianne.

'Gonnae fuck aff oot mah face, Josh?' Lianne snapped. 'Ah came oot fir a drink wi mah pals – yir no wan ay them.'

'Don't fuckin stert, Lianne, jist cos ye've a drink in ye.'

'Dae ye blame me – huvin tae look at your ugly coupon every time ah'm in here?'

Nathan leaned forward. 'I fink it's time we were goin,' he said to Karl, who didn't move. Nathan fixed him with a steely glare.

'Don't go cos ay *hum*!' said Lianne, looking at Josh as if he was something she'd just trodden in.

Josh grinned at them unpleasantly. 'See ye, boays. Don't stoap till ye git tae Carlisle.'

Karl stood up and edged his way between Josh and Moose.

'See you at work tomorrow, eh?' Nathan said, to Keighley and Lianne.

'See ya, girls,' said Karl. Lianne watched them as they shouldered their way through the crowd and out of the front door.

Josh pushed past Lianne and sat down beside Keighley. Gavin took Karl's seat, and Lianne tried to smile at him: he wasn't like the other two.

Keighley saw the triumphant look on Josh's face. She hadn't forgiven him for what he'd done earlier. 'Gonnae tell us whit that wis aw aboot?' she asked.

'Eight hunnert years of bein oppressed,' said Moose, then headed for the gents'.

'Yir anti-English,' said Lianne.

'Pro-Scottish darlin.' Josh drank some lager.

'Is that whit ye call it? Either way yir a racist.'

'Ah'm no a racist.' He looked to Gavin for support.

Keighley tried to think of one good reason why she should stay with Josh, but she couldn't. Lianne was right. He was a bully, a control freak, only happy when everyone else was dancing to his tune. He wanted to keep her in his pocket and bring her out when he felt like it. If she didn't fall in with his wishes she'd get a smack. Psychiatric nurse? She was more screwed up than most of her patients. It was as though her father was still here, but now in the figure of Josh. History was repeating itself: a man was wearing her down, chipping away at her self-esteem until she felt totally worthless and had to depend on him. Well, that was it, she thought. Self-diagnosis over. Time for some therapy.

'You want to stay out of that big bastard's road – and keep your mouth shut.' Nathan stomped along the road towards the guesthouse. He checked his watch: 9.10. Another early night. Fucking wonderful.

Karl followed behind him. He wasn't too bothered. He'd saved himself a few quid by coming home early – and he'd only missed ten minutes of the Channel 5 film. That Donna Mills bird was in it and she was all right, her. 'I'm not having some porridge-munching fuckin local givin me shit!' he said to the back of Nathan's head.

Nathan pushed open the gate, walked up the path, took out his keys and opened the front door. 'Yeah, well, just stay away from him, before we get in deep shit.'

'Fair enough. I'll stay away from him . . . and *you* stay away from *her*.'

Nathan avoided his eyes, walking off up the dark hall towards their room. Karl closed the front door. This job was getting more complicated by the day.

Josh sat up in bed and stretched. Keighley had slipped out this morning without a word. Her face was tripping her in the pub last night – she'd been hanging around with that Lianne for so long she was starting to act like her. He looked at the clock. Almost nine. Time to get up. Then it hit him. Get up for what? He had no work on today. In fact, he had no work on for the rest of the week. Panic set in.

His brain went into overdrive as the paranoia mounted. His first concern was the mortgage deal he'd struck when he bought this place – a fucking steal at the time, fixed at 3 per cent for two years. He was paying less for this flat than he'd been paying in rent back in Glasgow. But he was tied to the mortgage company for five years, and after two years at paying 3 per cent

they reviewed it and offered you the best deal they could
– the best deal for *them*. He'd been checking out the
newspapers lately, and now knew that in a couple of
months, when his two years were up, he'd be paying 7 or
8 per cent – more than twice what he was paying now. He
couldn't go elsewhere else either because he'd have to buy
himself out of this deal and he had fuck-all in the bank.

Then there was the van. He'd only bought it because
he was in the money at the time and the work was
flowing in, but now the work was drying up. He'd
wondered if someone else was nicking the jobs, but if
there was another spark on the patch he'd have heard
about him in no time. And these English bastards had
their hands full at the nut-house – they'd be hard pressed
to take on anything else. What was going on? A boycott?
But the cunts in the village couldn't even organise a
jumble sale. Sure he'd had words with a few of them, but
nothing that could sour his reputation to this extent.

His chest felt tight as he swung his legs out of the bed.
He stood up and walked over to the window. Keighley
wasn't helping matters either, spending money like it
was going out of fashion. He'd have a word with her
later but he knew what she'd say, that she had a wage,
didn't need his money. She didn't need all those fucking
clothes either, but it didn't stop her buying them, did it?

It was like some cruel joke: you work like a bastard
from when you leave school and the minute you start to
get ahead it all turns to shite.

He heard the post drop through the letterbox and he went into the hall to see a handful of envelopes on the floor. He often considered grabbing the postman's hand and hauling his arm through the letterbox shouting, 'you took yir time, ya basta!' Fucking gone nine o'clock and here he was only just meandering up to the door. Cunt was always too busy talking, that's why. Every time Josh saw him he was bumping his gums to someone on the street.

He bent down and picked up the letters. Two for her – one from the catalogue – a fucking bill probably and an application for a Barclaycard. He looked through his own – Reader's Digest – fuck me, he thought, *Open immediately – You may have already won Fifteen thousand pounds!* 'Aye, so ah fuckin huv.' He looked at the next envelope. Brown. TV Licensing. *Bastard.* He'd forgotten that was due. He looked at the next one and immediately wished he hadn't. It was another brown one with Inland Revenue on the front.

He ripped open the envelope and pulled out the letter. A Girobank slip. They didn't owe him money, surely? Then he read the letter. *Self Assessment – Statement of Account.* His eyes scanned the page. **How fucking much?**

He stared at the figure in the bottom right-hand corner.

Six grand?

He scanned the letter again – couldn't make head or tail of it. He thought he'd paid up to date. Then he remembered that fucking weasel of an accountant explaining the tax system to him. You paid an estimate based on the previous year. Last year he was minted, this year he was scratching his arse. **SIX GRAND, DUE NOW** – and that was only half of it: he'd owe double that in January. The pain came back in his chest. He considered phoning the tax office to say he was going to bill them for work *he* might be doing for *them* in the future. If they asked him what he was playing at he could tell them: same fucking thing as they were.

He threw the letters on to the kitchen unit and switched on the kettle. His head was pounding – it was too early for this shite. He'd have a shower and some breakfast, take his time and be down the Ptarmigan for eleven. Davie the butcher would be in for his lunchtime swallay. He always boasted that he paid fuck-all tax. It was time to find out how he did it.

Lianne unlocked the door of the storeroom to get some kitchen roll. A patient had puked their breakfast all over the place. She reached for the light switch.

(RACK! Her finger stuck to the metal casing. '*Aaaahhhh!!*' '*Ya basta!*' A bolt of pain ran up her right arm and across her chest.

She pulled her hand away from the switch. She was

shaking like a leaf and her chest was tingling. She tried to work out what had happened. It was those two. Too busy laughing keep their minds on what they were supposed to be doing. She slammed the door and marched up the corridor. Fuck the kitchen roll. It could wait.

'Whit ye dein?' The ginger werewolf had been standing behind Karl, tossing a brown ball in the air and catching it for the past five minutes. Nathan had gone to the van for a couple of drums of three-core and Karl wished he'd get a move on. This guy was making him uneasy.

'I'm putting new cable in and taking the old stuff out, mate.' He lay down and hauled a length of cable through the trunking, hoping the guy would take his ball elsewhere.

'Whit ye dein?'

For fuck sake. 'Ere, don't you have to be in the ward or somefink? Nurse Keighley was looking for you before.' He glanced at the guy as the ball landed **slap** in the palm of his hand.

'Whit ye dein?'

'I'm working, mate – *busy*, you know?'

'Whit ye dein?' Toss – **slap**.

Karl didn't answer. If he ignored him maybe he'd go away.

The door swung open and Nathan bounded in. He placed two drums of grey cable on the floor.

'Whit ye dein?' he asked Nathan. Toss – **slap**.

Karl glanced at Nathan. 'Fuckin hell, don't get him

talking – you'll never get away.' He cut the excess off the cable with a pair of pliers, then grabbed the insulation and pulled it back, exposing the red, blue and green wires inside.

'E's all right, aint you, mate? said Nathan, eyeing the ball as the guy threw it up in the air. Toss – **slap**.

'Ere, fling us your ball.' He clapped his hands together and backed up the corridor, putting a couple of metres between him and the werewolf, who tossed the brown ball into the air towards him.

Toss –

Nathan held out his hands to catch it. In the last quarter of a second, when the smell hit him in mid-air, he realised what it was, and caught it.

– **slap**.

It wasn't a brown ball at all. It was shit.

'Oh, fuckin hell!' He dropped the egg-shaped turd and it landed with a **slap** at his feet.

The werewolf, the game now over, shuffled past him and out through the swing door.

'I'm going to be sick.' Nathan held out his hands trying not to touch anything.

Karl caught a whiff of the clay mound on the floor and burst into uncontrollable laughter. 'He fuckin had you there, mate!'

Then Lianne stormed through the swing doors, one of which knocked Nathan's arm and brought his hand into contact with the front of his sweatshirt. 'Oh, fuck sake!'

He looked down at the brown handprint on his yellow Reebok top. Karl howled, and started coughing as though he were having a fit.

Lianne stood stony-faced in front of them. 'Ah want a word wi you two dickheids!' she snarled.

Nathan barged past her towards the door. 'Ave a word wiv im. I'm goin to the bathroom.'

Karl wiped his eyes and started to calm down. 'What's up, darlin?'

'Ah'll tell ye whit's up. Ah've bin electrocuted, so don't you *darlin* me, ya useless basta, ye!'

'Hey, hold on, hold on, what's goin on? What do you mean electrocuted? Where?'

'Follow me,' she said, trying to muster up some restraint. 'Ah'll show ye where.'

Karl took the circuit tester out of his pocket and touched the metal casing. It lit up. 'It's live,' he said.

'Ah know it's fuckin live – it's jist gied me a shock!'

'Yeah, all right, Lianne, there's no need for the language.'

'Fuck you! You've jist nearly kilt me an yir whingein aboot me swearin at ye?'

'I didn't nearly kill you. Something's gone wrong somewhere but I'll have it sorted out in no time,' he said, unscrewing the metal plate from the front of the box. He pulled a small torch out of his pocket and shone it on the back of the switch. He stared at it, puzzled. The live and earth wires were connected the wrong way round. 'Has anyone been in here?' he asked.

'Apart fae you two hof-wits, ye mean?' She folded her arms.

'Someone's been messing about wiv this.' He pointed to the wires with his screw-driver.

'Don't gies it,' she said. 'The door wis *loaked*. Me an Keighley are the only wans wi a key . . . an we're no electricians . . . neither are yous two by the looks ay things!'

'This was all right the other day,' he said, and unscrewed the live wire.

'Well, it's no noo, so ah suggest ye fix it – that's if ye know how.' She turned and stormed off up the corridor.

'Whit's black an broon an looks good oan a darkie?' Josh was holding court at the bar with Gavin, Moose and a couple of boys from the Forestry Commission. Brendan the barman was looking nervously at Nathan, who was sitting at a table with Karl and had turned round on the word 'darkie'.

'A Doberman Pinscher,' laughed Josh.

Moose threw his head back and cackled.

Gavin tried to look as if the joke was funny, but he was squirming with embarrassment.

Josh caught Nathan's reflection in the mirrored gantry. He hoped he'd take the bait, but he continued to talk to Karl.

*   *   *

'I'm goin to ave a word.' Karl began to stand up.

Nathan shook his head. It wasn't worth it. 'If I reacted every time someone made a stupid joke like that I'd go mental,' he said.

Fucking wind-up, that's what it was, thought Karl. He grabbed his bottle of lager and swigged it. 'He's the cunt who messed about with the switch.'

'How do you know?' asked Nathan.

'He was in looking for Keighley the day we started on the staffroom.'

'So?' asked Nathan, unconvinced.

'We'd already done the storeroom *and* tested it. It was okay when we left.'

'Maybe it was a patient.'

'Fuck off – *Patients*. They're only allowed *cutlery* under close supervision. They don't go round wiv screwdrivers on them.'

'Well, you were the one who wired the switch. I only raggled the cable.'

'What the fuck does that mean?' asked Karl, taking offence.

'Are you sure you tested it?'

'Of course I'm sure. If it was live I'd have got a belt off the metal casing when I screwed it back on, wouldn't I?' he said indignantly.

'Maybe you hadn't screwed the live in properly an it popped back out and touched the back of the plate.'

Karl pointed the neck of the bottle at his friend.

'Look, mate, I know what I saw. The live and the earth had been swapped round. It's not somethin I would have done.'

'Not if you were thinkin straight . . . but you haven't been since you got here, have you?'

'You fuckin what?' Karl looked at him incredulously.

'I've seen you – rushin about so's you can get it done and on to the next thing.' Nathan picked up his pint and took a mouthful.

'You cheeky cunt.' Karl was incensed. There's mates for you, he thought.

'Look, all I'm sayin is, your mind's elsewhere, isn't it? On Liz and the girls. I can understand that . . . but it's starting to show in your work.'

'There's fucking nothing wrong wiv my work,' said Karl, angrily. 'At least my mind isn't on fanny all the time.'

'Yeah, all right.' Nathan hoped Josh hadn't overheard that. 'But let's just slow down a bit, eh?' he said.

'So you can spin the job out and pull Keighley?'

'What makes you think that?' Nathan kept a wary eye on Josh.

Karl crossed his legs. 'Because you can't take your eyes off his bird.' He indicated Josh with his eyes. 'And,' he continued, 'you aven't once mentioned Angie since you've been here.'

'Do you fuckin blame me after what *she* did? You said yourself I needed a rest from her – decide what I'm going to do wiv meself.'

138

'Yeah,' said Karl, 'but I didn't know you were going to be chasing the triangle the minute you got up here.'

'I'm not,' said Nathan, unconvincingly.

'If you want to pull birds, mate, you wait till we're back home. At least you know where you are wiv London birds – not like this lot.'

'What do you mean by *this lot*?'

Karl leaned forward, as if dispensing information he wanted kept quiet. 'Scotch birds. They're fucking trouble, mate. You stay well clear, if you know what's good for you.'

Nathan snorted.

'What?'

'So are you saying that black should stick to black and white to white?'

'I'm not saying that at all.'

'Yes, you are – it's the same thing,' said Nathan, aware that he had Karl over a barrel.

'You trying to say I'm a racist?' How could he think that? Karl wondered. Nathan was his best mate and *he* was black.

'You've got racist views.'

Karl finished his lager and put down the bottle. 'Look, mate, if you want to meet a racist you only have to go over *there*.' He indicated Josh with a nod. 'But if you think I'm one just because I hate these cunts wiv a passion then, yeah, I hold me hand up, I'm a fuckin racist.' He cleared his throat. 'Same again?' He got up and went across to the bar.

Josh nudged Moose as Karl approached. Karl glanced at them without acknowledgement. 'Bottle of Bud and a pint of lager, please, mate,' he said to Brendan.

'Ye want tae go easy oan the sauce, pal, it's a big joab ye've goat oan there,' said Josh, patronisingly, for the benefit of his friends.

Karl looked at the grinning faces that hung on his every word. 'I can handle it thanks.'

'Ah'm jist telling ye cos ah've seen it aw before. Boys workin away, drinkin every night, the next day they go tae work wi a splittin hangover, minds no oan the joab. That's how mistakes are made, aren't they?'

The bastard *did* know about the switch. It *was* him. 'Yeah, well, you'd know all about that, wouldn't you?'

'Whit's that supposed tae mean?' Josh moved closer, Moose stepping out of his way.

Brendan put the bottle of Bud on the bar with the pint. Karl handed him a fiver and picked up the bottle, wondering if he was going to drink it or wrap it round this idiot's head. 'The brown wire's the live one, mate, not the green one,' he said.

Josh smiled broadly and looked at Gavin and Moose to make sure they were getting all this. 'Is that right? Well, it seems tae me ye've a bit ay trouble rememberin that yirsel. The way ah heard it Lianne copped a cracker ay a shock off wan ay they light switches ye fitted.'

Karl knew he had two options. He could walk away with the bastard's laughter ringing in his ears, or he could let the cunt know he was well and truly on to him. He settled for option two. 'I fitted it,' he said, 'but *you* fucked wiv it.'

Josh squared up to him. 'Oh, aye? Prove it, kin ye?'

'I'm working on it.' Karl stared at him. This was it. He'd been in this situation a few times before and had never once backed down. He knew he should this time but there was no way he was having anyone treat him like this. He'd rather have a go.

'Evenin, PC Gordon,' said Brendan, loudly. 'Large Grant's, is it?'

'Aye.'

Karl saw the expression on Josh's face change. He turned round. A man in his late thirties with brown wavy hair, like a Brillo pad, and a two-day growth was at the bar. He eyed Karl suspiciously, then turned to Brendan with a forced smile. 'Nae chance ay goin under cover wi you aboot, is there, Brendan?'

Karl saw his chance, took the drinks off the bar and made his way back to Nathan.

'What was that about?' asked Nathan.

Karl placed Nathan's pint in front of him and sat down. He took a long swig of the cold Budweiser to calm himself. 'You know what I was saying before about how much I hate these cunts?'

'Yeah?' asked Nathan.

'Well, times that by ten and you'll get a proper picture.'

Brendan put a large Grant's in front of Sandy Gordon, who picked it up and took a sip. 'Josh, ah wis hopin tae catch ye. Can ah huv a wee word?' he asked.

Josh nodded, panicking. The events of the past week turned over in his head. He'd done nothing illegal. Well, nothing much. Some old bag must have caught on to him ripping her off. Gordon, the fucking do-gooder, had probably said he'd have a word with Josh and get some money back for her. No chance. If he tried, Josh would baffle him with costs and overheads, the going rate and the difficulties he'd faced when he started the old bat's job. Gordon would soon see she didn't have a leg to stand on.

The policeman walked a few feet away from the bar. Josh followed him and waited expectantly.

'Ah wis wonderin, Josh,' he said, 'aboot how a young feller wid git sterted in yir gemme – mah boay, ah mean. He's seventeen.'

So he wanted advice, not to give him the third degree. Josh relaxed. 'Oh, right, well, er, his best bet is tae contact some ay the big companies an git himself an apprenticeship exam sorted oot.'

Gordon knocked back a quarter of his whisky. 'That how you sterted, is it?'

'Aye,' said Josh.

'Thing is, there's aywis a load ay other boays in fir these things, though, isn't there?'

Josh thought back to his own exam. He was amazed he'd ever passed. Just got through by the skin of his teeth, from what he remembered. 'Same wi everyhun, these days,' he said. 'A handful ay joabs an hunnerts ay kids chasin them.'

'Aye, yir no wrang there.' Gordon finished his whisky and grimaced. 'An he'd huv tae move tae Glesga or Edinburgh or somewhere. Hus ma'd no like that.' He raised his eyes to the ceiling as though searching for inspiration. 'See, ah've bin thinkin . . . Whit if he wis tae stert wi someone a bit nearer tae hame . . . someone local . . . a bit like yirsel?'

So that was his game, thought Josh. He'd had it all worked out before he came in here tonight. If he said no then Gordon could make his life hell. Best just to play along. 'Aye, ah see whit ye mean, bit ah'm no getting the work at the minute – ah'm scratchin ma erse lately.'

'Ah don't mean straight away, ah'm talkin aboot when things pick up, like?' Gordon looked at him, hopeful.

'Aye. *If* they pick up.'

'Aye, well, you huv a wee think aboot it an let me know, eh?'

Josh nodded, as though he'd mull it over and indicated Gordon's empty glass. 'Kin ah git ye another, Sandy?'

Gordon looked from the glass to his wristwatch. 'Thanks, bit ah've tae be oan duty . . . Gies a phone at the station when things pick up, eh?' He smiled at Josh, then turned and walked out of the bar.

'Aye, so ah fuckin will,' said Josh, under his breath.

Nathan heard a wolf whistle as he walked up the corridor carrying his toolkit. He thought about turning round then decided against it – probably a wind-up. Then it happened again – sounded like a woman. Best just to pretend he never heard it.

'Haw, sexy, gonnae wait fir me?'

Keighley. Nathan stopped and turned to see her hurrying up the corridor. A damp denim jacket hung limply over her uniform. She caught up with him, smiling mischievously. Her hair was wet and had been flattened by the morning drizzle.

'You're soaking,' he said, like a concerned parent. 'Don't tell me I passed you in the van and didn't see you?'

'I cut through the woods,' she said.

'Aint that a bit dodgy?'

She looked at him as if he had two heads. 'Ah'm a big lassie.' She wiped the rain off her forehead. Nathan thought that if she could look this good first thing in the morning she must be really something late at night wearing just a—

'Why'd ye no turn round?'

'I thought it might have been one of the patients.' He started to walk slowly up the corridor, making the most of the time he had alone with her.

'Did ye think it wis auld Lily?' She hitched her black leather bag over her shoulder. 'She says yir lovely,' she teased.

'Get lost.' He laughed.

'She dis. Sais ye look like a young Harry Belafonte.'

He threw back his head and laughed. 'My mum likes him – no way?'

'Hoanest!'

'You just love winding me up, don't you?'

'Aye, ah dae . . . cos you've goat a nice laugh.' Her eyes were fixed on the white polished tiles as she walked. She knew she shouldn't have said that but she couldn't help herself. He *did* have a nice laugh, an honest one.

'Thanks,' he said. 'I, er, thought you might have been in the pub last night. You only go out the one night a week, then?'

'A hud stuff tae dae,' she looked up at him, 'wash mah hair an that, ye know?'

Nathan guessed she was staying out of his way to avoid a repeat performance of the other night. 'We saw your boyfriend and his mates in there last night,' he said, as he pushed open the double doors and stood back to let her through. He caught a hint of her perfume as she brushed past him, the unmistakable smell of Lace. He remembered a girl he used to go out with, Melody – the only black girl he'd ever had sex with. She had worn it. It was inexpensive, but nice. On the rare occasions he smelt it now it brought back to him how they used to stay up all night in her parents' house. Fuck knows what they thought she was doing – playing tiddlywinks probably. Every night they had been butt-naked, rolling around the living room, on the furniture, under the table, in every position they could think of. He'd had to put the palm of his hand over her mouth to stop her screaming when she came. He'd have been lucky to escape with his balls on a plate if her mum and dad had ever walked in on them. Especially as most nights they fell asleep in each other's arms with the birds singing in the front garden.

'Aye he said he seen ye,' said Keighley.

Nathan knew that Josh would have filled her in on the details. 'Yeah . . . I don't think him and Karl are hitting it off too well.'

'You tell Karl no tae worry about hum. He's a basta.'

'Why do you go out wiv him then?'

'Habit?'

He could see she was unhappy. He wished he could sort it out for her. A girl like that didn't deserve to have an overbearing bullying bastard for a boyfriend. She deserved someone more like . . .

'Ye dae somehun fir so long it jist becomes second nature, disn't it?' she went on. He nodded resignedly, remembering Angie. He could see Keighley was looking for an easy way out. She deserved one.

'Sorry,' he said, 'I'm being nosy – it's none of my business.'

He swapped hands with the heavy toolbox as they approached the staffroom and went to push the door open.

She held his arm to stop him. 'No, listen, it's awright – ah want tae talk aboot it. Ah've only goat Lianne an she hates Josh's guts. Ah need someone to talk to – git mah heid straight, you know?'

Did he know? Did he fucking know? His head had been cabbaged since he met Angie. He knew only too well. 'Well, I'm here if you need me,' he said.

'Thanks. I might jist tek ye up oan that.' She took her hand off his arm.

'Hey, I mean it – any time,' he said.

She smiled sheepishly as though she had no intention of taking him up on his offer. He hoped she would. Half an hour, even ten minutes alone with her was all he needed. He'd get her to see sense. He pushed open the door and she smiled her thanks at him as she walked into the staffroom.

'Tommy's shat himsel again. Cunt's bin throwin balls ay it up the fuckin walls aw mornin.' Lianne was at the worktop, briskly stirring a mug of coffee. 'The minute ah think ah've goat it aw cleaned up the basta dis it again . . . Oh, an Lily's bein a right pain in the erse. Sais she's reportin me fir callin her a crabbit auld cunt. Gonnae gie hur a milligramme ay Lorazepam?' She glanced at

Keighley. 'If ah go in there ah'll only skelp hur roon the jaw!' She raised the mug to her lips.

Keighley looked at Nathan wryly. 'Back tae reality,' she said.

If he got his hands on the bastard who'd dented the door of his van he'd fucking swing for them. Now it would have to be garaged for the best part of the day and cost him well over a hundred quid into the bargain. Well, fuck it, it could wait. There was no way he was throwing money away like that. But he had appearances to consider. If anyone commented on it he could say he knew who'd done it and that he was going to give them a couple of days to come forward. If they did, he'd say nothing else about it. If not, they'd suffer the consequences. The place would soon be buzzing with stories about the big man being on the warpath and the guilty cunt would soon come up with the cash and an apology.

Josh sat at a table in the Ptarmigan and raised the double whisky to his lips. A pint of lager sat in front of him, untouched. Fuck it. He was on a mission to get pished. Besides, *The Pink Panther* was on this afternoon. He needed a laugh. He could sit here getting quietly arseholed and watch it on the pub TV.

He looked about. A couple of the old boys sat at a table in front of him playing draughts. He tried to imagine himself when he was fifty, whiling away the days with an old version of Gavin and Moose. Fuck that.

He'd have made his millions and be as far away from here as possible by then. With Keighley? Who knows? Probably not. She'd been staying out of his way. He knew it was because of the other night. He hadn't been able to stop himself. She was looking so fit lately and she hadn't been coming up with the goods as often as she used to. She always complained of him being drunk. What did she expect? It was the only way he could get a decent night's kip with all the fucking worry he had over work. She didn't have a clue – just carried on spending as if there were no tomorrow.

He drained the last of his whisky. He'd have to come up with something quick: it was no good sitting back and waiting for work to come to you, you had to go out and chase it. But where? He could get work in Glasgow, no problem, but it was nearly fifty-mile drive there and the same back. And he'd probably have to go through an agency, which would put him back where he started. No, it was better to ride out the storm. Tomorrow was another day.

He reached for the pint, thinking of ways to create work. He could always fuck about with someone's mains supply but you had to be in their house to do it. If he disconnected or cut through a cable outside it only meant that the council would dig it up and fix it. No, he'd have to be more fly than that.

Old Roddy jumped up and punched the air in victory. He'd cleared the board at draughts. Imagine being that excited over a game of draughts, Josh thought. What was his prize? A fucking dram?

'Right, who's next fir a thrashin?' said Roddy. He looked at Josh. 'Ye fancy a gemme?' Josh shook his head. 'Moan an sit ower here wi us,' said Roddy.

'Ah'm wantin tae watch the film, awright?' he said, indicating the news on the TV. It'd soon be on and he could escape from his problems for a good hour and a half. After that he'd be too pished to remember what they were.

'Oh, well, please yirsel.' Roddy saw that it would be best not to push his luck with the big feller. He felt as though he was still on probation after the carry-on the other night. Ignore him, he thought. His friend returned from the bar and handed him a double whisky. 'Cheers,' said Roddy, raising the glass to his lips. He took a sip and smacked his lips. 'Ahhh, nectar.'

Silly old cunt, thought Josh, and turned back to the TV.

'Fuckin battery's dead. Didn't you charge it last night?' Nathan pressed the trigger on the cordless drill. It spun pathetically.

'I thought *you* did it,' exclaimed Karl. 'It's your drill.' He pressed the trigger on his own and the bit bored through the brick in seconds.

Nathan waited till the noise stopped. 'Yeah, I know it's my drill, but last night you said to leave it out and you'd bung them both on charge.'

'Sorry, mate, must have forgot.' Karl put a Rawlplug into the hole.

'Fucking great.' Nathan looked about the floor for an extension lead: he'd have to use his back-up drill. He hated it. It had more power but it was a pain in the arse – cables everywhere for him to trip over.

Keighley came in, crossed to the fridge and took out a bottle of orange squash. She waved it at Nathan – did he want some? He shook his head.

'It's boilin in that ward,' she said, 'even wi the wind-aes open.' She took a glass out of the cupboard and rinsed it under the tap.

Nathan opened a case and took out his drill. He unscrewed the chuck and placed a bit inside, watching Keighley pour an inch of orange squash into the glass and fill it with water. He placed the key into the chuck and tightened the bit. She raised the glass to her lips and looked out of the window, admiring the red-hot day. A screw hit Nathan's leg. He glanced at Karl, who was looking at him with a mock-adoring expression. Nathan snapped to, annoyed at being caught staring at her. 'Do you know where the extension is?' he asked Karl.

'In the van, probably.' Karl put the bit against the wall and squeezed the trigger on the drill.

Nathan bent down and took the keys out of his toolbox. He trudged across the assortment of screws, Rawlplugs and bits of cable on the floor, through the swing door and into the corridor.

Keighley washed out the glass in the sink and placed it in the dish rack. She walked past Karl, who was oblivious to her as his drill screamed against the brick, and out through the door after Nathan. She watched him walking up the corridor. She liked the way he walked, tall, proud, not like Josh who waddled. If she didn't know better she'd swear Josh had webbed feet. She checked out Nathan's bum in his faded Levi's. Ten out of ten, maybe eleven. Lianne had caught her checking him out when he first arrived and laughed at her.

She wondered what he'd look like with no clothes on, what it would be like to be standing in the same dark room as him, naked. He'd gently kiss her lips, then down her neck and shoulders. He'd pick her up in his strong arms and carry her to the bed. He'd lay her down and kiss her breasts, her stomach, her hips and then . . .

'Are you following me?' Nathan asked suddenly.

'Eh? Oh, no,' she said, as though she'd been caught with her hands in the cookie jar.

'You all right?' he asked.

'Sure.' She stopped in front of him. 'No,' she admitted. 'Look, see – whit ye wis sayin before?'

'Yeah?'

'Did ye mean it?'

'Us talking, you mean?' She nodded. 'Course I meant it,' he said.

She stopped and looked up at the ceiling. 'Oh, whit a mess.'

'What is?'

'Everyhun.' She hung her head. Nathan glanced up and down the corridor to see if anyone was watching them.

She burst into tears. He put his arm round her and pulled her close to him. 'Come here,' he said. He could fell her hot breath against his chest, filtering through his white cotton T-shirt as she sobbed. 'You want to tell me about it?'

She tried to compose herself, wiping away the tears with her fingers. 'Ah'm jist so mixed up.' She took a shaky deep breath.

'Look, don't you think it would be better if we met up somewhere away from this place? I mean, if your boyfriend—'

'I know.' She didn't have to be reminded about Josh.

'What about tonight? Or are you washin your hair again?' he joked. She giggled reluctantly. 'That's better,' he said.

'Soarry.'

'Hey,' he touched her cheek, 'you've got nothing to be sorry about. It's not your fault. I mean, I've been in a relationship like that myself. I know it's not easy deciding what to do.' He pictured Angie, her bedraggled, matted hair as he hauled her out of bed after she'd taken the pills. A million miles away from where he was today.

'Whit did *you* dae?' she asked.

'Oh, I, er . . . I left her.' He nodded, as though confirming it to himself. They heard a key turn in a lock.

'Shit.' Keighley pulled out her keys and unlocked the storeroom door. 'It's Colin. If he catches me stonnin here greetin he'll think there's somehun goin oan between us.' She pulled Nathan into the dark room and closed the door quietly. They heard Colin come out of his office, lock his door and walk away.

Nathan breathed in the smells of disinfectant and air-freshener. He could detect Lace too. He felt her body push gently against his and she was holding his arm for reassurance in the dark. His heartbeat quickened.

'Do you think, er . . . he's gone now?' He kicked himself for sounding so stupid. Of course he'd fucking gone.

'Mmm,' she said, and he felt her breath on his chest as she moved closer to him. Maybe she just wanted a friend, a platonic relationship. Maybe she just felt safe with him? Yeah, that's what it was . . .

'Nathan, kin ah ask ye somehun?'

'Sure . . . what?'

'Kin ah . . . kiss ye?'

His mouth met hers. His tongue brushed her lips, tasting the orange squash and mint from a recent Wrigley's. He breathed deeply filling his lungs with Lace. She relaxed against him and put her arms around his neck, pulling him closer to her. His hands ran down her shoulders to rest on her hips. It would be wrong to go for a feel of her arse, he thought, when she'd only asked for a kiss. She pressed her hip into his groin and he

154

could feel his dick slowly hardening. He eased himself gently away for fear of embarrassment. There was no control over the bastard – it had a mind of its own and was guaranteed to show him up. She started to kiss him more passionately, and her hands slid down his back to rest on his arse. His hard-on dug into her stomach, threatening to pop over the waistband of his jeans and introduce itself to her. He slid his hands over her hips, caressed the outside of her thighs and her arse through her trousers. He could feel the outline of her skimpy knickers.

She pulled her mouth away and laid her head on his shoulder. 'I have to get back.'

'Yeah, me too. He'll be wonderin what's keepin me.'

'Ye still want tae meet up th'night?' she asked, as though she'd ruined the whole thing by making a move on him and he had every right to say no.

'Yeah, course I do,' he said. His dick was still straining to get out of his jeans and he considered going to the bog for a wank, then thought there might be cameras in there to keep an eye on the patients. Hopefully it would have gone down by the time he'd got the drill from the van. 'Where?' he asked.

'Ah'll tell ye where.'

'I'm just goin for a drive, that's all.' Nathan sat in the armchair and pulled on his trainers.

Karl was lying on his bed, eating a Pot Noodle and

flicking through the channels with the remote. He glanced at the TV guide – *A Woman Scorned* was the Channel 5 film. He scanned the page to see if it mentioned Donna Mills. 'What time are you coming back?'

'I don't know. Why?' Nathan straightened his clean Reebok T-shirt.

'There's a film on at nine.'

'So?'

'Well, I was thinking, if you're going to be back in time I might come wiv you.'

'I don't want you to come wiv me. I want to go on my own, all right? We fuckin work together, live together. We're not married, you know.'

'Please yourself.'

Nathan grabbed the van keys and opened the door.

'Give her one from me.' Karl grinned and scraped the bottom of the Pot Noodle carton with his fork.

He'd staggered in earlier and gone straight into the bedroom, demanding sex. He wobbled about, with a fish supper in his hand, and mumbled that it was his right. She'd been denying him for too long – that's why he'd done what he did the other night. Anyway she'd enjoyed it, hadn't she? He plonked himself on the bed and swung his legs up on the duvet, leering at her. A piece of batter fell out of his mouth and landed on the duvet. He disgusted her.

She decided against having a shower while he was in this state – he'd just reminded her what it had led to the other night. She'd get ready when he'd nodded off.

'Keighley . . .' He held out his arms. 'Gies a wee cuddle . . . *c'mere.*'

'Git some sleep, Josh,' she said, and left the room.

'Bit ah want ye.'

She closed the bedroom door and went into the living room, thinking he'd be lucky to raise a chip to his mouth, let alone anything else. She sat at the table and looked out of the open window. She was going to be unfaithful tonight, and she didn't give a damn. No pangs of guilt, no remorse, just pure excitement. He'd driven her to this. Anyway, she was young, wanted a life. Maybe Nathan was the boot up the arse she needed that would make her pack her bags and leave that bastard. If Josh took off tomorrow she'd be the happiest person alive. If she took off he'd come looking for her. It was easier said than done. He'd always said that if she ever left him he'd kill her. She believed he would.

She heard the noise coming from the bedroom. She stood up, crept over to the door and opened it.

Josh was snoring. Keighley went in and winced at the smell: a mixture of farts, alcohol and the fish supper, which now lay on the floor at the side of the bed. She opened the wardrobe and took out a blue micro-skirt and a white crop top. She would be bra-less tonight. And was going to give Nathan a treat he wouldn't forget in a hurry.

'That good, was it?' Karl glared at Nathan, who was on a ladder, absentmindedly screwing a cable into a connector block terminal.

'Hmm?' Nathan hadn't heard the question.

'The nurse – good ride, was she?'

The venomous bastard. He'd been in a mood ever since Nathan arrived home last night. The way he was carrying on you'd think he was his lover.

'It's fuck-all to do with you.' Nathan tightened the earth wire in the connector block and put the light-fitting in position, pushed a long screw through the hole and into the Rawlplug in the ceiling.

'I'm only saying cos it looks like your mind's still on last night's job instead of this one.'

Nathan put the second screw into the hole and started to tighten it.

'Only you've been at that for fifteen minutes. I'd like to get finished here in the not too distant future – get back home, you know. Unlike some.'

'Does your mouth bleed every twenty-eight days?' Nathan climbed down the ladder.

'Hey, you're the only cunt round here, mate,' snapped Karl. 'You want to get your mind on your work and off your dick.'

'Don't tell me what I should and shouldn't do,'

snarled Nathan, folding away the ladder and propping it against the wall.

'Well, someone should. I'm only trying to get you to see sense.' Karl screwed a socket into the wall.

'Yeah, well, *don't*.' Nathan started putting away some tools. 'You make me fucking laugh, you do. You're never happy, always whingeing about money. You get this job and you're still fucking whingeing. There's no pleasing you.' He rummaged for his cable strippers.

Karl pointed the screwdriver at him. 'It's only because I know what's going to happen.'

'Oh, fucking psychic now, are you? Mystic Karl, is it?' Nathan picked up a leftover length of cable and tossed it across the room towards a metal bin.

'I don't have to be a psychic to see that I'll be left to do all the work while you shag that fucking—' He stopped himself, and continued to screw the socket to the wall.

'Fucking *what*?' growled Nathan.

'You know what I mean,' said Karl, flatly.

'I'm afraid I don't, mate. Why don't you spell it out for me?' Nathan put his hands in his jeans pockets. Anger welled up in him. This ignorant bastard didn't know shit. This wasn't a holiday romance, a fling . . . If last night was anything to go by he was falling in love and there wasn't a thing he could do about it.

He'd met her at seven, at the clearing at the side of the woods. She had held his hand and led him deeper into the trees. She told him she always came here to think. It was peaceful. His heart was racing, partly through excitement, partly through fear of what would happen if they were seen together. She wasn't scared: she had it all planned out. They sat under a tree and talked for a while. She told him all about Josh, what a bastard he'd been and how she'd leave him if the right person came along.

Nathan talked about Angie, as though she were history, not sitting at home waiting for him. If Keighley knew the truth it would totally fuck up his chances . . . and tonight his chances were looking good. He studied her face as she talked: her soft complexion, her expressions, the way her top lip curled up when she spoke of her life with Josh. He knew she wanted him to say, 'Leave him and be with me,' but he couldn't. He hardly knew her. He lay back against the tree and she rested her head on his chest. He stroked her soft, shiny hair. She kissed him softly on the lips. He kissed her back, and soon it was as though they were welded together. She got up on to her knees, slid a leg across his, manoeuvred herself across him, and ground herself against him as her tongue searched his mouth.

He slid his hands up her skirt and along her smooth thighs to pull down the waistband of her knickers. She knelt up, allowing him to pull them down her thighs, then took his hand, put it between her legs, and massaged herself slowly against his palm. She pulled off her crop top and tossed it on to a tree stump.

She tilted her head backwards and ran her hand down his stomach to take hold of the bulge in his jeans. She fumbled for his zip, and he reached into his back pocket for a condom . . .

'She's fucking trouble, *all right*?' Karl glowered at him.

What did he know? She was beautiful, sexy. He could still smell her. 'Just mind your own business,' said Nathan, continuing the search for the cable strippers.

'When it starts to affect my work it *is* my business,' said Karl.

'Yeah,' mused Nathan. 'So you electrocuting people must be *my* business.'

'You cheeky bastard. Who do you think you are?'

Nathan looked at Karl's sneer, knowing what that expression meant. It was the same look that had preceded a number of drunken fights back home. Fuck him. He wasn't going to be intimidated.

'No, who do *you* think *you* are?' Nathan pointed a finger at him. 'You talk about me not havin my mind on the job? You're the one wiv his head back in London, makin mistakes cos he's dyin to get home!'

'And do you fuckin blame me, with you spinnin things out as long as you can just so's you can shag that bird?' Nathan snorted and turned away. 'Yeah, I fuckin thought so,' said Karl.

'Fuck off, cunt,' muttered Nathan, and bent back to his toolbox.

'You what!' Karl shoved his shoulder and Nathan fell across his toolbox. Nathan looked up at him with hate in his eyes. 'You fucking heard,' he said, and scrambled to his feet.

Karl pushed his face almost into Nathan's. 'No, *you* fuck off!' He stood there, waiting for a head-butt, but Nathan took a step back then headed for the door.

'That's right, walk away. Typical of you, that!'

'I'm going for my lunch,' said Nathan, and barged through the swing doors.

'And you wonder why Angie walks all over you!' taunted Karl. He kicked a hammer that lay at his feet. It slid across the floor and dented the skirting-board. He sat down on his toolbox, feeling as though he'd just beaten the crap out of his younger brother for no reason at all.

'Ye didnae?'

'Ah did.' Keighley poured water from a glass jug into the small plastic cups sitting on top of a metal trolley.

Lianne squealed. 'Whit wis it like?' she asked eagerly.

Keighley thought for a moment. 'It wis beautiful . . . He wis really gentle.'

'Where did ye dae it?'

'In the woods . . . twice.' Keighley put down the jug next to the cups and raised her eyebrows.

'Mah God, ya dirty midden!' Lianne laughed out loud.

'No, Ah'm no,' said Keighley, defensively. 'Ye've

aywis bin telling me ah should see other people – git away fae Josh. Well, noo ah huv.'

'Aye, but ah didnae mean ye tae go an git shagged in the woods by a workie.' Lianne made it sound ridiculous, like a fantasy.

'It wisnae like that,' said Keighley, almost hurt.

'Ah cannae believe it,' Lianne said.

'Well, believe it . . . ah'm in love.' Keighley wheeled the trolley into the ward.

Lianne stood transfixed. Excitement at last. A scandal in Glen Leven. Jerry Springer didn't have a look in! She wished it was her. She followed Keighley up the ward as a hundred and one questions sprung to mind.

Josh sat in the Ptarmigan nursing a pint, along with his bruised ego. He couldn't get over those bastards. You don't fuck about with Josh Strachan without getting hurt, and he knew exactly where to hurt them: in the pocket.

He'd spent the morning looking for them. Moose's missus had acted shifty, like she didn't want Josh to know where the wee shite was. Gavin wasn't at home either, so he deduced that, wherever they were, they were together.

He'd found them laying slabs up at old Mrs McNeil's place. They almost shat themselves when he walked round the back to catch them in the act. 'Awright, boays,' he said, leaning on the waist-high gate that kept an old cairn terrier from straying down the drive and on to the road.

'Oh, Josh,' said Gavin, less than happy to see him. 'How ye dein?'

'No bad,' said Josh, eyeing Moose as he walked the slabs on their corners and dropped them into place on the path. 'Awright, Moose?' he asked.

Moose forced a smile as he got his weight behind a slab propped up against the garden wall. His bare chest was scratched from the rough concrete edges, and every sinew in his body was stretched to the limit as he manoeuvred the slab along the path. Josh knew that smile. It said, 'I don't have the time to be standing chatting. If you've something to tell me you'd better say it while I'm working.' The man's attitude stank, but Josh knew he'd only himself to blame.

'Listen,' said Josh, 'Ah've jist goat us a couple ay days work wi Davie the butcher. Couple ay new counters goin in wi striplights oan them, tae light up that scabby meat he sells.' He expected them to laugh at the joke, but Gavin looked uneasy and glanced at Moose, as though he didn't know what to do. Moose dropped the slab into place and the cairn terrier jumped at the **whump!** Moose picked up a long-handled rubber mallet, which was almost as big as himself, and bounced it off the corners of the slab until it was in line with the others. He rested it on its head, took off his gloves and sauntered along the path to the gate where Josh stood.

164

'Cannae dae it, Josh.' He smiled another wee smile – this time it said, 'Tough shite.'

'Whit dae ye mean ye cannae dae it? It's good money,' said Josh. Gavin still wouldn't catch his eye: he looked like he was in the headmaster's study being told off for running in the corridors.

'We've work oan, mate. This place.' Moose's thin arm swept majestically along the half-finished path.

'How long's that gonnae tek ye?' asked Josh.

Moose bent down and picked up a bottle of Irn Bru. He unscrewed the top. 'Might be finished th'morra,' he said, and drank. He screwed the top back on, then put it down next to the dog.

'Aye, well, that's awright,' said Josh. 'Ah kin mek a stert oan it masel th'morra. Yous two kin turn up when yis git finished here, eh?' Gavin looked at Moose again. What was wrong with him, thought Josh. Had he taken a vow of silence? About fucking time – it was better than listening to his shite all day.

Moose scratched the back of his neck. 'Thing is, we're monoblockin hur drive after this,' he said.

'Tell hur ye'll dae it next week or somehun,' said Josh, starting to panic. His cheap labour had had a better offer and he was the last one to know about it.

'Ah cannae. Ah've awready telt hur ah'd dae it ower the next couple ay days.' He shrugged. End of story – like it or lump it.

'But . . .' Josh stammered. He was angry with himself

for not being able to find a solution. *Kill the old bag and bury her under the patio, that way you won't have to do the drive* was the only thing that sprang to mind.

'An we've goat some landscapin oan fir Boabby McVey after this,' Moose added.

'Whit?' Josh couldn't take it in.

Moose tilted his head at Gavin. 'Int that right, Gavin?'

'Eh? Oh, aye.' Gavin nodded to confirm it.

Josh looked at them. If anyone was going to pull the strings round here it would be him. Had they forgotten who paid their wages? 'Moan tae fuck, boays!' He held out his hands as though they should see reason. 'Ah've took this oan noo.' They stared at him, impassively. 'The only reason ah managed tae talk Davie intae gettin it done is because ah sais ah'd stert it oan the Saturday night an have it finished fir hum opening oan the Monday mornin. Ah wis countin oan you two helpin me oot,' he said. Moose shrugged again and looked back at the slabs, letting Josh know he had work to do. 'So, are yi sayin yir no gonnae dae it?'

'Josh,' said Gavin, 'it's no that we don't want tae dae it, we jist cannae. We've awready agreed tae other work.'

'You pair ay cunts.' Josh gripped the gate. 'Ah've bin gien yous two work since ah sterted here, an noo look at yis. Too fuckin good fir it, are ye?'

'No,' said Gavin.

'Whit fuckin work?' Moose put his thick gloves back on.

'Whit?' Josh snarled. Had this wee bastard lost his memory?

'Whit work? We've bin scratchin oor erses fir weeks – know whit ah mean?' said Moose.

'Aye, an yir no the only wan,' replied Josh, letting him know he was in the same boat and not hogging all the work for himself.

'Well, then. We hud tae dae somehun, din't we?' said Moose, 'ah've goat weans there, ye know.'

Oh, he'd remember his scrawny wee litter when it suited him, thought Josh. It wasn't like that when he was drinking the money as fast as it was handed to him. 'Jist as well yir missus gits family allowance, then, int it? Otherwise they'd aw starve – you keeping aw the money, ya selfish wee cunt!'

'Nae need tae be like that, Josh,' Moose said, and smiled another of those wee sarky smiles.

'Oh, ah think there *is* a need tae be like that,' said Josh. 'You pair ay diddies huv jist coast me that joab, so let's see how *you* like it.' He stormed off to his van, which was parked in the street.

Gavin shouted after him, with panic in his voice, 'Josh, mate, hoad oan a minute!'

Josh stopped in his tracks and turned to face him. 'Mate? *Mate*, is it? Yous cunts widnae know the meanin ay the word.' He stomped to the van and got in it.

'Arsehole,' said Moose. He hauled a slab on to its side, then glared at Gavin who was still standing at the gate watching Josh like a lovesick teenager. 'Gonnae forget aboot hum an git us some sand?'

Gavin picked up a bucket and shovel and headed towards the mound near the fence. He had a bad feeling about this. He knew what Josh could be like when he was angry.

Josh finished his lager. No matter how many times he played it over in his head he still couldn't figure out how he was going to do this job on his own and, more to the point, have it finished by Monday morning. He knew that if he told Davie the truth the deal would be off. He could have kicked himself for not getting any money off him up front. That way he could have done the job at his leisure and held the cunt to ransom. The trick was to get the money for materials, start the job and spin it out. You just had to keep your eye on the punter in case they got a bit stroppy and complained to Trading Standards. Few did. In fact, he'd already asked the red faced wee bastard for the money for materials but Davie had said he'd only pay up when the job was finished. Mindful of his financial predicament, Josh had had to agree. Gone were the days when he had had the upper hand. There was only one thing for it: get pished. Celtic was playing Aberdeen this afternoon. He hoped it would be a result for the Hoops: they were tanking everyone lately.

The door opened and Nathan came in. 'Lager, please,' he said to Brendan.

Josh waited for him to turn round to see who was in, but he didn't seem bothered, just gazed straight ahead as though something was on his mind. Brendan put the pint in front of him. Nathan handed over a tenner, raised the glass to his lips and swallowed half of his drink in one gulp. Something *was* bugging him. Time to find out what it was. Josh stood up, grabbed his empty glass, strolled over to the bar and put it down beside Nathan, who glanced up at him as Brendan put his change on the bar.

'Same again, Josh?' asked Brendan, reaching for a pint glass. Josh nodded.

'Awright?' said Nathan, acknowledging Josh casually. He took another long gulp of his pint.

'How's the joab goin?' asked Josh.

'Ah, you know . . . all right.' He took another mouthful, then coughed. 'You doin much?'

Josh wondered if he was taking the piss, but there was no way he could have heard about the job with Davie and that he'd been left in the lurch.

'Aye, dein a bit, ye know,' he said.

Brendan put the pint in front of him. Josh reached into his jeans pocket and pulled out a handful of coins. He looked at the forty-three pence in his palm then delved into his other pocket for some notes. *Nothing.* He checked his back pocket. *Nothing.* He pulled out his wallet and looked in that. *Fuck-all.* He glanced up at Brendan, trying not to be embarrassed. 'Hoad oan a minute.' He searched again. How the fuck had he managed to come out with only two quid and some change? He had been at the bar a number of times when Brendan had refused tick to regulars. He'd always said that Brendan was 'Quite fuckin right. Gie em it once an they'll expect it aw the time.' There was no way *he* was asking for it.

'Here, I'll get that.' Nathan picked up a fiver from his change on the bar and held it out to Brendan. Brendan looked at it, then at Josh, to see if he was going to pay for his own drink or let this guy foot his bill. Brendan didn't care who paid for it, as long as one of them did.

'Naw, naw, yir awright,' Josh protested, continuing the fruitless search of his wallet, flicking through old petrol receipts in search of a stray tenner.

'It's awright, mate, it's the least I can do after that business with the contract.' Brendan took the fiver and turned back to the till.

'Fuckin twenty quid in here this mornin,' said Josh, waving his wallet as though he'd been robbed. He stuffed it into his back pocket.

'Soon goes, doesn't it?' said Nathan, but Josh didn't answer. There was no point being too pally with him. All right, he'd stood him a pint, but he had a long way to go to make up for stealing Josh's livelihood.

Brendan turned to one of Roddy's old pals. 'Another Grouse?' he asked. The old boy nodded his head at Roddy, who had half a dozen double whiskies sitting around the draughts board in front of him. He was on a roll again and was getting noisier with each game he won.

Josh picked up his pint and glanced up at the TV. The match was due to start. He strained to hear it above Roddy's booming voice and the clacking draughts. 'Brendan, gonnae turn that up a bit?' he called down the bar. 'Ah cannae hear it fir aw these fuckin Jakeys.' He turned to let them know he was talking about them, but they were laughing like schoolboys and didn't see him.

Brendan picked up the remote control and pointed it at the TV. The blue volume bar appeared on the screen and went up a couple of notches.

'Who's playin?' asked Nathan.

'Celtic–Aberdeen. Who dae you support?'

'Chelsea,' Nathan replied.

'Full ay Ayeties that loat, are they no?' said Josh, as though Nathan should be supporting a good thoroughbred Scottish team.

'Some good players from Italy. Who do you support?' asked Nathan.

'Celtic,' said Josh, looking at him as though he had two heads.

'They all real Scotchmen, then, are they?'

'Scotch is a drink, mate, it's *Scots.*'

Nathan realised his gaffe. 'Oh, yeah, right.' He looked up at the screen as the Celtic team filed out on to the pitch. He pointed up at the TV. 'I've seen im in London

– he used to have long hair. Got his leg broke a while back, didn't he?'

'Hmmm,' said Josh, almost agreeably, studying the line-up as the names were superimposed over a shot of Pittodrie stadium.

'Same again?' Brendan pointed to Nathan's empty glass.

Nathan nodded. 'Do you think it was his leg or the shin guard sticking out?' he asked Josh. 'Looked bloody painful, didn't it?'

Josh pointed to an empty table. 'Ah'm gonnae git a seat.' He waddled over to it and plonked himself down.

Nathan took the hint, stood up and gathered his change off the bar. It was time he went back to work anyway. There was no point sitting brooding about his fall-out with Karl.

'Wan eighty, pal.'

'Eh?' Nathan turned, and Brendan placed a pint on the bar in front of him.

'Oh, right.' He'd forgotten about it. He handed Brendan two pound coins and settled himself to watch the game.

He was barely able to contain his joy when he saw them. Sean ran up the path and pushed at the gate, shouting, 'Dad,' while Jeanette walked along behind him, a flowery sarong wrapped round her waist and tied at the side. His eyes were drawn to her pink bikini bottoms and slender figure, which was visible through the thin material. Her flat tanned stomach showed no evidence of the three children she'd had. Two bows held her bikini top in place, one tied behind her slim brown back, the other at her neck. He thought of reaching out and gently pulling the bottom bow undone freeing her breasts, but checked himself – it was inappropriate with a two-year-old running around. What kind of example would that set the wee feller?

Sean was swinging on the gate. 'Ye comin in?' Gavin opened it. Sean ran down the path to where Moose was levelling sand with a long piece of wood. Gavin closed the gate, ambled over to the pile of sand and started shovelling it into a wheelbarrow, watching the family as he worked. Jeanette handed Moose a pack of sandwiches. He smiled and put them to one side. The dog woke up and sniffed at them, so Moose moved them out of its reach, to the top of a pile of slabs.

She was trying to feed him up, Gavin thought. That's what a good wife did – cared about you, fed you. That was the deal: you were the provider, went out to work and earned a crust; she did her bit at home, looking after the kids, making sure you got good meals to keep you healthy and strong so you could go back out the next day and keep providing for your family. It had been that way since caveman days. But something was wrong here. Moose didn't eat – one look at his body told you that – he just drank. And he wasn't a well man: his jaundiced complexion was a constant indicator of the state of his health.

Sean ran over to him and Moose ruffled his hair while Jeanette chatted away. Then Sean spotted the pile of sand by Gavin and came across to it. He held out his hand for Gavin to help him climb up it.

There was a rap on the window. Jeanette turned and waved at old Mrs McNeil, indicating the pack of sandwiches to let the old woman know what she was doing there. She reached out theatrically to pinch what flesh she could grip at Moose's waist, miming that she was here to feed her man. Mrs McNeil shook her head despairingly. She'd tried on a number of occasions to get him to take a piece of cake, a sandwich, anything, but he waved her away politely and said he'd already had a big breakfast. Gavin knew what Moose's *big breakfast* consisted of: a cup of weak tea and half a dozen fags.

Gavin knew why Jeanette was really here. Moose had told her he was getting paid today, tomorrow at the latest. She wanted some sort of guarantee that he'd be home with the money. They had bills to pay. Gavin had heard this conversation between them a million times before and had tried to get Moose to see it from Jeanette's point of view. She didn't begrudge him a pint, she just wanted to be able to count on him. Moose always laughed and said Gavin should take up marriage-guidance counselling.

Just over two years ago Moose had driven her to the point of despair when he landed some work on the roads. He'd hit it off with the Tarmac boys in the pub and got himself a cash-in-hand labouring job. At first they were reluctant to take him on until he told them he'd laid roads before. In an attempt to prove how good he was, he said he'd work the first day for free. What did they have to lose? They gave him a start and it didn't take them long to see that this wee guy worked like a bastard. Hardly stopped for a break. A wee drink from an Irn Bru bottle and the occasional fag, which he usually smoked while he worked, then he was off again with his rake and barrow, as happy as a sand-boy. Put the rest of them to shame. After the shift they'd all go for a few beers, and Moose would get home *eventually*, as black as the ace of spades, then slide into bed smelling of tar, beer, sweat and vomit.

It had all got too much for Jeanette. Then one night she and Gavin had bumped into each other when she was at a much-needed Ladies' Night at the Glen Tavern. A stripper from Glasgow was appearing and her friend had persuaded her to come out and let her hair down. She'd also provided a babysitter, in the form of her own teenage daughter.

Gavin had been having a quiet drink in the bar, while in the function room the women screamed and whooped as a guy called Big Dirk lathered himself in whipped cream from a can then invited them to lick it off. Tina had appeared in the bar on her way back from the ladies' and spotted Gavin. She went over to him, smiled and asked if he needed company. Delighted, Gavin bought her a drink and they sat at a quiet table in the corner. This was what she really needed, she told him, not some stripper waving his tackle over her drink. She talked about the kids, and about Moose, while Gavin listened. She asked him for his honest opinion about what she should do. He let her know that Moose was a fool. He had a beautiful wife and two boys to be proud of.

'Dae ye really think ah'm beautiful?' she asked.

Gavin's heart raced. She'd had a bit too much to drink, and so had he. They were both vulnerable. But she was being treated like shit and didn't deserve it. He wanted to hold her, kiss her, take her and the boys away somewhere where they could all be happy. But she was Moose's wife and they were his boys. It was wrong even to think it.

'The most beautiful woman ah've ever seen,' he said, with complete honesty. He could see she was thinking the same as he was, but it could never happen. Never in a million years.

'Kin Ah ask ye somethin?' she said.

'Aye, anyhun.' He picked up his pint and took a drink to wet his lips, which were bone dry with nerves.

'Did you used tae fancy me? When ah wiz younger ah mean. Mah pals aywis said ye did.'

He nodded, as though it were no secret.

'Ah thought so,' she said.

'Ah still dae.' He looked directly at her.

She dropped her eyes, and looked away, not knowing what to say.

'Soarry,' he said. 'Forget ah ever said it.'

'No, it's awright.' She took his hand.

He glanced about the room to see if anyone was watching. They weren't. The old men at the bar, telling tales of misspent youth, were in a world of their own. Gavin was in paradise. He kept his hand still on the table. He wanted this moment to last for ever.

'Ah like you too, Gavin . . . a lot.'

He shrugged, as though accepting he'd come second best. 'Thanks . . . like a brother, eh?'

She shook her head slowly, then pulled away her hand. He took it as a hint that he'd overstepped the mark. 'Dae ye want tae git oot ay here?' She stood up and pulled her bag over her shoulder.

He didn't have to be asked twice.

They walked through the quiet village, discussing Moose and the kids again. Jeanette said she had no idea where he was tonight. She didn't care. She told Gavin that she couldn't bear to let Moose touch her – he hadn't washed in a fortnight.

He helped her over a stile, into one of the fields high up on the outskirts of the village. They walked up a hill, stopped briefly to get their breath back, and turned to look down at the twinkling streetlights and the warm glow from the Glen Tavern. She sat down on the grass and he sat next to her like a shy schoolboy. She turned his head towards her and kissed him.

He was in a dream. Limbo. It was better than he'd ever imagined, and he'd imagined it over and over again. She pulled herself away and lay back on the grass, unbuttoning her flowery blue dress and pulling it open. He stared down at her, illuminated by the light of the moon. A pair of tiny white briefs was all she had on under the dress. 'Make love tae me, Gavin,' she whispered.

Gavin touched her smooth stomach gently as if to prove to himself that she was real, that *this* was real, that it was really happening. She arched her back, raising her buttocks off the ground, and slipped off her briefs.

Gavin cast his eyes over her. He was going to remember this for the rest of his life.

His hand moved slowly across her belly as she breathed deeply in anticipation. It was all too much for him. He was overwhelmed. Tears formed in his eyes. 'God, Jeanette . . . ah love you, ah really, really love you,' he blurted out, and the tears flowed.

She sat up, put her arms round his neck and pulled him close to comfort him.

What a big daft bastard he was, thought Gavin. Here he was with the woman of his dreams and he was greeting like a baby while she rocked and shushed him and stroked his hair. What was wrong with him? He took a deep breath and wiped his eyes. 'Ah'm soarry,' he said, 'ye must think ah'm a . . .'

She put her finger to his lips to stop him talking. *She* knew what Gavin was. He was the guy she should have married. She took her finger away and kissed him. He put his hand behind the back of her neck and laid her gently on the cool soft grass. She pulled off his jacket, then his T-shirt, and he knelt above her, unbuckling his belt, unzipping his fly, pulling his jeans down to his knees . . .

'Dad, look at me!' Sean stood on top of the pile of sand. Gavin was still holding his hand.

'Sean, git doon fae there!' shouted Moose, irritated.

'Ah'm the king of the castle!' said Sean, to Gavin.

'Aye, you are that, son,' said Gavin. 'You are that.'

Gavin looked down at him proudly. He had Gavin's mum's eyes and his old man's forehead. God, he was beautiful. If only they were alive to see him.

CLACK   **CLACK** – Ha!
       CLACK   **CLACK**
     CLACK.

Roddy clapped his hands in glee, reached over and pulled his opponent's hat down over his eyes.

'Gonnae fuckin wrap it?' shouted Josh.

Roddy and the old boys looked at him, indignant.

'Needs tae learn some manners,' one of them muttered.

Roddy leaned past his friend to get a look at Josh. 'Whit is it?' he asked.

'Ah'm tryin tae watch the gemme!' Josh pointed at the TV. What fucking planet were they on? Celtic were playing, for God's sake. They were already one–nil down to the Dons.

'We're only *playin* a gemme.' Roddy straightened in his seat.

Josh glared at him. Cocky wee bastard. He noticed the empty whisky glasses piling up on Roddy's table. He was getting too mouthy with the drink and because his Jakey pals were all around him. Josh thought he would have learned his lesson after the other night. If he didn't shut it he'd have to put the old man in his place. 'Jist keep it doon a bit, eh?' he said.

'Aye, aye,' someone mumbled, and laughed.

Josh tried to see who it was but the four of them all looked and sounded the same. Doddering old bastards.

Nathan tipped his glass to his lips. Every time a draught hit the board Josh stared over at the old blokes, irritated. Nathan reminded himself to stay out of his way in future: Josh was definitely unstable. If he ever found out about him and Keighley . . . He shuddered at the thought and took another swig of his pint. He'd finish this and get back to work. He could see Karl's point now, but there was a way of speaking to someone about these things. You didn't just drop sarky comments all the time, and it wasn't as though Nathan wasn't pulling his weight on the job.

CLACK
        CLACK

Josh fumed and stared at Roddy as he took another two of his opponent's draughts off the board. Then he heard the excited noise from the crowd on the TV and looked up to see Aberdeen break through the Celtic defence. Winters had a clear shot at the goal. He staged a bogus kick, sending the goalie the wrong way and flat on his arse, then hooked the ball in towards him. It bounced a couple of times, once on each knee, before he regained control and volleyed it into the back of the net. Two–nil. *Two-fucking-nil to Aberdeen*. Aberdeen, for fuck sake. What were the Hoops coming to? They were a total embarrassment.

CLACK
       CLACK
              CLACK

Roddy's opponent sank back in his chair and sighed deeply. Another Grouse was soon on the cards.

   'Ah fuckin telt you, din't ah?! Pack it in!' Josh bellowed at them.

   Roddy looked at the veins sticking out of Josh's neck. This guy was a candidate for a heart-attack, getting worked up about nothing. He decided not to say anything. The mood Josh was in, you could give him fifty quid and a written apology and he'd still want to fight. Daft spoilt wee boy, that's all he was. Used to getting his own way. Roddy glanced at his friends and raised his eyebrows at them as Josh turned back to the TV.

Nathan thought it was time for a sharp exit. He finished his lager, noticing the stuffed bird on display beneath the gantry. He'd seen it the last time he was in and wondered what it was. You never saw a bird like that in London.

'What *is* that, mate?' He pointed to the bird.

'Eh?' Brendan took the empty pint glass off the bar and dunked it in the washer. 'The bird?' he asked.

'Yeah.'

'A ptarmigan – a kind ay grouse.'

'Oh, so *that*'s a ptarmigan,' said Nathan. The penny had finally dropped. 'I wondered what a ptarmigan was.'

'Well, now ye know, eh?' Brendan winked.

'See you later, then.' Nathan considered saying goodbye to Josh but decided against it.

'Cheers, son,' said Brendan, drying a glass.

Nathan walked to the gents', pushed open the door and went inside.

CLACK. There was that noise again. Josh glanced from the board to the TV. One of the Celtic players had been red-carded but he couldn't hear who it was.

'Brendan, gonnae turn it up a bit?' he shouted. Brendan reached once more for the remote control.

Nathan stood at the urinal and sighed as the piss hit the metal trough and ran like a yellow river through the running water and around the white cakes of disinfectant. What the hell was he doing? He'd only come here to work, get away from Angie for a while, sort himself out and hopefully give her a chance to do the same. The last thing he'd expected was to start seeing someone. What now? Continue to see Keighley on the sly and keep up the pretence that everything between him and Angie was over? It would be worth it for the sex, but she deserved better than that. He'd have to come clean. And what if she finished with Josh? Fuck, he'd have to leave the country. They both would. And then there was Angie. If she found out he was leaving her for someone younger . . .

He zipped up his fly. He'd created a monster and it was about to turn nasty on him.

CLACK. Josh drank some of his pint, trying to make it last. He tried to work out how much money he had in the bank and if a trip to the cash machine would prove fruitless. He suspected it would. He looked at the date on his watch and remembered that the payment for the van would come off his account today. Was there enough in his account to cover it? Probably not. It would mean another smartarse letter from the bank asking if he needed 'financial advice' and they'd charge him twenty quid for sending it. Maybe he'd reply to it charging them *thirty* quid – see what they had to say about *that*, the cheeky bastards.

Nathan splashed some water on his face and looked at his reflection in the mirror. *A young Harry Belafonte.* He laughed to himself as he thought of her smile. She was gorgeous – there was no denying it. Imagine the boys back home if he told them he'd been shagging a nurse. No, he wouldn't do that. It was private what they had between them. When they were making love it was just him and Keighley – nobody else mattered. They didn't shag, or fuck, or hump. They made love, and it was special. Beautiful. Man, you could search your whole life for a bird like that and not even come close. Oh, Christ, what was he going to do?

CLACK. Josh was irritated beyond belief. It was that board. That fucking home-made wooden board, laminated with a hard shiny plastic that grated on his nerves when they whacked the pieces down on it. Why couldn't they use a cardboard one like everyone else?

CLACK

   CLACK

He looked over at smug Roddy. How many times did he have to tell him not to bang them down so hard? He was getting smart in front of his pals because he had a drink in him. Josh should have given him a smack in the dish the other night – that would have put him in his place. One more time, just one more time. Do it, go on, do it – I dare you, he thought.

Nathan dried his face and hands on the towel and turned to the door. There was nothing for it but to come clean. He'd sit her down and tell her that he hadn't been entirely truthful the other day. His marriage was as good as over in his eyes, but in Angie's . . .

He pulled open the door.

CLACK

      CLACK

            CLACK

            CLACK

      CLACK

CLACK

'Ha-ha!' Roddy punched the air.

'BAAAASSSSTTTAAAAAA!' Josh leaped out of his seat, knocking over the table and his half-finished pint, and shot across to Roddy.

Roddy had had enough of this. He rose to his feet and stood his ground, staring back.

'Whit did ah tell ye, eh? Whit did ah tell ye?!' Josh screamed in his face, as though he were losing the plot.

'Ah don't care *whit* ye've telt me, son.' Roddy wagged his finger in Josh's face. 'Ah'm here enjoyin a wee drink wi ma pals and a gemme ay draughts, an if ye don't like it ye kin lump it.'

Josh reached out, grabbed the board and pulled it off the table. The draughts scattered and rolled under the table.

Roddy refused to be intimidated. He reached out for his glass of whisky, which he raised calmly to his lips. 'Aye that's right, son, huv a tantrum. Ah'd expect nuthin less fae a big spoilt basta like yirsel.' He took a sip, then glanced up at his friends with a half-smile that suggested they pretend this moron wasn't here.

Nathan was watching from the door, not knowing what to do. He could slip away unseen, leave the pub now before the trouble started, but what would that make him look like? A pussy, that's what. Like a scared little girl who runs away from a fight in the playground. Or he could stay like a man. It was as he watched Josh swing the draughts board through the air that he knew he'd made the wrong decision.

Josh swiped the wooden board sideways, like a machete cutting through bamboo. It made contact with Roddy's scalp with a sickening crunch. Blood spurted across it and ran in rivulets down its smooth waxy surface.

Roddy fell backwards, landing on the carpet and banging the back of his head on the jukebox. His friends sprang out of their seats to help him. One bravely pushed Josh out of the way and stood between him and Roddy to protect him from any further punishment.

Josh stood back. The old boy's hair was matted with blood from a two-inch wide gash on his scalp. Josh winced. He'd warned him, he didn't know how many times. 'Ah telt ye!' he said. 'You fuckin brought that oan yirsel so don't go greetin tae any cunt, right?' He looked wildly about the bar for some understanding of why he'd done it.

Brendan was as white as a sheet. He grabbed a clean beer towel and turned the cold tap on full blast. Josh glanced across to the gents' where Nathan was rooted in the doorway. Nathan directed his gaze to where Roddy was sprawled on the floor, with blood up the side of the jukebox and his pals tending to him. Brendan was holding the towel to the cut. One old man ran to the phone at the corner of the bar and dialled 999. Josh realised he'd outstayed his welcome. He about-turned and marched out.

'I'm comin home.' Karl put another tenpence in the callbox and waited for the pips to stop and the line to clear.

'You're what?' said Liz.

'Comin home.' He pulled out a handful of change and

put it on the shelf, sifting through it for a fifty-pence piece.

'Great. Is the job finished already?' she asked.

'No . . .' BEEP, BEEP, BEEP, BEEP, BEEP, BEEP, BEEP. 'Fuck.' He slid twenty pence off the shelf and pushed it into the slot. He'd probably get longer for his money if he were calling from Spain.

'No?' she asked.

'It'll be another couple of days yet. Maybe a week – I don't know.'

'Well, why don't you wait till you've finished? It doesn't make any sense you coming all the way home for a few days then having to go back up there again, does it?'

The voice of reason. Why did she always have to be so sensible? thought Karl.

'Karl?'

'Yeah, I'm here . . .'

'Well?'

'I miss you.' He turned sideways and stared out of the callbox. Ben Leven loomed threateningly above him, a constant reminder that he was nowhere near London.

'I miss you too. So do the girls.' Her voice sounded distant. Sad. They weren't meant to be apart, none of them. He wished the girls were here now. What he wouldn't give for a hug.

'Is everything all right?' she sounded concerned. She knew him better than he knew himself.

'Yeah, yeah,' he said, matter-of-fact. 'Course it is. I'm just a bit homesick.' BEEP, BEEP, BEEP, BEEP, BEEP, BEEP, BEEP. 'Oh, for fuck sake!' He grabbed at the money on the shelf, knocking some coins on to the floor. He stooped down to pick up twenty pence and banged his forehead on the front of the phone. 'Fuck!'

'Karl?'

He pushed the twenty pence into the slot, rubbing his forehead. 'Look, I'm running out of change,' he said.

'You're not coming home, then?'

'No, I'll stick it out till we're finished. I'll phone.'

'Use your mobile next time – that's why I bought you it.'

'It costs too much. I don't even know if they sell the cards up here.'

'Of course they do,' she said. 'Buy one and phone me tomorrow. The girls are off school – you can speak to them too. You're earning enough money, Karl, treat yourself.'

'Yeah, yeah, all right,' he conceded. She'd bought him the phone in case anything happened at work, in case the van broke down. He'd only used it a couple of times and it had swallowed up a five-pound card. Fuck that, he thought. He only kept it switched on in case she needed to contact him in an emergency, but what he'd be able to do stuck up here God only knew. He'd be as much use as tits on a bull.

BEEP, BEEP, BEEP, BEEP, BEEP, BEEP, BEEP.

'Look, I'll have to go – there's the pips.' An old lady

with a bag of messages was approaching, looking like she wanted to use the phone.

'Put some more money in – I never told you what Jade came out with yesterday.' She laughed.

'I've run out of change,' he lied, wedging the phone to his ear with his shoulder and scooping the money off the shelf into his palm. It was time he got back to work. The job wasn't going to do itself.

'What's the number? I'll call you back,' she shouted, before he got cut off. He knew she'd already have the pen in her hand and would be turning to a blank page in the pad they kept by the phone.

'I can't, darlin – someone's waitin. I'll call tonight when I buy—' BEEEP! He replaced the handset, pushed open the door and stepped out into the street. He held the door open for the old lady but she walked past him as though he wasn't there and carried on up the street.

The petrol gauge was low. He couldn't even go for a drive if he wanted to. He'd have to tap Keighley for some cash till he got the money from wee Davie for the job on the shop. He drove the van up the courtyard and pulled into his parking space outside the block of flats where he lived. Well, that was one mouthy cunt dealt with today. Time to get shot of another. He pulled out his mobile, pressed the phone-book key and scrolled down to D. Ah, there it was. He pressed the button with the green handset icon on it and the phone autodialled.

'Good afternoon, DSS,' said a voice.

Josh leaned back in his seat. 'Afternoon,' he said. 'Ah jist thought ah'd let ye know that ah've seen a couple ay people who sign oan working today.'

'Jist a minute. There's a free phone number ah kin give ye . . .' Josh grabbed a pen from the glove compartment. Fucking inconvenience. You'd think they'd be glad of the tip-off.

'Hello?' The voice was back, and dictated the number.

Josh grabbed a half-empty pack of cigarettes off the dash and scribbled it down. He opened the packet and looked inside. Moose's emergency supply. Wee cunt would need more than a fag once he'd finished with him. He took one out and sniffed it. It smelt inviting, bringing back memories of when he used to smoke twenty a day. After those two diddies this morning, and now that cunt in the pub, he needed something to settle his nerves. Why not? He pushed the cigarette lighter into the dash and placed the fag in his mouth. He looked at himself in the rear-view mirror. Hard as fuck. Cool as a cucumber and hard as fuck. No one messes with Josh Strachan. The lighter popped out. He pulled it out of its socket and the red-hot element glowed dangerously in front of him. He wondered what Moose would look like with a red circle branded on his forehead for his cheek. He placed it on the end of the fag and drew deeply, then blew a thick blue plume of smoke from the corner of his mouth. It wafted up to the roof of the van. He replaced the lighter in its socket and inhaled. It felt good, like an old flame who had a calming effect on him. They'd been apart for too long. He slipped the packet into his pocket.

It had been the perfect opportunity, the one he'd been waiting for. Josh would have been out of his life. Keighley would be free. Everyone would be happy. All he had to do was say the word. He couldn't.

Nathan watched PC Harvey scratch his head and look about the bar as though he was searching for that one piece of incriminating evidence that would prove his theory and get someone, anyone, to spill the beans. But they were as thick as thieves this lot. A flock of frightened sheep who stuck together.

PC Harvey knew that whatever he did would prove fruitless. The finger was pointing at one man. The trick was to get them to point their fingers at him too.

He placed his hat on a table and ambled about the bar in a white open-necked police shirt and black trousers. His baton, CS gas and cuffs were displayed on his belt like a warning. He glanced at Nathan and strolled across the room in his direction. He rubbed his hand across his jaw. A thin oily strand of black hair fell across his face and he swept it back.

He glanced across to his colleague PC Gordon as he came out of the gents' wiping his wet hands on his trousers. Gordon took out his pocketbook and nodded at Harvey to let him know he was ready. Harvey pulled out his pocketbook, too, and tossed it on to the table next to his hat. He'd already spent a good ten or fifteen minutes expressing his disgust to the occupants of the bar at such a cowardly attack. He knew they felt the same and the code of silence between them had to be broken. They had nothing to fear but the big man himself.

Experience told him that Josh Strachan was the only man in the village who would have carried out such an attack. You didn't have to be a criminal profiler to work that out. Harvey had studied Strachan's arrest sheet the first time he had picked him up in the village for putting one of the boys from the Forestry Commission in hospital with a broken nose – the lad had been winding him up good-naturedly about his name, saying it sounded like something out of the Bible. 'Joshua.' He had insisted on calling him Joshua all night till *Joshua* stuck the nut on him. Strachan had committed other violent offences: GBH, aggravated assault, concealing a weapon – he'd been pulled over for a minor traffic incident in Glasgow and they'd found he was carrying a baseball bat in his boot – criminal damage to a vehicle, criminal damage to property, criminal damage to business premises (the last place he worked at) . . . and now this. Collaring him in the act would have made Harvey's day. Scum like Strachan shouldn't be walking the streets of Glen Leven. This was a quiet village. Okay, so some of the Forestry boys went a bit nuts at the weekend but they were only kids – they worked hard and played hard. Harvey had known most of them since they were wee and he could still get their respect, even if they were rolling about shit-faced drunk.

'How ye dein?' Harvey pulled up a chair and sat down opposite Nathan.

Nathan nodded at him, then glanced up at the concerned faces of the lunchtime drinkers who now looked more like hostages. Roddy's mates sat together, looking scared, their hands and clothes flecked with their pal's blood. They'd wanted to go in the ambulance with Roddy but the police wanted statements before anyone went anywhere.

'So,' Harvey lifted up his pocketbook and turned to a new page, 'are you gonnae tell me ye were in the toilet as well when this happened?'

'I was, as it happens.' Nathan looked him in the eye. Harvey took a deep breath and sighed dramatically. Nathan caught the unmistakable whiff of cheese and onion.

'Must huv bin pretty busy in there?' said Harvey, for the benefit of anyone else in the bar who was considering using the same alibi. Nathan raised his eyebrows in confirmation that it had been.

'Name?' Harvey poised his pen over the page.

'Nathan Weller.'

'Weller,' mused Harvey, writing it down.

'Yeah, as in Paul.'

Harvey looked up, puzzled. Nathan realised the guy didn't know what he was talking about, probably thought he was taking the piss. 'The musician,' he said quickly.

'Whit did ye see, Nathan?' Harvey asked, as though he meant, 'Let's cut the shit.'

'I didn't see nuffin.' Nathan tried to sound convincing.

Harvey leaned forward in his seat. 'Ye *didnae see nuthin*? So, that must mean you saw *something*, then.' He smiled a half-smile, playing an intellectual game with Nathan. One–nil to PC Harvey.

'What?' Nathan wasn't sure he understood the question.

'If ye say ye didnae see *nuthin*, it means ye must have seen *something*. It's a double negative, Mr Weller.' He waited for Nathan's answer.

Nathan started to get annoyed. Smart bastard. Is that what they taught them at Hendon? 'Look, mate, I don't care what it is. I didn't see *anything* cos I was havin a slash at the time. When I came out the bog the old bloke was lyin on the ground an his mates was seein to him. Why don't you ask them what they saw?'

Harvey scribbled in his book. 'Oh, ah will Mr Weller, ah will.' He took his time writing down what Nathan had just told him, then raised his eyes, as though searching for the correct way to put the next question.

'Dis the name *Josh Strachan* mean anyhun tae ye?' He stared Nathan in the eye.

Nathan knew. Harvey knew. They all fucking knew. All it was going to take was somebody to say the word and Josh would be history. Nathan thought there was no point denying it. 'Yeah, electrician bloke. I've seen his name on the van,' he said nonchalantly.

'Aye, but did ye see him in here today?'

Nathan glanced at Brendan, who avoided his eye and busied himself behind the bar. The big shitebag. If anyone should be saying anything it should be Brendan – He'd served Josh for God's sake.

'Don't look at hum fir yir answer, ah'm askin you,' said Harvey.

Nathan turned to face him again. 'No . . . I never saw him.'

Harvey stared through him. The Jedi mind trick, thought Nathan. He could stare as long as he fucking liked, but he wasn't going to spill the beans. If this lot hated Josh so much they should be the ones to do it. Nathan wasn't going to be a scapegoat just because they were all too shit-scared.

'Right, then . . . you can go.'

Nathan stood up. 'Thanks.'

Harvey held out his arm as though to stop Nathan walking past him. 'Yir stayin at Mrs Grant's place, aren't ye?' he asked.

Nathan nodded.

'Good . . .' said Harvey, and scribbled down the address. 'We might need tae talk tae ye again.' He moved his arm, and Nathan walked past him and out of the front door of the pub. He stood outside in the street and breathed a sigh of relief.

The door opened again and old Pat McBain came out. 'Whit dae ye mek ay that?' he asked, conspiratorially, glancing back to make sure they weren't being listened to.

'Why didn't one of you say something?' Nathan stared, bewildered, at the old man, whose shirt was smudged with blood from when he'd helped Roddy up. They were obviously mates, and Nathan thought he, at least, should have said something.

'Are ye mad, son?' Pat started walking up the road. 'Ah'm no fit for the likes ay Josh Strachan. Ye seen whit he did in there.'

Nathan followed him. 'Then phone the police up and tell them. You don't have to give your name.'

'If yir so bothered aboot it *you* phone them,' said Pat.

'Does this kind of thing happen a lot around here?' Nathan asked.

'It niver used tae.' Pat stopped in his tracks. 'It only sterted happenin when outsiders came tae live here.' He sniffed, and turned to walk away.

Outsiders? thought Nathan.

Pat stopped and turned again, as though he'd remembered something. He looked Nathan up and down as if he was trying to measure his integrity. 'How did *you* no say anyhun?' he asked.

'Cos . . .' Nathan studied the pavement, trying to find the right words to justify himself, but he couldn't. Why hadn't he said anything? Out of fear? Because he felt it wasn't his place? Pure stupidity? What? He hadn't a clue. He looked up at Pat, who was now smiling slyly at him.

'Aye . . . ah thought so,' Pat tottered off up the street.

It was always the same whenever he went for a shit: the phone would ring or there'd be someone banging on the door. He wiped his arse and pulled up his jeans. This had better be important, he thought, rinsing his hands under the cold tap and drying them on his jeans. He bounded through the living room and opened the front door. PC Harvey stood at the top of the steps with a grin on his face. His apologetic-looking sidekick, PC Gordon, stood on the step behind him.

'Awright, boays, whit kin ah dae fir ye?' Josh asked innocently. News travels fast, he thought. But not as fast as his brain could conjure up an alibi.

'A wee word, Josh, if ye don't mind?' Harvey tried to step over the threshold.

Josh blocked his way and leaned on the doorframe. 'Oh, aye?' he asked.

'Aye.' Harvey took the hint and stepped back. 'We'd like tae ask ye a couple ay questions, if that's awright?'

'Depends whit they are,' said Josh.

'Kin we come in a minute, Josh?' Gordon asked.

'No,' replied Josh, flatly.

Harvey sighed. 'Where were ye today at wan forty-five?'

'Glesga.'

'Glesga.' Harvey nodded, amused. Of course he was. Where else? 'An ye've somewan who kin verify this, huv ye?'

'Aye,' said Josh. He'd already called Big Alan and told him if the polis phoned he was to say Josh had been with him. Big Alan was a bit put out that his so-called pal hadn't phoned before today, but Josh explained that he'd been really busy. Alan asked where he was but he just said, 'Ayr.' He'd give him his full address and phone number the next time he saw him – he'd be in Glasgow next week and they could maybe meet up for a pint. Alan seemed happy with that and was itching to fill him in on a forthcoming contract in Ireland. No tax. They'd be minted. Josh said he'd hear all about it when he was next in the town.

'Ye widnae happen tae know anyhun about draughts, wid ye?' Harvey queried. Josh stifled a smirk. Harvey was a right dry bastard when he wanted to be. He could drop his little one-liners all day if it kept him amused – but there was no way he'd get anything out of Josh.

'No a thing,' said Josh. 'It's no my gemme.'

'No auld Roddy McIntyre's gemme either. No since he had the tap ay hus heid teken aff by a draughts board.' He looked at Josh for a reaction.

'Shame, that,' Josh said, in mock sorrow for old Roddy's predicament.

'Int it?' Harvey turned to Gordon, standing behind him, looking like Stan Laurel.

'Ah know ye did it,' Harvey went on.

Josh snorted, amused. 'Dae us a favour, eh? Piss aff an git a witness.'

'Oh, ah will,' said Harvey, confidently. He watched Josh for a moment or two, then turned and headed down the steps to the car sitting in the parking bay.

'That it, then?' Josh called after him.

'For now, aye.'

Gordon watched him unlock the car and get in. 'See, the thing is, Josh,' he said, as though he was trying to explain, 'someone attacked auld Roddy.'

'An he thinks it's me, right?' said Josh, indignantly.

'Ye know he disnae like ye – no since that time ye nutted Stevie MacPherson. Ye could huv picked someone else tae nut instead of hus wee cousin.' Gordon glanced back at the car as Harvey started the engine. 'Ye any idea who it could be?'

'Ye could try talking tae they London boays – everyhun wis quiet roon here till they showed up.' Josh folded his arms and leaned on the doorframe again.

'The black guy?' asked Gordon.

'Aye, an hus pal – he's no right in the heid, that cunt.'

'Ah'll huv a word,' Gordon said. 'Keep mah eye oan them, ye know.'

'Aye, you dae that.' Josh narrowed his eyes.

'Listen, Josh . . . huv ye given any thought tae whit we were talking aboot the other day, you know, mah laddie an that?' he asked, almost apologetically.

The bastard never missed an opportunity, did he? thought Josh.

'Aye, aye, ah huv,' he lied. 'Ah've jist bin a bit busy, ye know?' Gordon's eyes lit up. Josh realised that Gordon had thought he meant busy-at-work, snowed-under, need-all-the-help-I-can-get, course-I-can-give-your-boy-a-job kind of busy.

'Naw, naw, ah don't mean wi mah job,' said Josh, trying to put him straight, 'that's still the same. Ah meant wi other things.'

'Oh,' Gordon said, deflated.

Harvey sounded the horn and Gordon waved to let him know he'd only be a minute.

'But ah'll look intae it, eh?' said Josh, making sure that Gordon was still interested in the carrot dangling before him.

'Aye, right ye are, then, Josh. Ah'll let mah laddie know, eh?' He turned and started down the stairs, then looked back at Josh, pointing a mock-threatening finger at him. 'An try to keep yir nose clean, eh?'

'Tossa,' Josh muttered, as he shut the door.

'We're just good friends.' Nathan hauled the cable through the conduit that ran down the wall.

'Right,' said Karl, not believing a word as he knelt beside his toolbox and rummaged about for his mole grips.

'We are,' said Nathan, as though he was trying to convince himself too. 'We just enjoy each other's company – have a laugh together, you know.'

'Well, that's not how it looks.' Karl picked up the mole grips and walked over to the length of old cable that swung precariously against the wall.

Nathan watched him as he used the grips to yank the cable down from the ceiling. It landed on the stone floor. Nathan considered telling him the truth, then realised that Karl would only nag him to keep away from her. Karl didn't know Keighley like he did. Nobody did. Especially Josh. Fear coursed through him and he shuddered at the thought of Josh finding out about them. Nathan knew he was on his own – he couldn't even discuss the situation with his best friend.

'I'm just sayin it looks suss, that's all, you bein so friendly wiv another bloke's bird. He's not right, that bloke – got a screw missin.' Karl picked up the cable and tossed it on to a pile of scrap in the corner of the room. A screw missing? thought Nathan, Josh had a whole toolkit missing.

'Just do yourself a favour and don't do anyfink stupid . . . all right?' Karl pointed the mole grips at him, and Nathan nodded amicably.

*   *   *

'Oh, God . . . Oh, don't stop, Nathan – ah'm comin!' She held on to his shoulders and pulled him closer to her, wrapping her legs around his back. Nathan gripped her hips and tried to pull his head upwards to get some air but she wouldn't let go of his back. Her hips followed him upwards with every stroke, her arse occasionally making contact with the sleeping-bag on the floor of the van. Not the ideal place for a meeting with a lady, thought Nathan, but it was dark in these woods and was away from prying eyes.

She screamed and dug her nails into his back, burying her head in his neck and biting his shoulder. He felt himself coming and pushed deeper into her. She moaned and stuck her nails into his arse. He fell on top of her, exhausted. She stroked his hair and the back of his neck. He lay still for a minute while he got his breath back.

'We're taking a risk, aren't we?' he asked thoughtfully, as he pulled off the condom and tied a knot in it. He dropped it behind the driver's seat, and reminded himself to dump it before he got back to the guesthouse. The last thing he needed was Karl coming across it.

'No as long as yir usin condoms. Mah doctor says ah hud tae come off the pill fir a while before he'd change it – it'll no be long afore ah'm oan it again.' She sat up and put her arms around him.

'No, I don't mean that, I mean with Josh. I can't stop thinking about what he did to that bloke today.' He watched her as she leaned back on the sleeping-bag and

reached about in the dark for her knickers. The moon-
light glistened on her moist body, showing the curve of
her waist and the contours of her ribs as she raised her
hips in the air and pulled her knickers up over her thighs.

'He's a madman,' she said. The elastic snapped
against her hips. 'Anyway, ah don't want tae talk aboot
hum . . . ah want tae talk aboot *us*.'

Nathan started pulling on his jeans. 'Oh, yeah?' he
asked, non-committal.

She sat up and ran her finger gently down his back-
bone. His shoulder-blades stuck out automatically. She
was already finding out his ticklish spots. 'Nathan . . .
how dae ye feel aboot me?'

'How do you think I feel?' he asked, as though she'd
just asked the stupidest question on the planet. 'Do you
think I'd be sitting here, wiv that mad boyfriend of yours
running about out there, if I didn't want to be with you?'

'Aye, ah know but . . .'

'What is it?'

She was playing with the zip on the sleeping-bag, as
though she had a confession to make. 'Ah think ah'm in
love wi ye,' she said.

Nathan didn't know what to say. What was he supposed to say? That he loved her too? That would just
complicate things even more. If he didn't say anything
she'd get moody – women were like that. The minute they
committed to something you had to follow suit. It was like
putting your money where your mouth was.

'It's the first time I've seen you stuck fir words,' she observed.

'I just don't know what to say wiv you sayin it out of the blue like that.'

'How could anyone no love ye?' She wrapped her arms around his waist and laid her head on his shoulder. He stroked the back of her neck. 'Yir gentle, yir kind . . . great in the sack.' She smiled.

'I'd love to spend the night wiv you,' he said, 'wake up in the morning and see you still there . . . I dream about you all the time, you know.' He kissed her forehead.

'Ah huv tae leave hum,' she said, as though thinking aloud. 'Ah jist cannae bring masel tae dae it th'noo . . .' She raised her head off his shoulder and looked him in the eyes. 'Whit's wrang wi me?'

'There's nothing wrong wiv you. You're scared, that's all.' He stroked her cheek.

She flicked the zip on the sleeping-bag as she thought. 'If ah left hum . . .' There was a prolonged silence. Nathan waited. 'If Ah left hum . . . could ah come tae London wi you?'

Fuck, Angie would love that, he thought. Keighley thought *she* was in a difficult position. Well, she should try being him.

'Er, yeah, it's just that, er . . .' He searched for the right words, anything that would give him a decent reason to say that it wasn't the best idea right now, but he couldn't find any. His mind was blank.

'Well, ye don't seem very convinced.' She reached for her top and pulled it on. He noticed the way her tone had changed.

'No, I mean, what about your job?' He tried to imply that she should think things through before making rash decisions.

'Ah kin git wan in London easy enough – wi mah qualifications.' She reached for her skirt. Nathan sighed inwardly. The ball was in his court. How the fuck would he get himself out of this one? There was only one thing for it. Come clean. She wasn't going to like it one bit – but if he worded it right?

'Look, Keighley—' He stopped himself and thought about how to say it. Just come out with it. I'm married. No, he'd have to be subtler than that, dress it up, and conceal the fact that his 'ex-girlfriend' was really his wife. He looked at her. She'd stopped pulling up her skirt and seemed frozen to the spot, staring straight ahead through the windscreen. He turned and looked out to see what she was scared of. It couldn't be Josh, could it? 'What is it?' he asked, with panic in his voice.

'Please tell me that's no the right time?' She pointed to the clock on the dash. Nathan breathed a sigh of relief. He pressed the light on his watch. 'Yeah, half twelve,' he said.

'Omigod.' She pulled her skirt up. 'Ah telt hum ah'd be hame fir eleven! 'He'll be goin mental. I hope he husnae phoned Lianne – she's a crap liar.' She reached for her shoes and pulled them on. Nathan climbed into the driver's seat. She crouched down to avoid banging her head, wriggled over the sleeping-bag and fell into the passenger seat.

'Don't worry – he's probably asleep by now,' he said, and started the engine.

'Ah hope tae God he is.' She wiped the condensation off the window and looked out at the woods.

Gordon sat in the car outside Harvey's house, eating a bag of chips and listening to Clan FM on his Walkman. The music was a bit young for his taste but the songs were growing on him. They were the songs his laddie listened to. He was glad that at last they had something in common – something they could talk about. He hoped Josh would come across with that job. Bringing home a wage was just what the lad needed.

He watched Harvey's front door for signs of him coming out. Still nothing. He'd told him to take his time, and he always did when he went for a shit. He could spend half a shift on the bogs. The sound of the Verve's 'Lucky Man' played in Gordon's ears. He liked the sound the Walkman produced: crisp, clear, not like that big stereo he had at home.

He tossed a green chip out of the open window and watched as the blue Escort van came round the corner at the top of the road and parked a good hundred yards in front of him. He put the chip paper down on the passenger seat and squinted as he made out her shape. There was no mistaking her, even from this distance. It was the wee nurse Josh went out with. He watched her get out of the van, lean in at the driver's side and give the black guy a kiss that said a hell of a lot more than 'Thanks for the lift'. If Josh knew about this . . . he thought. Well, *he* sure as fuck wasn't going to be the one to tell him. He watched her dart round the corner, her shoes click-clicking on the pavement as she ran. She was obviously in a hurry – trying to get home before Josh got back from the pub, no doubt. The van did a three-point turn and headed back the way it had come.

Gordon looked at the clock on the dash: 00.41. There weren't many places Josh could be tonight, he thought, unless he was up at Gavin Ritchie's or Moose's. Maybe the Ptarmigan was having a lock-in. Bastards, he thought, as Harvey came out of his house and shut the front door. There was no way he was having that, not without them inviting him – his shift would be finished in a couple of hours. He'd suggest it to Harvey, a quick drive by the place to see if things were locked up okay.

Harvey opened the passenger door and eased himself in. He looked at Gordon with a puzzled expression.

'Whit?' Gordon slipped off his headphones. Harvey sat up in his seat and reached behind him, took out the chip paper and threw it into Gordon's lap.

'Oh, soarry aboot that,' said Gordon, balled it and tossed it out of the open window into the gutter.

'Five hunnert pounds fine fir that,' said Harvey.

'Well, ye'll huv tae whistle, yir honour, ah've no goat it.' He started up the engine, put the car into gear and cruised off down the street in the direction of the Ptarmigan.

'Yir a fuckin slag!' Josh paced the room in his boxer shorts, fuming, barely able to contain his anger.

'Ah wis at Lianne's,' she said, nervously, as she sat on the edge of the bed and took off her shoes.

'Till whit time, eh?' He barged over and stared her in the eye.

'Till er, aboot . . . ah cannae remember. We went back tae hurs after the pub.'

He nodded as though he'd caught her out. She'd hanged herself with just one sentence. 'The pub, eh?' he said. 'Well, ah phoned the Ptarmigan an Brendan said—'

'Ah didnae say we went to the Ptarmigan. We were in the Glen.' She looked at the floor in case he saw the lies behind her eyes.

'The Glen? When the fuck huv you ever drank in the Glen? It's an auld man's pub – ye said so yirsel.'

She'd have to convince him quickly or she knew what would come next. 'We fancied a wee change, that's aw.'

'You an Lianne?' he asked.

'Aye.'

'Well, that's funny,' he said. 'Ye see, ah phoned Lianne an she said she never seen ye th'night.'

She scrunched up her face, puzzled, as though trying to figure out how Lianne could have been at home answering the phone to the likes of him when she was really out with her. 'Whit?' she asked, as though he were a half-wit.

'Don't you fuckin *whit* me. You've bin seein someone else!'

'Oh, Josh, don't start aw that again. Look,' she said, 'Ah'll no be late again . . . awright?'

He continued to pace the room. 'Don't you fuckin patronise me, okay?' He gave her a look intended to put her in her place. The please-don't-insult-my-intelligence look. The kind of look a Mafia boss gives someone who's been stealing from him. 'Ah want tae know who it is.' He glared at her.

She stared back. Surely he didn't know? How could he? No one had seen them together. 'Who *whit* is?' she asked, as innocently as she could. She was quaking with fear and her breathing was shaky. Had he spotted the signs?

He stormed forward and jabbed his finger in her cheek. 'Laist fuckin chance!' he shouted. She knew the choices: she could come clean or she could deny it. Either way there was a price to pay.

'Ah'm no seein *anyone*.'

'Fuckin liar!' He swung a fist at her, catching her on the cheekbone.

She screamed and reeled backwards with the force, fell off the bed and landed with a thud on the floor.

'Yir fuckin at it! Ah telt ye before – if ah ever catch ye . . .'

'Ah've hud enough ay this, Josh,' she said quietly, rocking gently on the bed like a child trying to comfort herself.

'You've whit?' He stepped forward like a bull who'd just been shown a red rag.

She turned to him with hatred in her watering eyes. A purple patch had formed on her cheek and was beginning to swell. 'Ye've hud enough, huv ye?' he asked. 'Well, whit ye gonnae dae aboot it?'

'*Ah'm leavin ye!*' she screamed.

'Is that right?' He clenched his fist.

She flinched, expecting another punch.

'Try it. Go oan, jist fuckin try it,' he said, as he squatted down and stared into her white, scared face. She turned her head away but he grabbed her jaw and pulled her round to face him. 'If you ever – *ever* – leave me, ah'll find ye an ah'll *kill* ye,' he said, as though it were the only logical thing for him to do. He stood up and marched out of the door, into the spare room, and slammed the bedroom door shut behind him.

Keighley lay face down on the bed, held her throbbing cheek and sobbed.

Josh sat down at the multi-gym and grabbed the bar above his head. He gritted his teeth and pulled it down until it touched the back of his neck. The cable hoisted the eighty-kilo weights smoothly up the frame then down again to land with a **CLANK**. He breathed deeply and pulled on the bar once more. He could hear her sobbing in the next room. Fuck her, she'd brought this on herself. There was no way he was going to let any woman treat him like that. He pondered if he'd been wrong, to lash out like that, but, he remembered the signs too well.

He thought back to the nights he'd look out of the back window when he was a kid. His mum would be dolled up and climbing over the fence in her high heels and short skirt. Duncan Thompson, their neighbour from up the street, would be helping her over, putting a friendly hand on her arse and copping a feel of the goods he was going to sample that night. Josh would go back to the TV, thinking about what he would tell his dad if he phoned from the night shift.

He'd felt guilty, knowing what was going on all that time. The seeds of family break-up had been sown before his eyes and he had been either too stupid or too disinterested to put a stop to it.

He pulled the bar down again and it hit him on the back of the neck, leaving a small red mark between his shoulders. He clenched his teeth and took the strain as the weights fell back to the pile with another **CLANK**. He felt his shoulder muscles burn – he should have done some warm-up exercises first, but he'd been too angry to bother with all that shite.

He'd always said that if any woman treated him the

way his ma had treated his da she'd be for the fucking chop. He'd told Keighley the score and thought she understood, yet here she was, flaunting herself with other men, making him look a cunt in the process. He stood up and paced the room, swinging his arms in a circular motion, trying to loosen up his stiff torso and shoulders. He took the metal peg out of the weights and moved it up two places. A hundred kilos. He sat down and grunted as he took the tension on the bar, straining to lever his arms down. The weights edged up the frame and teetered near the top before they slammed down. Josh took a deep breath and heaved again, thinking of how his dad must have felt when his mum told him she was leaving to go and live with that Duncan Thompson. The poor old bastard. He still carried a torch for her after all these years. Josh had lost contact with her a few years back, after he'd bumped into Thompson in a pub and wiped the bar with him. Cheeky bastard! He'd tried to shake Josh's hand as though everything was all right. Things were far from all right. That arsehole had made sure of that. Within a week of the business in the bar he'd heard that Thompson and his mum had uprooted and moved to Edinburgh.

Josh lowered the bar and stood up. What now? Where did they go from here? He imagined she'd probably have seen sense by now and would apologise in the morning. With a bit of luck it wouldn't be mentioned again.

*   *   *

Thirty quid return. That was the business. In a couple of hours he'd be in Euston. He'd taken Liz's advice and bought himself a phone card. Trouble was, he'd used it all up in one call to her. The girls were off school when he phoned and he talked to them too. God, he missed them. That's what swung it for him, their little voices. When Jade said, 'Daddy, I miss you,' he'd thought his heart was going to break. Instead he asked her to put Mum on and told Liz he was coming home – no arguments. He reminded her that he was earning decent money and of her advice to him – 'Treat yourself.' He bought a train ticket to go and see his girls.

Karl looked about the compartment, observing the passengers: families going to visit relatives down south, Scottish businessmen swotting up on reports so they could argue their corner when they joined their London colleagues for their quarterly arse-whipping over low sales figures. He watched as people got their belongings together, hauling jackets and bags down from the over-head storage shelf and edging past others standing in the middle of the aisle. They'd just pulled into Oxenholme and a couple of young American girls were easing off their enormous rucksacks and trying to wedge them between the seats. They looked like sisters, had the same features, same hair, and seemed to get on together. He imagined Jade and Lucy at their age, travelling the world. Christ, he'd be about fifty.

A young black guy at the end of the platform caught

his eye as the train pulled out of the station. He thought of Nathan, working away on his own, and felt guilty for leaving him. Then again, Nathan hadn't opposed his plan. In fact, it had been as though he were pushing him to go. He'd said it was about time he got some work done instead of letting Karl do it all.

Karl knew he was shagging Keighley, and he could understand where he was coming from. It was about time he got a break. Angie was as mad as a cuckoo's arsehole and she didn't deserve him. Nathan was far too good-natured, easy-going. Sometimes Karl wished he'd stand up for himself. He'd seen it a few times when they'd been out together. Some cunt would be showing out and Karl would get into a spot of potential bother. Nathan always took the role of mediator, rather than take it outside. It always ended with Nathan making them shake hands. Karl knew that sometimes a good ruck was needed to clear the air. It did both parties the world of good. People had problems at work, in their family life, whatever; they needed a release. Besides, they were adults and knew what they were getting themselves into. There was always a chance they might get hurt but it went with the territory. If some cunt noised you up you dealt with it. If it meant you took a whipping then so be it, but at least you didn't lose face. People understood. If they saw you fight, give it your best shot then it didn't matter who the fuck won. You still got patted on the back if you lost because you were in the right so either way you came out the hero. Karl wondered when Nathan last had a fight. Not in all the time he'd known him. The guy had a lot to learn about life.

'Enjoy yir meal.' The barman of the Glen Tavern placed a ploughman's lunch in front of Nathan.

'Thanks.' Nathan picked up his cutlery and un-wrapped the red paper napkin that enveloped it. Out of the corner of his eye he saw Josh lumber in and plonk himself on a bar stool. The warm sunlight filtered through the open door and into the room, lighting up the specks of dust that hung in the air.

Nathan forked a slice of cheese covered with Branston pickle into his mouth and opened his copy of the *Daily Record*, turning to the TV section. There was a new series called *Sharks*, a sitcom he'd never heard of on BBC 1 and the second of a two-part drama that looked okay on STV. Pity he'd missed the first part, but he'd been too busy shagging . . .

'Awright?' said Josh, putting his pint on the table and sitting down opposite Nathan.

Nathan almost choked as a pickled onion caught the back of his throat. 'How's it going?' he replied, and tried to put all thoughts of shagging Keighley out of his mind.

'No bad.'

Nathan buttered a slice of French bread and glanced at his paper, wondering what Josh wanted. Usually he wouldn't give Nathan the time of day and now here he was as though he wanted to be mates or something.

'Listen,' said Josh. Nathan looked up from his paper. Someone must have seen them in the woods and decided to spill the beans. The world was full of evil, twisted . . .

'That business the other day,' continued Josh. 'Er, cheers fir no sayin anyhun, like.'

'Oh, right,' said Nathan, relieved. He was still disgusted with himself for not speaking out.

'Mouthy wee cunt that Roddy. Someone should huv done it ages ago.' Josh drank some lager and looked about the room. Old Pat McBain sat in the corner and busied himself flicking ash off the table with a beer mat. Josh turned back to Nathan with a sneer that said he was glad people knew their place now – they'd think twice about messing with him in future.

'So,' Josh eyed Nathan's lunch, 'ye goat lucky since ye goat here?'

'Sorry, mate, you've lost me.' Nathan was genuinely puzzled by the question. What did he mean? With work? He wasn't going to bang on about that again, surely.

'Goat yir end away yet?' Josh leaned forward as though spelling it out.

Nathan felt sick, but then saw Josh's amused expression – he didn't know about him and Keighley, didn't have a clue. If he did he wouldn't be sitting here grinning and asking about his sex life. Anyway, what kind of question was that? If he said yes, he *was* getting his end away, the nosy bastard would expect him to say who with and tell him what it was like. If he said no he'd think he was gay or just unlucky. If he said he was married and not interested, it might get back to Keighley and he was already up to his arse in it as things were.

'Er, not exactly,' Nathan said, as though he was hinting that he was working on something.

'Goat yir eye oan anyone?' asked Josh.

Nathan scratched his ear. He had to think fast, throw him off the scent. If Josh suspected for one minute that he fancied Keighley Nathan's guilty face would give the game away. 'Well, there is that little dark-haired bird at the post office,' he said. She'd smiled at him a couple of times when he was in there, posting letters to Angie to which she'd still to reply. The girl was nice-looking although her enormous arse was out of proportion with the rest of her body. Not her fault, though – and it was something you could live with. He had a mate, Dougie, who would have thought it an asset . . .

'Wee Morag?' Josh put down his glass. 'Aye, she likes the boabby awright.' He grinned. 'Still, you'll be awright there, eh?' Josh jerked his head towards Nathan's groin. Nathan smiled, even though he hadn't understood a word of what Josh had just said. He'd only mentioned the girl to make him think he was looking elsewhere. Who was Bobby anyway? Some guy she was going out with? Good luck to him. He watched as Josh finished his pint and got up.

'Goat tae go. See ye.'

'Yeah, be lucky.' Nathan looked at his meal and put down his knife and fork. He'd lost his appetite.

He'd hoped to bump into her on her day off but could only imagine she'd spent the day indoors hiding away from people. She was wearing more makeup than usual, but that wasn't what shocked him: it was the black eye she'd tried to conceal.

Keighley walked through the door of the ward and gave him a faint smile. He knew his face must have shown his concern: he was trying to figure out what she'd been through, and what other injuries she might have sustained. He glanced about the ward: Eddie the nurse was at the other end and Lianne was in Colin's office. Now was as good a time as any. He walked over, took her by the arm and turned her away from the patients.

'What happened?' he asked. Her eye was badly swollen underneath the thick brown foundation she'd applied. The white was a startling red, as though she was wearing a joke contact lense.

'Whit dae ye think?' she replied. 'Ah telt ye he widnae be happy aboot me stayin oot.'

'Oh, God, Keighley, I'm sorry.' He felt more than partly responsible for the state she was in. Then reality hit home. Maybe Josh had been biding his time, playing games with him yesterday. 'He doesn't know about us, does he?' he asked.

'No,' she replied, with a faraway look in her eyes. He could see the tears welling up, threatening to cascade over her cheeks. He considered how his last question must have sounded. Selfish. Here she was, taking a beating for something he'd been part of and it seemed as though he just wanted to save his own skin. 'Sorry, I didn't mean for that to sound like I was only worried about myself . . .'

'It's awright.'

'What are you going to do?'

'Ah don't know.' A tear brimmed over. She sniffed.

He felt as though he'd intruded on her life and turned it upside down, then left her alone to pick up the pieces. Within a week or so he'd be out of here and their relationship would be over because he would have come clean about Angie. Keighley would go back to a man she despised. Sometimes it was a case of *better the devil you know*, but her particular devil could be a right evil bastard, and Angie was no angel either.

'Whit dae you think ah should dae?' she asked, wiping her face and taking a deep breath. She looked into his eyes.

Was this a trick question? Women had a knack of asking the right question at the right time. You had to have the right answer ready and deliver it, without hesitation and with tons of conviction. He'd known this for years but he still hadn't mastered it. 'I think we should cool things for a while,' he said, and her face dropped. Wrong answer.

She pursed her lips.

'I don't like seeing you like this,' he said, trying to make his feelings clear.

'So, ye'd rather no see me at aw, is that it?'

Fuck. Another trick question. 'No,' he said, 'that's not what I mean. It's for your own safety.'

She looked at him incredulously. 'Oh, come oan,' she said, disbelievingly, and shook her head as if to say she'd heard some crap excuses in the past but this one just took the biscuit.

'I mean it. He could kill you next time.'

'He will if ah stay wi hum.'

He knew what she would say next, but he decided to play dumb.

'Nathan . . . yir the only good thing tae huv come intae mah life in years. Ah don't want tae lose that.' She looked at him for an answer, but he stared at the floor. She went on, 'Ye know, these patients huv bin evaluated as mentally ill, but wi aw the stuff ah put up wi in mah life, it probably makes me madder than them.'

'I don't know what to say,' said Nathan. He thought back to the first time he'd seen her and wished he'd resisted temptation, kept himself to himself instead of flirting with her. Now he was in it up to his neck. He saw her lip tremble and knew then that he was wrong to think this. He *did* love her – he wanted to protect her, take her away from Josh and all the madness in her life . . . but to what? A situation that was just as mad in London?

'Ye could tell me how ye feel aboot me.' She wiped away a tear and looked into his eyes for some sign that he understood what she was going through. Even if he didn't have the answer to their predicament he could at least tell her he felt the same way about her.

'I love you, Keighley – you *know* that,' he said.

Her face broke into a smile.

He'd said the right thing at last. Maybe he was beginning to understand women. Nah, there was no chance of that. Guys had spent their whole lives trying to and had failed miserably.

'Dae ye know how ah think aboot you?' she asked. She didn't wait for a reply, just went on, 'Ah see you as mah rehabilitation,' she said. 'Ah kin only be strong enough to leave Josh if yir wi me. Ah want tae huv a normal relationship fir once in mah life.'

A normal relationship? he thought. If only there were such a thing. Maybe there was and he didn't know it. The difference between Keighley and Angie was night and day. He pictured Keighley in his flat, sleeping in his bed, making love to him in the shower . . . Angie's mad face staring through the steam-covered glass, holding up a carving knife . . .

'Look, let me think of something,' he said. 'I promise I'll sort it out, okay?' She sniffed, unconvinced. 'I mean it,' he said. 'Now, stop worrying.'

*　　*　　*

Harvey looked up through the glass panel in the door and saw Nathan. Immediately he thought that this would be about another petty crime, the outsiders being picked on by the locals, but he knew that only a handful of blokes were narrow-minded enough to carry on like that. Josh Strachan was top of the list. But as Nathan approached the counter, Harvey reread his expression, and thought it might be something to do with his van. Maybe someone had nicked it, let down the tyres, smashed the headlights. Again, Josh Strachan sprang to mind. It was only when Nathan stood in front of him and said, 'In the pub, the other day . . . I saw it all . . . it's Josh you want,' then looked down at his shoes as though he were Judas Iscariot blowing the whistle on Christ, that Harvey realised there was indeed a Santa Claus and that all his Christmases had come at once.

'Are ye prepared tae mek a statement tae that effect?' he asked cautiously. Nathan nodded. 'Good man,' said Harvey. He raised the hatch on the counter and smiled at Nathan, indicating that he should come through into the back of the station. He laid a friendly hand on Nathan's shoulders as he showed him the way to an open office and indicated a seat. 'Here ye go. You sit yirsel doon an ah'll git the paperwork. Kin ah git ye a tea, coffee?' he asked.

'Coffee, please – white, two sugars,' said Nathan.

Harvey began to leave the room. Suddenly he stopped and turned as though he'd remembered something.

'Ah'm glad someone's had the balls tae ston up tae this idiot. Stuff like this hus bin goin oan fir far too long around here.'

'Will he go down for this?' asked Nathan.

'Oh, aye.' Harvey laughed, as though he'd been looking forward to putting Josh away for a long time.

Nathan sat at the black laminated table, studying the posters on the lime-green walls. *Shop the Dealers* and an *AA* poster faced him. *Zero Tolerance* was on the wall next to him with a picture of a badly beaten young woman with a black eye and a cut across her nose. He thought of Keighley, and any ideas he had about not doing the right thing left him – although he could imagine only too clearly what the consequence might be when Josh found out that he'd grassed him up. He wondered what police protection they might offer him. He couldn't remember hearing of anyone he knew getting a police guard, but the issue of his and Keighley's safety should be enough to buy them some sort of guarantee. He realised he probably shouldn't mention her: if the police got wind of them being an item it would cast doubt on the credibility of his statement. But what if Josh *didn't* get banged up? Some of these coppers were incompetent bastards – particularly village bobbies. Their idea of crime was someone's milk getting nicked from their doorstep. He hoped Harvey knew his job and wouldn't make a complete arse of this.

'Right, then.' Harvey breezed back into the room with

two steaming plastic cups and some official-looking paperwork under his arm, 'Ye ready?' He hooked his foot behind the door and pulled it shut, then sat down opposite Nathan.

'Yeah,' said Nathan. 'Ready as I'll ever be.'

'He's dein it so's he can tek hus woman affay hum. Ah seen them th'gether the other night,' said Sandy Gordon as they drove along in the police car, approaching Josh's flat. The tyres crunched on the quartz pebbles in the driveway as Harvey turned the wheel and swung the Mondeo alongside Josh's van.

'It's a sworn statement,' said Harvey, switching off the engine and opening the door.

'It's no worth the paper it's printed oan,' snorted Gordon, slamming the door, hoping Josh would hear it and get wind of what was going on. He knew what Josh was capable of, but he'd thought he'd got through to him in the past about keeping that temper of his in check. If the charge stuck, it meant that, with Josh's track record, he'd get jail this time. And where would that leave Gordon's laddie? His one chance of a career snatched away from him by a dodgy statement from an English bastard.

They walked up the stone steps to Josh's front door and Gordon coughed loudly, as though he had a tickle in his throat, trying anything he could think of to let Josh know of his unwelcome visitors.

* * *

Josh glanced out of the window and saw the police Mondeo parked next to his van. He could hear their boots scuffing up the stairs, and knew it was Harvey. The cunt must have got his statement. But who from? He didn't think the English boy would have blown the whistle on him. Londoners were streetwise, like Glasgow guys or Scousers. They didn't shop anyone because they knew what the consequences would be. It only left the cronies, old Roddy's mates. Could have been them – they were too daft to understand what havoc Josh was capable of. He imagined them all huddled together in the pub, firing each other up about Josh having no respect for his elders and all that shite. That was why old Pat couldn't look the road he was on the other day. The auld cunt. Just wait till he saw him. Then there was Brendan. He knew what a shifty wee shite he could be. Aberdonian Davie was just as bad: a right wee sweetie-wife. A couple of drams and he'd be bumping his gums to Harvey, no problem.

Josh slid down the side of the bed where Keighley had landed the other night. The bell rang and he ducked as he saw Harvey's face peering through one of the patterned glass panels in the front door. He'd have to lie low for a while until he knew what the score was. Right now it was too dodgy to chance staying around here. Harvey would have him banged up faster than his feet could touch the ground.

Harvey hammered on the door again and pressed the

bell, making it ring for what seemed an eternity. Josh snorted, amused to himself. What, did he think he could irritate him with the doorbell so Josh would jump up and wrench the door open and ask him what the fuck he was playing at? He'd have to be a lot cleverer than that to get Josh Strachan.

The paintwork scratched on a tree branch as Josh pushed the van into the dry ditch. Between that and the dent in the door it was just as well he was leaving the fucking thing here for the insurance company to collect. He wondered how long it would take them to find it. He wished he'd thought of this earlier – it was cheaper to have it repossessed than make the payments. Especially now, as there was less than a hundred quid in his account and no prospect of work on the horizon.

He'd left Keighley a note on the kitchen table, saying he thought it was a good idea that they spent some time apart. He knew he'd been a bastard lately but the pressure of work was getting to him and he'd be a different guy when he came back from Ireland in a few months' time. He'd have money then and they'd be sorted.

He hauled his tent and rucksack out of the back of the van, slammed the door and trudged off through the dark woods in the direction of Ben Leven.

When she found the note she'd thought it was some sort of sick joke. Ireland? Then she remembered he'd mentioned something about a friend going to work over there. But she'd never considered for a moment that he would just uproot and take off like that, not until Nathan filled her in on what Josh had done to old Roddy. Then it made sense. Out of all the shitebags in the village who saw Josh attack him that day, Nathan was the only one man enough to do the right thing and go to the police, despite the likely consequences when Josh found out. That was when she knew that he loved her . . . *really* loved her. If he was willing to stand up to Josh, he was definitely the man for her. She wanted the whole world to know how happy she was.

The topic of conversation in the Ptarmigan that night was Josh's attack on Roddy, and how Josh wouldn't be stupid enough to show his face around here again. As the night wore on, Keighley got pissed enough to think it would be safe to let more than a couple of the regulars know just how she felt about the new man in her life. 'Ah love hum. He's the bravest man ah know.' She pulled Nathan's face towards her and planted a kiss on his lips. Nathan was embarrassed: this was unfamiliar territory. Not only was a beautiful woman paying him compliments, but the locals were treating him like a celebrity. He looked down at the drinks on the table in front of him and indicated the two whiskies that sat among the pints of lager. 'Lianne, do you want to help me out wiv those? I'm half pissed.'

Lianne smiled and shook her head. Keighley looked as

though the weight that had been hanging around her neck had been cut free. She was glad that bastard was out of the way. He'd pissed off just as quickly as he'd arrived, and now that he was gone Glen Leven would be a better place.

The door swung open, and she saw Keighley's eyes flick towards it. Moose and Gavin breezed in. *No Josh.* Thank God. Lianne realised this was something both she and Keighley would have to get used to. Moose and Gavin walked up to the bar, joking with each other. 'Thank fuck,' Moose said, when Keighley told them that Josh was away in Ireland. Lianne didn't suppose there was anyone around here who'd miss him.

Nathan sipped his lager, feeling conspicuous. Keighley hadn't been able to keep her hands off him all night, rubbing the inside of his thigh or tickling the back of his neck. She didn't care who saw her. As she put it, 'Ah'm in love wi ye, Nathan, an ah don't care who knows aboot it.'

'Come on, let's get you home,' he said now.

'Ah don't want tae go hame, ah want tae be wi you.' She looked longingly into his eyes. 'Whit wis aw that talk aboot wantin tae wek up wi me?' she asked.

Nathan recalled stifling Melody's screams of passion, and he knew he'd have to do the same tonight. Somehow he couldn't see his landlady tolerating the idea of her no-guests rule being broken.

*　　*　　*

Josh awoke with a shiver and pulled the sleeping-bag around his neck. He wondered if the damp inside it was due to the early-morning dew or his sweat. He huddled into a ball – it definitely wasn't the latter. How many more nights could he put up with this? It had only been one and already he felt like his joints had seized. And this was the middle of summer! He opened the tent flap and peered out. The dense trees enveloped the woods, allowing only meagre patches of sunlight through, and he considered moving his camp to a warmer spot but that would blow his cover. He looked at his watch: eight fifteen. He tried to remember what shift Keighley was on. He'd spent the night thinking about her, dreaming of making love to her.

He reached for the small camping stove, amused that he was fantasising about shagging his girlfriend instead of that dark-haired lap-dancer from the Channel Four documentary he'd seen recently. It must be love if Stella never got a look in last night.

He struck a match and lit the stove, turned up the gas and cupped his hands above it for some warmth. A couple of blankets wouldn't go amiss. That big spare double duvet was lying in the bedroom cupboard doing nothing. He could have done with it last night. He thought about going back for it but Harvey was prob-ably watching his place. No, this definitely wasn't the life for him. He'd been camping a few times but he was too used to his home comfort now. *The Sopranos* was on last night and he'd missed it, having to hide out here. It was the only TV show he really liked. That Tony Soprano was a gallus cunt – reminded him a bit of himself.

He poured some water from a five-gallon container into a metal cup and placed it on the stove. He'd have to get some supplies soon: he'd only managed to grab the essentials on his way out of the door yesterday.

Then Keighley sprang to his mind again. He could meet her. She always walked through the woods on her way to work. It would give him a chance to explain what was going on and, more to the point, what a complete cunt he'd been lately. He thought about the things he'd done to her. She hadn't deserved any of it. He knew he was insecure – his ma and that arsehole Duncan Thompson had made him like that. He didn't need a psychiatrist to tell him he was scared that the woman he loved would walk out on him. When she said she was leaving him the other night that sick, empty feeling had come back worse than ever in the pit of his stomach. He cast his mind back to his teenage years and remembered how he felt – his poor old da not knowing his missus was having an affair. His ma treating his da like shite, and making him leave the house, then Thompson moving in a couple of days later. The anger rose inside him and Josh swore for the millionth time that no woman was ever going to do that to him.

Keighley knew only too well what his problem was – she

was a psychiatric nurse, for God's sake. So why had he never trusted her? Too scared to open up, probably. Scared it would shatter his macho image. Imagine big Josh Strachan sitting greeting in front of his bird about his childhood problems. Fuck that. But they weren't his childhood problems any more, they were his adulthood problems. They were happening *now*. They were the reason behind his rage – the fact that he thought people would rather fuck him over than do him a good turn. It was all very nice to see the good in people, like Keighley did, but at the end of the day it didn't hurt to be wary, on your guard. The world was full of arseholes and there was no way they were going to take the piss out of him any more.

He placed a teabag in the boiling water and pulled the sleeping-bag around his shoulders. He'd have his tea, then scout about for some wood before heading off to the stream Keighley always passed. He knew she'd be glad to see him. Especially now he'd decided to turn over a new leaf. He was glad she was the way she was. He'd misjudged her – had seen it as a weakness in her character. Fuck, she was stronger than he was. He'd tell her that, tell her how much he admired her, how sorry he was for what he'd done. She'd forgive him and they could start again. Maybe Ireland wasn't such a bad idea, after all.

Nathan sat in the van, thinking over the previous night's events. He'd had to sneak Keighley in through the window, hauling her, drunk and giggling, over the windowsill and collapsing in a heap on the floor. It was great to be able to spend the night together in a bed – even if it was only a single one. He'd had to haul it away from the wall to stop the headboard banging. Keighley had ended up lying on her stomach with her face in a pillow to muffle her moans. Nathan felt himself starting to get hard as he thought about it.

Keighley came out of the newsagent's and jumped into the van. She slammed the creaky door shut and winced as the noise reverberated in her head, making her wish she hadn't done it.

'How you feelin now?' asked Nathan.

'Rough.' She unscrewed the top off the bottle of Irn Bru and took a long, satisfying drink, then offered it to Nathan.

'What is it?' he asked, looking at the bright orange liquid.

'Ginger.' She handed him the bottle.

'Doesn't look like ginger beer – it's the wrong colour,' he said, examining the contents.

'No ginger beer – ginger . . . *juice*.'

'Why's it called ginger, then, if it's not ginger flavour?'

'Just is,' she said.

He raised it to his mouth and took a swig. 'Urgh.' He handed it back to her.

'Don't ye like it?' she asked.

'No, it's horrible. How can you drink that first thing in the morning?'

'Best cure fir a hangover.' She let out another burp and held her hand to her mouth. 'Oops!'

Karl looked across the restaurant to the ball pit, where Jade bounced a bright pink ball off Lucy's head then climbed, laughing, up a rope ladder to a padded platform from which she teased Lucy to chase her. Karl laughed as Lucy took the bait and hurled a ball back at her sister then started her ascent up the rope-ladder. He turned his eyes back to Liz, who smiled and raised a forkful of salad to her mouth. 'You miss us?' she asked, knowing the answer, but wanting him to confirm it.

'What do you think?' Karl sliced into his steak. Liz cut a small piece of hers and dipped it into the peppercorn sauce.

'You not looking forward to going back, then, or is that a daft question?' She put the meat into her mouth and chewed. It had been a while since they'd done anything like this. These places were great when you had kids: they'd play for ages in the ball pit, leaving you to have a meal in peace. Then they'd wolf down a plate of chicken nuggets and chips, a quick slurp of a Coke and run back screaming to the madness of the ball pit.

'Yeah, it *is* a daft question. The sooner I get finished the sooner I can come home.'

'Well, we've missed you . . . I can hardly wait for you to be back. I don't like you working away. I don't feel safe unless you're in the house.' Liz looked up from her

234

plate and saw the expression on his face. His narrowed eyes and clenched jaw. The last time she saw a look like that was just before he'd had a fight with a guy in a pub. She didn't want a repeat of that, not with the girls about. 'What is it?' she asked.

'Over there – don't look now,' he said, indicating the bar.

She hated it when people said that. It made you want to do the opposite. She half turned and saw the unmistakable bleached-blonde mane of Angie Weller as she tossed it over her sunbed-tanned shoulders and waited for her change. She wore a pair of faded jeans and a low-slung powder blue halter-top.

'Angie?' said Liz, as she turned back to Karl. Covertly Liz checked out the tall black guy who accompanied her. He slung a thick muscular arm around her slender waist and whispered something in her ear, which made her laugh. His hair was shaved almost to the wood, leaving a millimetre or so of shiny black growth. His meticulously trimmed goatee was of the same length. Liz watched while Angie ran her eyes down his frame, as though he were her trophy. A waitress came back from the till and gave Angie her change. She put it away and hooked her thumb into the back pocket of her companion's jeans. They headed for the door.

'Stevie,' said Karl, pushing away his plate.

'You know him?' asked Liz.

'He's a bouncer. Works in the same club as her.'

'Well, he's big enough . . .' Liz mused.

Karl wondered what the hell she meant by that. Did she find him attractive – think there was nothing wrong with what Angie was doing?

'. . . to be a bouncer,' continued Liz. She could see from his look that he'd picked her up wrong. 'You going to tell him?' she asked, knowing the answer.

'Course I'm going to tell him. He's my mate, aint he?'

Keighley's shoes crunched along the red stone chips of the Ptarmigan car park to Nathan's van. She tripped then regained her balance. 'Bloody shoes,' was all she could think of to say.

Nathan unlocked the door, jumped inside and leaned across to open the passenger door for her. She'd continued to celebrate her new-found freedom tonight, but knew now that she had to stop: this was the way things were going to be around here from now on. Josh was history. She was proud of Nathan, and wanted to be seen with him, but she would be sober. She would face the villagers without a drink inside her. She'd made an arse out of herself tonight by telling the whole pub she was in love with Nathan and had seen the sneer on Moose's face. He'd told her she wouldn't be saying that if Josh were there. She said she would, she wasn't scared of him – not like Moose who'd always lived his life in Josh's shadow and was probably the only one around here who actually missed him. She mused that it was time he got a life, then left him standing at the bar, fuming.

Keighley closed the van door and pulled the seatbelt around her. Lianne had gone home an hour ago: she was being sensible for a change, wanted a clear head for work in the morning. She'd kept going on about how having to change shitey bedclothes with a hangover was a fate worse than death. Nathan had been on orange juice all night after the previous evening's bender, preferring to drive rather than walk as it was raining. Keighley had suggested a drive to a little spot she knew. It was the place where they'd first made love. The thought of being naked in the woods with Nathan and the cool wet rain on her skin was already making her body tingle with anticipation.

'Where to, madam?' asked Nathan, as he started the engine and switched on the headlights.

'Somewhere where no one kin hear ye scream,' she replied mischievously.

'I like the sound of that.' He grinned.

He'd been too deep in thought to notice it at first and he didn't know what had made him look. A squeak, a stifled laugh? Someone was definitely having sex in that van.

Josh approached cautiously, trying not to be seen. Imagine how it would look if the couple caught him staring at them through the windows? He was the last person you could call a pervert. He recognised the rocking blue Escort as the one owned by the English guys. He hadn't seen the white bloke for a couple of days, and guessed he was away home, so that left the black guy.

The moans of pleasure from the girl brought his thoughts back to Keighley.

He watched as the Southend Electrical motif swayed back and forth on the van's creaky chassis, while inside the steamed-up windows he could just make out the shape of an arse going ten to the dozen. He sniggered: wee Morag from the post office was getting more than she'd bargained for. He wished things were different so that he could go into the post office just to see her face. He could hint to her over the counter that he'd seen her in the woods. Her expression would be priceless. He shuffled through the trees that lined the clearing and headed for the village. 'Dirty English bastard.' He grinned.

'Ow, ow, ow . . .' Keighley lay on the floor of the van, with Nathan on top of her.

'What? Sorry, was I hurting you?'

'It's yir watchstrap. It's caught in mah hair.'

'Sorry.' He took it off and continued where he'd left off.

'Oooooh, God!' Keighley dug her nails into Nathan's back as she felt him coming. He thrust deep into her, arched his back and clasped her waist. The hot spurts inside her were too much to bear and her whole body shuddered as she, too, came to a climax.

She lay still for a moment, wondering if she'd imagined what she'd just felt, but it was soon confirmed when Nathan pulled out of her and examined the condom.

'Oh, fuck!'

'Whit?'

'Condom's bust – split in half.'

She fumbled in the dark for her knickers. 'So?'

'So much for safe sex,' he said, wiping a sticky hand on his boxer shorts.

'Whit ye so worried aboot?' said Keighley. 'It's no as though ah'm goin wi everywan, is it?'

'No, of course not,' he said.

'An you telt me ye've only bin wi the wan person fir a couple ay years?'

'Yeah, I know, but . . .' He pulled his jeans on, wondering how to word it.

'Well, then, whit ye goat tae be worried aboot? Neither ay us sleeps aboot or dis smack so there's little or nae chance ay gittin Aids.' She felt about for her knickers again and decided to forget it. They'd turn up.

'I don't mean that,' he said, fastening the belt on his jeans. 'I mean, what if you got pregnant?'

'Whit if ah did?' she smiled. 'Ah quite like the idea of huvin a wee Nathan aboot.' She reached out and tickled his ribs, but he pulled away.

He reached for his socks, thinking what a coward he

was. He felt as though he'd been using her. She deserved to know the truth. If things were to work out for them – and God knows how that was going to be possible – he'd have to tell her about Angie. He looked at her in the eye and took a deep breath.

'Look, Keighley . . . there's something I should have told you . . . I haven't been totally straight . . .' He paused, knowing that however carefully he crafted the words in his head there was no way that they'd come out of his mouth the same way.

'Whit dae ye mean by no straight? Yir no bi?'

'No, no,' he replied, and almost laughed, but thought better of it in the circumstances. 'I mean about my relationship . . . with Angie.'

'Yir girlfriend?' She pulled on a shoe slowly and looked at him questioningly.

Fuck, this was going to be even harder than he thought. His heart was hammering behind his ribs. He swallowed. 'She's not my girlfriend . . . she's my wife . . .'

'But ye've left her?' she asked, hopefully, searching his features for the truth. He bit his bottom lip and reached for his T-shirt, examining the creases in the Nike tick across the front. 'Not . . . totally.'

'Whit dae ye mean, *no totally*?' she asked. He realised she wanted answers, and she deserved them.

'Look, it's a bit rocky . . . I want to leave her but . . .'

'But whit?' Keighley stared at him. Was she hearing things?

'She said she'd kill herself if I leave her.'

She snorted as though he'd fallen for the oldest trick in the book. 'Yir jist mekin excuses, Nathan.'

'I'm not, honest.'

'Hoanest? Hoanest, is it? Ah cannae believe a word that comes oot yir mooth! You telt me ye'd split up wi hur!'

He was ashamed. 'Yeah, I know . . . That was before I fell in love with you.'

Keighley sat up and grabbed her bag. 'Ach, don't gies it . . . *Love me*? You *used* me, Nathan.'

'No, I didn't!' he protested, and reached out to take her arm. She pulled away, opened the back door of the van and climbed out. Nathan shuffled after her on his knees. 'Keighley, nuffin's changed. All I need is a bit of time to break it off wiv her *gently*. If I went back and told her I'd met someone else she'd top herself – I couldn't deal wiv that.'

'So, ye still love hur, then?' she asked, rearranging her skirt.

He could see he was getting nowhere fast. If he'd laid his cards on the table in the beginning he wouldn't have stood a chance, and now that he'd decided to come clean he still couldn't win.

'Course I don't love her,' he said. 'It's took me three years to work that out. I just need a bit of time to finish it. She deserves that at least.' He stepped out of the van and pulled on his white Nike T-shirt.

'An whit dae ah deserve, eh? Tae be used?' She stepped forward, threateningly. 'I didn't use you, Ange – *Keighley*,' he corrected himself.

She looked at him as though she'd just been enlightened. She bit her bottom lip. 'Ange am ah noo? It's no bad enough that ye treat me like an idiot but ye cannae even remember mah name. Thanks, Nathan, thanks very much.' She turned to walk away but he grabbed her arm.

'You've got me that confused I don't know *what* I'm sayin. It was a slip of the tongue, that's all, thinkin about her. Her name just came out. Don't mean nuffin, Keighley.' He looked deep into her glistening eyes.

'Ah wonder how long ye would huv kept this up fir . . . Till ye goat hame? Kept me hangin oan by the phone, no answerin mah letters – that's assumin ye'd give me the right address in the furst place. Don't want *Angie* finding oot noo, dae we?' she spat.

Nathan wondered how to make her believe him. This was the first step: admitting the problem. The second was dealing with it. 'Keighley, I'm going to finish it, I promise. I don't want her, I want you.'

She pulled her arm away from his grasp. 'But there's nuthin ye kin dae aboot it, int that right? Cos if she *is* suicidal, like ye say, an she teks an overdose it'll be *you* who's put the pills in hur hand, won't it?

'Yeah, that's what the problem is.' He was glad she could understand.

'That's bollocks, Nathan. Absolute bollocks. Yir no responsible fir anyone but yirsel. If she wants tae kill hursel there's nuthin you can dae aboot it, so git aff the guilt trip.' She walked about in circles like an agitated boxer before a title fight.

He knew she was right – Karl had said the same thing – but it wasn't as easy as that. And people who dispensed this kind of advice were never likely to be in such a position in the first place. Bastards. He tried a different approach. 'It's the same as you, though, innit?' he said. 'You said if you left Josh he'd come looking for you and he'd kill you. That's why you stayed wiv him so long. You were trapped too.'

'Aye . . . bit at least ah wis strong enough tae dae somehun aboot it. No like you. You cannae ston up tae hur – she's goat you danglin oan a string!'

He was speechless. She was absolutely right. He *was* a spineless bastard. The easiest thing to do would be to go back to London next week and carry on where he'd left off.

'See ye, Nathan. It wis nice knowin ye.' A tear ran down her cheek and she hurried away.

He gazed at the broken twigs lying at his feet. 'Fuck!' He hated himself. He sprang into action and ran after her. 'Keighley, wait! I'll do it. I'll go home and finish wiv her – just as soon as Karl gets back.'

She stormed towards the dense dark trees as though he wasn't there. 'If you go back tae London that's the laist ah'll see ay ye, so ah'll save ye the bother. It's over – the noo!'

Nathan followed, catching his leg on a broken branch that dug into his thigh. 'Keighley, wait!' he shouted, 'I can't see where I'm going. Hold on a minute – *please*!' He saw the white figure stop. She waited a second or two then marched back towards him. That's better, he thought. 'Look, this is stupid . . . let me drive you home,' he pleaded.

'Ah don't want anyhun fae you, Nathan. Stay away fae me!' she warned.

'You're being stupid,' he said.

'Aye, stupid tae let masel git used by you. Well, it'll no happen again!' She tried to barge past him, but he grabbed her by the arm and pulled her over to the van.

'Git yir hons affay me!' She tried to wriggle free but he held on tight. There was no way he was going to leave her to walk home on her own – anything might happen. If she didn't want to talk to him, fine, but he could at least see her home safely. 'Ah sais git yir hons aff!'

'I'm taking you home. We can talk about this when you've had time to calm down.' He dragged her round the side of the van and held her tightly as he opened the passenger door.

'Fuckin let go ay me!' she screamed. He held her firmer and tried to push her into the van.

'Ah sais let go!' She lunged at him like a trapped cat, clawing his cheek with her painted claws. He felt the

244

searing pain on his face and instantly let go of her, clapping his hand over the wound, feeling the blood run from it. He stood beside the van and watched her stumble towards the clearing.

A minute or so passed before the woods were quiet again. He heard a twig snap and a shiver ran down his spine. He didn't like this – he'd never been the same since *The Blair Witch Project*. He climbed into the van and drove away, shaking his head at the bravado of the Scottish woman.

Stuart looked down at the image forming on the ten-by-eight as he gently rocked the tray. The developer swished backwards and forwards over the print like a small wave. He glanced over his shoulder, double-checking that the snib was on the door. There was no way he wanted James, the photographer, coming in and seeing this.

He grabbed the print by one corner with a pair of plastic tongs and slid it into the stop bath. Another quick swish and then into a larger tray of water among a bunch of similar prints.

He looked down at the image of Keighley and felt sorry for her, but there was nothing he could do. If there was one thing he hated it was violence – he'd been on the receiving end of it enough times and knew what it was like. But it was a part of everyday life and sometimes you just couldn't avoid these things.

He pulled the print from the tray and ran a squeegee over it, examining the detail. It didn't look like the Keighley he knew, not the gentle, caring girl who would take him for a drink and treat him as an equal, sing him to sleep and assure him everything was going to be all right. She seemed a million miles away, as the Keighley of late hadn't had time for him since Nathan had appeared on the scene. He cast his eyes over the photo of her sprawled over a felled tree. He diverted his eyes from her crotch and her spreadeagled legs; embarrassed that she wasn't wearing any knickers and that he'd taken this shot of her in a most unflattering pose. Yet the pose wasn't important, he reminded himself, it was the recording of the event. The time and date. Especially as it had occurred when the moon was full. He didn't expect she'd understand the significance of that. Nobody did. They all thought he was mad, but this would make them see him in a different light.

Little did they know it but the moon affected everything. There were thirteen lunar months in the year; almost every animal took its navigation from the moon. That was why fishermen always swore the fishing was best when there was a full moon – they worked out the tides from lunar charts. He remembered telling Gavin in the pub once that the spring tides are the highest when the gravitational pull of the sun and the moon line up along the same axis. Gavin had seemed genuinely interested, but then started to go on about planets and *Star*

Trek. Stuart knew he wasn't really interested, but Karl had told him an interesting fact: that the word *lunatic* came from *lunacy*, meaning *affected by the moon*. It was true that people went a bit crazier when the moon was full. You only had to check police records to confirm that. And Keighley, lying there in that state, just proved the already tried and tested theory. The moon was a more powerful influence on people than they could ever imagine.

His eyes scanned the print, taking in the bruising to her face and legs. Her T-shirt was ripped and showed a large proportion of her right breast, but no nipple was visible. Stuart was glad of that. It might have looked as though he'd purposely positioned her that way for the sake of a photo and he didn't want people labelling him a sicko.

There were scratches on her upper body where she'd tried to fight him off, but he had been too strong for her. The bruises on her inner thighs were a reminder of how he had pinned her down and repeatedly thrust into her, mouthing obscenities about what a dirty bitch she was and how she'd brought this upon herself for being such a slag. Was this what she wanted? He'd kept asking, but she'd never answered, just kicked and bit and fought back. Stuart was amazed at her resilience and thought she would never give in. But she did . . . eventually.

He switched on the dryer and laid the print on the roller. Warm air belched from the back of the machine as the fan whirred into life and the rollers turned. He watched Keighley's image being pulled slowly into the machine. He took a second print out of the water tray and gave it a quick run over with the squeegee, examining it for faults. This had to be his best work yet, but no one was likely to see it. It would have to be for his private collection. If this fell into the wrong hands . . . The police? God forbid! He shuddered at the very thought and placed the second print on the roller as he heard James, the photographer, talking to a member of staff in the corridor. He would have to be quick and get them dry. If James saw this he'd never understand.

It wasn't so much being woken up at five o'clock in the morning by the police, or that they gave him little or no indication of why he was wanted for questioning back in Glen Leven. Or why they'd escorted him from the house in front of his upset wife and crying children on to the train with people looking at him as though he were a bank robber. No, it was the fact that he was expected to give a sample of semen – wank off into a plastic cup – just like that, as if there were nothing to it. They'd already taken hair, blood samples and his clothes for examination – and now they expected this?

He sat in the interview room, wearing a white boiler suit made out of what could only be described as processed paper, fuming as they slowly and deliberately questioned him. He sneered at them with disdain. Completely out of their depth – they reeked of incompetence. These stupid hick-town coppers didn't have a clue. He could see them mentally jerking off because this was the biggest thing in years to have happened in this shitty little village.

They said Keighley had been attacked: raped and beaten. And because early DNA tests had indicated that she was attacked by more than one man – the main suspect in this case being Nathan, as he was the last person to have been seen with her – they arrived at the obvious conclusion that his accomplice had been his friend, Karl.

He told them he had been in London when it happened but they smiled sarcastically and said, 'We'll see.' They asked him what his relationship was with Keighley. He said he didn't particularly like her, and that he'd told Nathan on a number of occasions to stay away from her as she was trouble, but they just kept messing with his head and misconstruing his sentences.

She was *trouble*? Needed to be taught a lesson? Did *you* teach her a lesson, Karl?

You say you didn't like her? Did she *laugh* at you, reject your advances, make you feel *sexually inadequate*? Did you feel the need to pay her back, Karl?

Why didn't you want your friend to have a relationship with her? Did you want a relationship with her yourself? Or did you feel rejected by *your friend* when she stole him away from you?

That was the best one yet. They were way off-course. Dickheads. He told them it didn't matter what he said, they had their minds made up. He said if they had something to go on they should charge him; if not, they should fuck off and leave him alone. It was the good-cop bad-cop act. The one called Harvey questioned him as though he understood Karl's motive for attacking her. All he had to do was tell Harvey, unburden himself. The other one, Gordon, was a clown and reacted to every move and gesture Karl made. Karl could see he was itching to have a go at him and wondered when Harvey would leave the room and Gordon would set about him with a length of hosepipe. He continued to shake his head and say, 'Charge me, if you're going to – I've told you all I know.' They said he could go. No charge – they just told him not to leave Glen Leven till they'd satisfied themselves with their enquiries. He felt as though they were still playing games with him, wanted to observe him, see what he got up to. Well, they'd have a fucking long wait, he thought, as he got up off the seat and left the room.

He was starting to wish he hadn't refused a solicitor but, as he put it, he had nothing to hide. However, he'd forgotten what a crap liar he was and was soon reminded of his inability to think on his feet.

Nathan shuffled in his seat and unstuck the white paper boiler suit from his arse.

'We've goat witness statements that say you left the pub wi hur,' said Harvey.

'Look, I offered to drive her home,' said Nathan, trying to keep calm. His stomach was churning and his heart was beating like a jackhammer. He remembered the police did that thing where they approached you gently as if you were their mate, placed a hand on your chest and felt the beat of your heart. Many a man who'd allowed them to do that had consequently hanged themselves. Nathan knew he couldn't rely on his body to help him out at a time like this and hoped they wouldn't pull that one on him. They didn't have to. From the expression on their faces they had more than one ace up their sleeve.

'She said she didn't want a lift and walked off through the woods,' added Nathan.

'An whit did you dae?' asked Gordon.

'I went home – back to the guest-house.'

Harvey looked at his notes. 'Did you go into the woods?'

'No,' replied Nathan. Best to keep the answers short, he thought. Don't tell them any more than they need to know.

'Yir landlady sais she didnae hear ye comin in till after hof twelve.' Harvey looked at Nathan for his response.

'Old ladies tend tae sleep light, don't they? Good joab,' mused Gordon to Harvey. Nathan sat and tried to think. What time had Keighley stormed off? It was much earlier than that – the pub was still open. What was that batty old trout on about – *half twelve*?

'Look, Mrs Grant must be mistaken. I came back a lot earlier than that. She was in bed.' He glanced at them for some recognition of what he was telling them but they stared back, stony-faced.

'Did Keighley git in the van wi ye?' asked Harvey.

'No. I've already told you,' said Nathan, affirmatively.

Gordon leaned forward in his chair. 'Then how dae ye account fir hur knickers bein in there?' Nathan hadn't thought of that. 'Well?' asked Gordon.

Nathan shrugged as if it was the first he'd heard about it, but inside he was mentally kicking himself. He was getting lazy. With Karl being away he hadn't felt the need to cover his tracks. He wished he'd been a bit more careful.

'Fir the benefit ay the tape Mr Weller has shrugged his shoulders,' said Gordon. Nathan glanced at the double tape deck whirring away and pictured himself at the end of the interview choosing which tape would be his. What the fuck was he supposed to do with it? Invite friends round to listen to it on his home stereo? There'd be no stereo where he was going.

'There wis a used condom doon the back ay the driver's seat an aw,' said Harvey, with an air of relish. 'Looks like it hud seen a but ay action but we'll be able tae git DNA fae it.'

Well, hip, hip, hooray, thought Nathan.

'Ye could save us the bother?' suggested Harvey.

'How dae ye explain the used condom?' asked Gordon.

'It's a works van – I'm not the only one to have used it, you know.' He felt annoyed. They had him now so he could be as cheeky as he liked. Maybe it would boost his confidence if he looked as though he didn't give a fuck.

'The strands ay hair found oan yir watchstrap have already come back as a match . . . They belong tae Keighley.' Harvey glanced up, awaiting Nathan's answer.

'I might have put my arm around her in the pub,' said Nathan confidently, as though he had nothing to hide, but he was aware that his feeble answers were making him look as guilty as sin.

'We've hud yir pal in. He sais ye were aw fir goin back tae London wi hum fir a few days bit ye suddenly changed yir mind. Whit made ye dae that, Nathan?' Harvey relaxed back in his chair; ready to listen to whatever crap excuse Nathan could give him, just so he could shoot it down in flames.

'I don't remember saying that. Anyway, what if I did? There's no law against changing your mind, is there?' He tried to sound cocksure, but his legs felt like jelly and his heart was beating in his mouth.

'Look, Nathan, we're aw men ay the world here . . . Why don't ye tell us whit happened? If ye were gien the lassie wan ye kin tell us.' Nathan looked at the simper on Gordon's face. He knew he couldn't trust him as far as he could throw him.

'She's just a friend,' Nathan lied. 'We get on . . . that's all.'

'Bit she *has* bin in yir van before? Ye cannae deny that?' asked Gordon.

'I've given her a lift to work, if that's what you mean,' replied Nathan, trying to look puzzled at their line of questioning.

'Oh, but yir relationship wi Keighley goes a wee bit further than bein workmates, though, disn't it?

Nathan shrugged his shoulders.

'We saw hur gittin oot yir van. Couple ay nights ago.' Gordon raised his eyebrows in triumph. Nathan stared at him. Had they? Or were they bluffing? The best thing for him to do would be to come clean – tell them they *were* having an affair . . . but he couldn't. It would mean changing his story, and then they wouldn't believe a word he said as he'd already spent the best part of an hour lying through his teeth to them. No, he would have to stick to his original story and see it through. The thought of Angie getting wind of this was giving him palpitations. Every time he answered their questions, sat silent, or even pleaded ignorance he knew he was digging a deeper hole for himself. He couldn't do a thing right. His fear of the process hadn't done him any favours. Here he was in an interview room with the shit about to run down his legs and he was sure he would have a heart-attack.

There was a knock on the door. Harvey stood up to answer it. Nathan watched as a guy in a brown suit whispered to him and indicated a report he was holding. The guy in the suit looked at Nathan as though he were the latest in a long line of felons and he just wanted to get a quick glimpse of him before they sent him to the electric chair.

Harvey took the report from the guy, followed him out and closed the door leaving Nathan with Gordon. A few minutes later Harvey came back, laid the report on the desk and slid it across to Gordon. Nathan watched Gordon's face as he took in the content.

'The DNA report oan the condom,' said Harvey, indicating the report. 'Ah'm afraid ah'm gonnae huv tae charge ye, Mr Weller.'

Nathan tried to take in what was happening. Somewhere in the distance he could hear Harvey's voice: 'Mr Weller, ah'm chargin you with the rape an battery ay wan Keighley Fraser. Ye do not have tae say anyhun . . .' He felt as if he was having an out-of-body experience – as though this were happening to someone else. He wondered when it would hit him. When he was sitting in a cell? If only he'd told a different story, got legal representation. It was too late now. The evidence was weighted firmly against him. They knew it. He knew it. The scratch on his face was a dead giveaway. The hair under his watch that they'd taken off him the minute he was brought in was more than enough to hang him. And now this, his semen inside her, the used condom in the van. He was fucked – well and truly. He wished he'd listened to Karl about Scotch girls being trouble.

He'd waited in the woods for an hour that morning but didn't even catch a glimpse of her. He'd spent the rest of the day calculating the risks of going back into the village to try to find her, but as he stood at the clearing, looking towards the deserted estate, he came to the conclusion that as it was the weekend, the filth – in the form of Harvey and his sidekick Gordon – would be cruising about near the chip shop, looking for potential troublemakers with a drink in them. It would give him enough time to nip into the Ptarmigan, get Keighley to come outside and away from that nosy bitch Lianne so he could have a word with her. Ten minutes was all he'd need. He was even prepared to turn on the waterworks if it made her believe him. He just had to be alone with her without any distractions. Then he could convince her that everything would be all right and they could plan their future in Ireland. He hoped she had enough savings. She could sell the flat, the furniture, the whole fucking lot. They both needed a fresh start.

But it had been the sneaky wee smile on Moose's face that did it. The pleasure it must have given him to see Josh's expression was incalculable. Josh had breezed into the Ptarmigan as though nothing had happened, walked up to the bar and smiled at Brendan, who looked as though he'd just seen a ghost.

'Pint, is it?' Brendan stuttered. Josh looked about for Keighley and Lianne. 'Naw thanks, Brendan – ye seen Keighley?' He searched the crowd of drinkers at the bar and saw Moose nudge Gavin.

'Er, she was in here earlier.' Brendan eyed Josh's mud-stained jeans and boots.

Moose sauntered towards him, grinning that sneaky wee grin as though he had one up on him. 'Ye looking fir Keighley, Josh?'

'Aye, ye seen hur?'

'Oh, ah've seen hur.' He smirked.

'Gonnae stoap actin like a wee diddy an tell me where she is then?' asked Josh, in no mood for Moose's infantile games.

'Left aboot hof an oor ago.' Moose raised the pint of Guinness to his lips and took a slow, deliberate swig. He lowered the glass and wiped the foam off his mouth. 'Wi that English boay – the black wan.'

'Eh?' Josh craned forward as though he hadn't heard him above the chatter of the crowd.

'Didnae tek hum long, did it?' said the smug-looking Moose, as he took another swig of his drink and raised his eyebrows at Gavin. Josh looked at Gavin for confirmation but all Gavin could do was give an apologetic smile. Josh stared at Brendan, who was trying to avoid his eye. He turned and stormed out with Moose's cackling laughter ringing in his ears.

The worst part was not remembering. The policewoman called her Keighley as if she knew her. She thought the name sounded familiar, as though it belonged to her, but she couldn't be sure. The strange thing was that comfortable feeling she had had when she came in here, of who she was, what her name was, as though it was all there in the back of her mind, just ready to be plucked from among all the other information as usual. But when she came to find it, to rely on it, she found she couldn't. It wasn't there any more. That was the most frustrating part. She felt as though her name was on the tip of her tongue and she laughed out loud at how ludicrous the situation was, saying, 'Imagine forgettin yir aen name,' but nobody else found it amusing. They were far more intent on treating her injuries.

She'd found herself in the woods, unable to remember how or why she was there. She'd tried to sit up but her back throbbed as though she'd fallen down a flight of stairs. Dried blood had stuck her matted hair to the side of her head, which now felt as though a lead weight was inside it when she tilted it forward. She rubbed her swollen jaw and neck, and pulled down her short white earth-stained skirt in case anyone passing by got a glimpse of her without any knickers. She wondered where her knickers might be, but couldn't for the life of her remember.

She was sore between her legs. Just as painful was her backside. Perhaps she'd participated in something she'd never done before. She wondered if she'd been drugged. She felt dehydrated as though she was awakening from an almighty night on the tiles, but no matter how hard she tried she couldn't remember a thing.

She'd got up and staggered about the woods barefoot on wobbly legs, looking for a way out, trying to get her bearings through the tears that blinded her, but she was hopelessly lost. She wanted her mum, and hoped she would be at home when she got there, although she had no idea where home was. She just knew she had an overwhelming urge to get to her. Her mum would be worried sick. She wasn't in any fit state to take care of herself. She felt guilty for letting her down.

The female doctor shone a light in her eyes and gave her a reassuring smile. 'Kin ye remember anything yet?' she asked. The policewoman at the side of the bed leaned forward with a sympathetic smile. 'About who attacked you?'

'Attacked me?' Had she been in a fight? She read their serious faces and knew what they were thinking – they were hoping she could remember so they wouldn't have to tell her. She wished they would.

'Sit up, please.' The doctor eased her head upwards. Keighley swung her legs over the edge of the bed and sat up while the doctor felt along her vertebrae, pressing and digging in her fingers. She glanced across to the small mirrored cabinet above the sink. A purple-faced hunchback with split and swollen lips stared back at her. She ran her tongue along the inside of her mouth and felt the jagged remains of two broken front teeth. The creature in the mirror looked at her shiftily through its good eye, while the lids of the other seemed to have been inflated from the inside and were set to burst at any minute. Its hair stuck out in all directions and looked like a bad henna job done by a blasé junior stylist in a cheap salon. It pulled its gown from its black and blue neck, showing her the extent of its bruising and the scratches around its throat. A lonely earring remained in one dirty lobe. The other must have freed itself from the bloody tear in the creature's other ear.

She felt the stabbing pain in her groin again and put her hand between her legs to see what it was, but there was some sort of pad or folded bandage in the way, taped down across her stomach and up the cheeks of her arse. She felt the tape tugging at her skin and lifted the gown to see if she could fix it but the nurse took away her hand firmly but gently. 'That's all right – ah'll dae that fir ye. Is it jaggin intae ye?'

She nodded. In the mirror the creature nodded, too, as though confirming it for her. She felt her eyes closing again and she began to fall slowly backwards. A pair of hands caught and supported her. She opened her eyes briefly to see the creature's head lolling to one side. It smiled a drunken smile at her and closed its good eye.

She felt sorry for it – it must be tired. She knew exactly how it felt.

'*Raped?* What the hell's been going on, Karl?'

Karl pulled the mobile away from his ear as Liz shrieked at him. He looked across the hospital car park and saw Lianne watching him from the window. She shook her head at him as though in disgust. He mouthed, 'What?' although he could tell that he'd been tarred with the same brush as Nathan. He leaned back on the van and sighed. 'I don't know. Police wouldn't tell me much.'

'But why did they drag you back like that? That's what I can't understand. What have you got to do with it?' There was an accusatory tone in her voice that she couldn't disguise. He felt himself getting uptight, thinking that maybe she suspected him too. This thing was far too complex to explain over the phone – he had less than three pounds left on his phone card and he needed to save some of that to call Ellis – he wanted to get off this job pronto. 'Cos I'm his mate, aren't I?' he said, through gritted teeth. 'This whole fucking place, Liz, it's so tight-knit – it's like the village of the damned or something. The minute something happens they come looking to the strangers!' He paced along the path, kicking the gravel. Pebbles rattled against the stone steps of the hospital.

'What the hell have you two been getting up to up there?' Her voice was shaky, as though *he*'d been the one playing away. Surely she knew him better than that? He looked across to the hospital window again – Lianne was talking to Eddie the male nurse. He thought back to the night in the pub when he had been drinking out of her glass. He'd been tempted then . . . but he hadn't done anything about it. Thank fuck. Nathan had, and look what had happened to him.

'I haven't been doing anything,' he said wearily. 'I'm just trying to do my fucking job!'

'Don't you snap at me – I'm not the one being sneaky!' she hissed.

He glanced at his watch, aware that she'd be struggling to get the girls ready for school, standing in the kitchen trying to keep her voice down.

'Liz,' he said, 'I'm not being sneaky. I haven't done a thing. It's Nathan – he's gone off the rails if you ask me, all this business with Angie.'

'Are you saying that when you told him he went off and did this?'

'No.' He tried to think of a way to reword it. 'I didn't get a chance to tell him about Angie – I haven't even seen him since I got back. The police questioned me, let me go and the next thing I know he gets banged up in Kilmarnock.'

There was silence at the other end of the line for what seemed like eternity. 'Liz?' He looked at the credit on the phone's display: £2.87 remained.

'Did he do it?' she asked.

That was the million-dollar question. You think you know somebody . . . He shook his head as he answered her: 'I don't know, Liz . . . I really don't know.'

'What do you mean *you don't know*? He's your mate. Surely you must have some idea what he's capable of?'

'Yeah, I know but—'

'Then tell me what you think. Did he or didn't he rape this girl?'

'It's possible,' was all he could think of to say.

'You've goat a visitor.' The guard opened the cell door and stood back to let him out. About fucking time. He hoped it would be his solicitor with some good news, or Karl to let him know what the hell was going on. Why hadn't he been to see him? Some mate he was. When he next saw him he'd let him know exactly what he thought of him.

He trudged along the metal landing and looked down at the mesh net below. Screwed-up paper and other rubbish rested across the gaps, occasionally falling to the ground.

This place was full of animals – he didn't belong here. Much less on a wing that had so many violent prisoners in cells on either side of him. He remembered their faces when he was brought in. As though he were fresh meat. They already knew what he was in for. How the hell had they found out? The newspapers? Some glared at him and turned their backs as though they had a score to settle and had all the time in the world to do it. Others smiled knowingly, as if he were the newest recruit in their sick little club. Chick, the bloke in the next cell, was the only person he felt he could trust in here, although he knew little or nothing about him. What he did know was that Chick had been sentenced for car crimes – the police had been after him for some time and finally nabbed him trying to hot-wire a souped-up Calibra in Glasgow. The way he'd explained it to Nathan was as though he was public enemy number one in Glasgow and they'd mounted a huge operation to get him. He'd tried to resist arrest and stuck the nut on one of the coppers, which had increased his sentence – as had the numerous sets of car keys, spare parts and illegal car-breaking devices that were found in his flat, not to mention a number of chipped mobiles. He was now coming to the end of his three-month sentence and was already talking about getting back out there and making some real money. He said he believed in Nathan's innocence: he knew how devious women could be. He thought Keighley had played Nathan like a sucker. In his book women were all the same. Nathan explained that Keighley probably didn't know what she was saying as she had lost her memory.

'Disnae matter,' said Chick. 'As long as the polis huv goat some cunt, that's aw they're interested in.'

The guard swung open the doors of the visiting room and Nathan's eyes focused on the thin blonde sitting in the corner of the room. His heart sank. Angie turned a look of determination on him. Her hair was at least two shades lighter than he remembered and she'd obviously been catching some sun. She looked tired and drawn, and all of her thirty-eight years, plus ten. He strolled over and leaned down to kiss her but she pulled away.

'You're looking well,' he said. She tutted and shook her head.

'What?' he asked. 'Look, this isn't what you think, Ange. I'll be out of here before you know it.'

'I hope not.' She pulled a cigarette out of the packet that sat in front of her on the small Formica-covered table, and lit it with a cheap red disposable lighter. He watched her as she blew smoke a foot above his head. Had he heard her right? Was this some sort of sick joke?

'What do you mean?'

She looked him up and down. 'I don't want to be associated wiv a rapist,' she said, drawing on her cigarette. The corners of her mouth turned down, making her look older still. Age was her greatest fear, and yet here she was cooking her leathery skin in the sun and pulling ugly faces.

'I'm not a rapist!' he snapped. The guard in the corner of the room glanced at him, and he realised he should cool it. 'I'm innocent . . . It was some other bloke – her boyfriend, I think,' he said. She was staring across the room as though the other prisoners were infinitely more interesting than him. 'Ange!' he said, tapping her wrist.

She looked at him as if he was a piece of crap. 'So where is he, then? In here wiv you, is he?' She tapped her cigarette on the ashtray.

'No, he's on the run from the police. Ireland, I think. Look, I didn't touch her.'

'You fucking liar. Don't you lie to me, Nathan. I'm not stupid, you know.' She drew shakily on the cigarette, trying to calm her nerves.

She had every right to be upset. He wondered how he could convince her of his innocence.

She sat back on the worn orange plastic chair and blew smoke out of the corner of her mouth. 'You did fuck her, though, didn't you?' she said, her steely blue eyes narrowing as she looked into his soul.

There was no denying it. A fling, that's all it was . . . She would understand. God knows, *she* hadn't been faithful. 'I had sex wiv her, that's all it was – sex,' he admitted, and watched as she smirked and drew heavily on the cigarette.

'I don't love her, Ange,' he lied. He did love her, that was the problem. When the police had shown him photos of the extent of her injuries he had felt as sick as a pig and known instantly that Josh was responsible. Who else could it have been? He'd asked to be able to speak to her but they wouldn't let him anywhere near her and said she was suffering from amnesia. She didn't know who *she* was, so she sure as hell wouldn't recognise him.

'I've packed up your stuff – your dad's coming for it tonight.' Angie tapped the ash off her cigarette again.

'What?' he asked, incredulous. 'Look, you've got it all wrong – I didn't touch her!' He stared at her, mock-amused. 'What did you tell my dad for?' He knew that nothing else would have given her greater pleasure.

'Somebody had to. He wanted to come right up but I told him I needed to see you first. I think you'd better give them a call, don't you?' She scraped a long red fingernail along a groove in the Formica.

'You needed to see me first? Why? To tell me you're throwing me out? It's not like that when you're slagging about, is it? The crap that I've had to put up with!' She wagged her head at him as if he was a pathetic little boy who couldn't handle the pressure. 'I told you what I'd do if I ever found out you'd been seeing someone else, didn't I?' She leaned forward until she was a few inches from his face. 'Good fuck, was she? Younger than me? I bet she was. Well, you and your little tart are welcome to each other. Let's see if she comes to visit you in here, cos I won't.'

He took in her manic expression. So this was it – the final threat. She was going to take her life and she wanted his stuff out of the flat to make it look like he'd gone and left her and she couldn't take it any more. The calculating bitch. There was nothing he could do about it either as he'd be banged up over four hundred miles away.

'Ange . . . look, I love you – you know that,' he pleaded.

She stubbed out the cigarette. 'It's too late for that.' She picked up her bag.

Time was running out. He had to do something – make her see sense. 'Ange, don't do it – I'm sorry. She didn't mean anything to me. You're my wife – I love you!' Tears were starting to run down his face, but he was crying from fear rather than anything else. She stood up and looked at him disdainfully.

'You should have thought of that before you got your dick out. Bye, Nathan.'

He stood up. 'Ange, don't do anything stupid – please.'

She stopped in her tracks. 'Oh, I've got you scared, have I? Scared of what I'll do to myself?' He was unable to speak because of the lump in his throat. A tear ran down his cheek and dropped on to the table.

'Get a life, Nathan. I wouldn't waste the pills on you.' She turned and walked one.

Nathan slumped back into the chair and held his head in his hands as the tears of relief flowed through his fingers.

She lay on the hospital bed, staring at the ceiling, wondering when her mum was going to come. How long had she been in here? A day, maybe two? Her face was still swollen and the purple bruising had now changed to yellow and black.

She'd had another visit from the policewoman who'd sat at the side of the bed and asked her the same questions. She still couldn't answer them. Besides, it sounded as though all the stuff the policewoman was talking about had happened to someone else. She'd asked if she remembered Nathan, a black guy from London she'd been working with at the hospital, but she didn't know anyone from London, let alone a black guy. They asked her about Josh. Ditto. He could be anyone for all she knew. Apparently he was her boyfriend. That's nice, she thought. She looked forward to seeing him and was already picturing the kind of hunk he was. They told her she was a nurse, an RMN trained to work with the mentally ill, but it all seemed a bit far-fetched to her. She was all set for a career as a surgeon and told them she'd had to put it on hold for a year while she took care of her mum. She knew that much. There it was again. Whenever she mentioned her mum the policewoman looked uncomfortable and changed the subject. Maybe Alzheimer's was a sore point with her.

Every time she asked the doctors when she could leave they said 'soon'. As though they were humouring her. She wished she could remember where home was. She glanced at the cards on the bedside table, took one down and read the message inside. 'Get well soon, missing you, love Lianne X X.' Keighley shrugged and put it back. Lianne who? Maybe she was her sister. She'd have to ask the nurse when she came back in. Imagine having a sister. Maybe they wore each other's clothes. She took down another card with a picture of two cats looking up at the moon. She opened it and saw that the printed message had been scribbled over with felt pen. She could just make out that it had previously said 'Love is, blah blah blah'. Underneath that was, 'Get well – Stuart.' She looked at the two cats again, obviously in love.

But there was something about the picture, the big white moon hovering in the sky above them. Its craters. The significance. She looked at the name again, trying to remember who Stuart was. An old boyfriend? A relative? She couldn't think straight – probably something to do with that bloody tune that was still going round and round in the back of her head. She wished someone could turn it off. Frank Sinatra was beginning to get on her tits. She replaced the card on the bedside table and lay back on the pillow to join the two cats staring up at the moon.

'I want off it – now!' Karl checked the display on his mobile. Credit remaining: £1.20. He knew he should have bought another phonecard before calling Ellis. He wound down the window of the van to get some air and gazed at the picturesque loch that lay before him.

'It's not as easy as that,' said Ellis. 'I sent you two up there in good faith to get this job done and—'

'Now, wait a minute—'

'No, *you* wait a minute – I've got the reputation of my firm to consider here. If I knew you two dickheads were going to go up there and cause me this amount of fucking trouble do you think I'd have sent you?'

Karl tried to compose himself. 'All I'm saying is I want someone else to come up here and finish it. I can wait till they arrive if it's only going to be a day or two. Any more and I'm—'

'You're what?' spat Ellis. 'Walking off the job? I dare you – go on I've got your contract right here in front of me, mate, and what it tells me is I've got your balls the minute you break it!'

'Have a bit of sympathy!' said Karl.

'I'm a fucking businessman, not an agony aunt. Get it sorted, you stupid tart!'

Karl was aware of how his bleating must sound but he didn't give a fuck about the job any more, he just wanted to get back to the safety and comfort of his home. Ellis had spent the past ten minutes telling him he'd better not show his face in London till the job was finished and the satisfied client had signed a job-release form. Karl had considered cutting his losses and walking off the job, but Ellis had told him if he did he'd blacklist him. The devious bastard had him in a stranglehold.

'Just send someone else up to give me a hand, will you?' said Karl, impatiently.

'I've already told you there's no one available,' replied the irate Ellis.

'There must be someone – a few more days and I'll have it finished.'

'Then get your fucking finger out and stop moaning about it. I'll see you when you get back.' Ellis hung up. Karl looked at his mobile: 50p credit. He drew back his arm to hurl it into the loch, but Liz would want to know what he'd done with it – and he could hardly tell her he'd lobbed it out of the van window. He needed to speak to her – she was always the voice of reason at a time like this. He dialled home.

It rang twice and she picked it up. 'Hello?'

He could hear the TV in the background. The *Postman Pat* theme was a giveaway. He knew that Jade would be lying on the floor watching it. Lucy would be reading a book on the settee next to Liz. Maybe even drawing a picture at the kitchen table. A picture for him.

'Hello?' said Liz again.

He imagined her cuddling up to him in bed in the early hours of the morning when she'd wrap a leg around him – a sign that she wanted to make love. He'd start kissing her while he was still half asleep, and run his hands up her nightie.

'Hello? Is anyone there?'

He heard the panic in her voice. She probably thought it was a crank call. He tried to speak but his throat felt as though it were about to shut. He realised he was crying. He cleared his throat. 'Liz?' he said. 'It's me.'

'I was just about to hang up there,' she said. 'How are you doing?'

'I miss you . . . I want to come home, Liz.' He started to sob.

'Karl?'

'But I can't.' He put the phone on the passenger seat. He could hear her voice coming from the earpiece but he was unable to speak: he sat and blubbered like a baby, then reached across to the phone and switched it off.

Nathan shovelled the earth into the wheelbarrow and looked at the allotment shed where the guard sat reading a newspaper. If someone had told him a week ago that he'd be on remand, awaiting trial for rape, he would have laughed. He plunged the spade into the earth and leaned on it. He hadn't stopped thinking about Keighley since he came in here. Last night he'd woken up with a hard-on after dreaming they were in bed together, but reality kicked in when he felt the rough prison blanket and heard Chick fart in the cell next door. He lay awake for the rest of the night, thinking about her injuries. If Josh had wanted to take it out on someone it should have been him.

He shuddered at the thought of how easily he could become prey in this place. He'd always thought of himself as streetwise but that counted for nothing in here. He'd been befriended by a couple of guys, Brian and Scott. They were in for embezzlement, so they said, and had been a couple of friendly faces in an otherwise hostile environment. Like Chick they seemed to believe in Nathan's innocence and said if he ever needed someone to talk to they would lend a sympathetic ear. They put him straight on prison life and said guys like them should stick together, look out for each other. Brian took him to one side in the TV room and asked if he'd like to come to his cell for a smoke – Scott had got his hands on some blow. Nathan declined, saying he was in enough trouble as it was, but as Brian explained, 'If yir gonnae git caught fir stealin a sheep ye might as well shag it too.' That had made Nathan laugh, so he agreed and went along.

While Scott made coffee Brian passed the joint and told Nathan he was glad they were mates – they should keep in touch when they were on the outside. Nathan said he couldn't see himself on the outside ever again. Brian sat beside him and put a friendly arm around his shoulder, saying he shouldn't be thinking like that. It would only be a matter of time and Josh would get what was coming to him.

Nathan nodded as he drank his coffee. It was strong with an unusual flavour. Scott said it was Colombian, like the hash. Nathan handed back the joint as it was going straight to his head. He looked up at Scott as he felt the palpitations in his chest and suddenly felt uneasy. He remembered why he'd stopped smoking dope: it sometimes made him paranoid. He thought it would be a good idea to go back to his own cell and he stood up to leave but Scott, still smiling, blocked his path. Nathan wobbled on his feet and could think of nothing more inviting than his bed and a well-deserved kip. All that working outside must have got to him – his legs were giving way. Brian caught him as he swayed, almost crashing against the wall.

'Here, you huv yirsel a wee lie-doon,' said Brian, helping him on to the bed. Nathan lay back and felt as though he were falling through it into a pile of soft pillows. His breathing eased and the palpitations had gone. He hadn't been so relaxed in years. Whatever was in that joint had knocked him for six. He turned his head and focused on Scott, who had picked up his coffee cup and was emptying it down the sink.

Scott glanced outside the cell then closed the door and came back in, grinning. Nathan struggled to keep awake as he felt his trousers being unfastened and his zip pulled down. He reached down to hold on to them but they were already around his ankles. Another pair of hands pulled off his shoes. He knew something was wrong and tried to open his eyes but he couldn't – all he wanted to do was sleep. It would have been so easy just to drift off but he knew what would happen if he did. He felt himself being roughly turned over and could make out their eager, hissing voices as they set about their strategy. He could feel one of them lying on top of him and Nathan tried to turn over and flip him off but they were too strong for him and held his arms down, pinning him to the bed.

'Hoad hum doon, will ye?' said the urgent voice behind him. He felt his arms being pulled out in front of him to the end of the bed while the man on top of him hastily freed himself of his clothing. The last thing he remembered was the feel of flesh on flesh then Chick's angry voice and the weight on top of him being hauled off amid shouting and scuffling.

Later he awoke in his cell with a sore head. Chick was eyeing him with concern from the other side of the cell. He reached down and felt his arse but it felt normal.

'Aye, it's still there ya daft cunt' said Chick, shaking his head at Nathan's stupidity.

'What happened?' Nathan had tried to sit up, then decided against it as the pain in his temples over-whelmed him.

'Ye were nearly jelly-banged, that's whit happened. Ye huv tae watch oot fir cunts like that. Dirty bastards.'

'Haw you!' The guard lowered his paper and nodded at Nathan's shovel. 'Git a move oan!'

'Sorry.' Nathan scooped up another shovelful of earth and hurled it into the barrow.

He knew it had been a mistake the minute the car came into view. By the time he'd run down the embankment and was half-way across the field Harvey and the two special coppers were on him like a pack of dogs. The plan had seemed sensible enough – pack up and hitch back to Glasgow in search of civilisation – but in reality it had probably been the stupidest thing he could have done. He'd waited at the side of the road for what seemed an eternity with cars whizzing past him, and his concentration lapsed. He longed for a hot bath, some clean clothes and a pint with a few old mates. If he'd been watching the road instead of a fox padding about in the field next to him he would have seen the occupants of the police Mondeo before they'd seen him. It was slowing down to a halt when he turned to see that the person pulling over to give him a lift was a grinning Harvey, accompanied by a couple of young uniformed idiots.

Josh sat in his cell and stared at the floor. He'd got off lightly by all accounts. When he was charged with the actual bodily harm of Roddy McIntyre he'd awaited the next charge of rape and battery but it had never come. He wondered why they hadn't charged him. But if they weren't going to mention it he sure as fuck wasn't. He wondered if Keighley was okay. He'd left her for dead, but the next day when his conscience got the better of him he'd returned to the spot but she'd gone. She must have made her way home. He sat and contemplated what he'd done to her, remembering that that night he had been like a man possessed. It had all been too much for him – the thought of her being fucked by another man. The sounds that came from the van still echoed in his head and he pictured her laughing at him while sucking the black guy's cock. The dirty bitch had got what she deserved, he'd made sure of that. He wondered if this made him a rapist, or if he'd felt what rapists feel that night – the power of being able to do whatever you liked to another human being, to use them for your own pleasure . . . Anyway, he reminded himself that it hadn't been the Keighley he knew. The one he'd come across was a hissing, spitting bitch, who wanted to claw his eyes out.

He'd only gone to confront her about what Moose had said, and things had just got out of control. She'd said she wasn't answerable to him any more and told him it was all over. He told her she was getting too big for her boots and needed taking down a peg or two so he gave her a slap. She looked at him defiantly and said that was the last time he'd ever touch her.

'Aye, we'll see aboot that,' said Josh.

'You think I did it?' Nathan searched Karl's face for a clue, but his friend was unable to look him in the eye.

'I don't know.'

'Oh, thanks very much, mate. It's nice to know I can count on you at a time like this.' He'd spent the last fifteen minutes going over what had happened that night and thought at least Karl would believe him, but Karl's face was telling a different story.

'I don't know what to think, do I?' Karl shrugged his shoulders and looked about at the other prisoners in the visiting room. 'I just know I want to go home – I've had it with this place.'

278

'*You*'ve had it? I was nearly—' He stopped himself before enlightening Karl about his near buggering incident.

'What?' asked Karl.

'Nothing . . . it doesn't matter. Look, you're going to have to get some evidence on Josh to get me out of here.'

'Who the fuck do you think I am? Columbo?' asked Karl.

'I don't know what else I can do. I know it was him but I just can't prove it, especially not in here.'

'I'll have a think and see what I can come up with,' said Karl, half-heartedly.

'Have you seen Keighley?'

Karl shook his head. 'Lianne's been in a couple of times. Came back upset cos she didn't know who she was.'

'Fuck.' Nathan tried to understand what she must have gone through. 'I hope she's going to be all right . . . That fucking bastard.' He gritted his teeth.

'Yeah, I know. Lianne said her face was in some state. She doesn't want to go up there any more till she's well again.'

'Why don't you go up?'

'Me?'

'Yeah, see if she remembers anything.'

'She won't.'

'Well, you won't know till you've been up there, will you?'

'I fucking hate hospitals.'

'Look, do it as a favour to me. Tell her I'm sorry for . . . you know.'

'No . . . I don't.' Karl looked at him vacantly.

'Tell her I'm sorry for throwing her feelings back in her face.'

'She won't understand,' said Karl.

'Tell her it's all over between Angie and me and it's her I want.'

'Waste of time, mate.'

'Just tell her I love her, hey?'

It was all getting to be too much to handle. She wondered how much more she could take. First Keighley and now this. Lianne sat in the staffroom and glanced at the letter on the table. She tried to pick up her coffee but her hands were shaking. This morning she'd been watching Karl through the window, talking on his mobile, when old Agnes came into the ward to tell her and Eddie that she couldn't wake Lily.

Lianne went in and found that the old lady had died in her sleep. That didn't freak her, it was part of the job: elderly patients died all the time. What did freak her was the locket in Lily's hand, as though she had known she was going to die and hadn't wanted to be parted from it. Lianne prised it from her grasp and examined it. The imaginary necklace? So it existed after all. This was what Lily had spent her days misplacing and relocating.

Lianne opened it and saw a picture of a youthful Lily on one side and a handsome young man on the other. She shuddered and closed it, as though something was telling her to leave it alone.

What freaked her even more was the letter on the bed side unit addressed to *her*. The envelope read 'Nurse L. Crooks.'

Lianne knew she'd been a right bitch to the old woman in the past. Lily had been someone's mother, someone's husband and daughter, but to Lianne she'd been a major pain in the arse since she arrived on the ward, always fussing and whingeing over the slightest thing. Lianne knew she wasn't the most patient of nurses but the necklace business always got on her tits. She'd always doubted the woman's past too, that she had once been a writer, because the geriatric that shuffled through the ward, mumbling and moaning was barely able to string a sentence together. Lianne had always called her a crabbit old woman whenever she kicked off. Now Lily had got her own back.

The letter was a warning – a message from beyond the grave. It was Lianne's last chance to become a better person. She vowed she'd treat the patients with the respect they deserved in future . . . just as soon as she calmed down. She picked up the letter again and read it a second time.

What do you see, nurse, what do you see?
Are you thinking when you're looking at me?
A crabbit old woman, not very wise
Uncertain of habit, with faraway eyes
Who dribbles her food and makes no reply
When you say in a loud voice, 'I do wish you'd try,'
Who seems not to notice the things that you do,
And forever is losing a stocking or shoe,
Who unresisting or not, lets you do as you will,
With bathing and feeding the long day to fill.
Is that what you're thinking, is that what you see?
Then open your eyes, nurse, you're not looking at me.
I'll tell you who I am as I sit here so still,
As I use at your bidding, as I eat at your will.
I'm a small child of ten with a father and mother,
Brothers and sisters, who love one another,
A young girl of sixteen with wings on her feet,
Dreaming that soon now a lover she'll meet,
A bride soon at twenty my heart gives a leap,
Remembering the vows that I promised to keep.
At twenty-five now I have young of my own,
Who need me to build a secure, happy home.
A woman of thirty, my young now grow fast,
Bound to each other with ties that should last.
At forty, my young sons now grown will be gone,
But my man stays beside me to see I don't mourn.
At fifty once more babies play round my knee,
Again we know children, my loved one and me.

Dark days are upon me, my husband is dead,
I look at the future, I shudder with dread,
For my young are all rearing the young of their own,
And I think of the years and the love that I've known.
I'm an old woman now and nature is cruel—
'Tis her jest to make old age look like a fool.
The body it crumbles, grace and vigour depart,
There is now a stone where I once had a heart.
But inside this old carcase a young girl still dwells,
And now and again my battered heart swells.
I remember the joys, I remember the pain,
And I'm loving and living life all over again.
I think of the years all too few gone too fast,
And accept the stark fact that nothing can last.
So open your eyes, nurse, open and see,
Not a crabbit old woman, look closer – see *me*!

Lianne threw it on the table and breathed deeply to try
to calm herself.

He thought it must be a flashback to whatever drugs
Scott and Brian had put in his coffee the other night,
or that he was just plain seeing things, but there was
no mistaking the bulldog neck bent over the sink in
the cell along the block. Nathan watched as Josh
dried his face, and slowly turned his head, aware that
he was being watched. His eyes narrowed as he
caught Nathan's. 'Whit you dein in here?' he asked.

Then the penny dropped. 'You've bin charged wi rape, haven't ye?'

'Yeah, and it was you who did it, wasn't it?'

'Ah'll ask the questions, cunt!' Josh waded through the doorway, grabbed Nathan by the scruff of the neck and hauled him into the cell, sending him reeling backwards to hit the wall with a slap. He slid to the floor. Josh stood over him, then glowered briefly at another prisoner standing outside to let him know he wasn't welcome. The guy took the hint and moved on. 'You went tae the polis an gied them a statement, din't ye?'

Nathan rubbed the back of his head and stood up. 'What you did to that old bloke was a fucking disgrace – not to mention what you did to Keighley.'

'Oh, aye? Well, I'm no the wan in here fir rapin hur, pal. That's you.'

'They'll get you for what you did to her – I'll make sure of it.' Nathan's heart was rebounding off his ribs, and the top of his head felt like the pressure was going to blow it off at any minute. Josh would only have to punch him and he'd be knocked through the wall. He considered moving away from it but any sudden moves might make the already twitchy Josh strike out first and ask questions later.

'Do you want tae know whit ah did tae hur? Eh, dae ye? She wis like putty in mah hons . . . best ride ah've hud affay hur in years.' Josh grinned, revealing a set of chipped and stained teeth.

'You sick bastard!'

'Don't knock it till ye've tried it. Anyway, she's no the issue here – it's you an that fuckin statement. Ye kin git it retracted fuckin pronto – tell them ye made the whole thing up or ye'll be oan tae the beatin ay yir life, right?'

Nathan stared up at him. The mad bastard really thought that everyone was going to do whatever he told them to.

'Ah said *right*?' Josh jabbed a finger between Nathan's eyes, causing the back of his head to bump off the tiled wall. 'Are you fuckin listenin tae me . . . *boay*?' he growled.

'Fuck you!' Nathan sprang up on his heels and slammed his forehead between Josh's eyes. Josh reeled back and grabbed his nose with one hand while trying to swing a punch at Nathan with the other. Nathan stepped aside to dodge the blow and swiftly kicked Josh in the ribs but it had little effect. Josh took his hand away from his nose. Blood ran from it and dripped on to the floor. He grabbed his towel, wiped his watery eyes, and flung it back on a sink before moving towards Nathan with a look on his face that said Nathan should prepare to meet his Maker. Nathan tried to get into the middle of the small cell but Josh was already there and he was trapped between the bed and the wall. He was all set to come out with fists flying when two guards burst in.

'Right, Strachan, back aff!' The first waved his baton.

Josh walked back to the sink and picked up his towel, wiped his bloodied face with it and examined the split at the bridge of his nose in the mirror.

'Whit's goin oan?' asked the other guard, looking at Nathan.

'Just a wee bit ay a misunderstandin, int that right?' Josh said, dabbing the towel at his nostrils.

Nathan nodded dumbly to the guards.

'Right, you – git.' The first guard pointed at Nathan with his baton, then indicated the door. Nathan didn't have to be asked twice.

Stuart sat on his bed with ten-by-eights of the moon strewn all over it. Under his pillow was a photographic paper box that contained his most recent work. He reached under the pillow, pulled out the corner of the box and thought about opening it. But how was he supposed to look at his work if he had to keep it a secret? How was anyone else supposed to see it?

He watched Karl screwing the light switch cover back into place and considered asking him if he'd like to see his photos. Karl was okay, wasn't a threat, but he wasn't that interested either. Stuart pushed the box back under the pillow. He'd have to give this some thought.

Karl dropped the screwdriver back into his toolkit and set about picking up the cable cuttings. He thought about his run-in that morning with the local police. He'd gone to the local station and said that he had some information about the attack on Keighley. Gordon eyed him with disdain and asked him what *information* he could possibly have. Karl told him it was Josh who had attacked her, but Gordon just shook his head. Karl said they should be questioning Josh and testing him for DNA, but Gordon said that Karl had been watching too many episodes of *The Bill* and they already had their man. When Karl mentioned that it was the wrong one, Gordon turned nasty and said he should piss off back to London, if he knew what was good for him, and warned him that if he didn't keep his nose out of their business he'd be in bigger trouble than he already was. Karl realised he was wasting his breath. The guy was a moron.

He threw the cable clippings into the bin and picked up his toolbox. He had a final look round to see if he'd left anything behind and noticed that Stuart, sitting on the edge of his bed with a flat box, was watching him. 'You all right, mate?' he asked.

Stuart nodded, looked down at the box, then up at Karl. 'Dae ye want tae see mah photies?' he asked.

'Some other time, hey? I'm a bit busy at the minute.' Karl strolled out into the corridor. If you've seen one photo of the moon you've seen them all, he thought.

He'd spent the morning planting fuchsias while he thought about how to get Josh done for attacking Keighley. He planned to have a word with his brief about him when he came to visit in a day or two. But his main concern at the moment was the unfinished business with Josh in the cell. The next time he crossed Josh's path would probably be his last. He'd have to buy himself some time. But how? It was only when he took the plant pots back to the shed that inspiration struck. In the far corner of the shed sat a plastic dish with bright blue grains of rat poison in it. He looked about and saw that the guard was having a cigarette and talking to a couple of other prisoners, so he walked into the shed, put the plant pots on a shelf, bent down and scooped up a few grains of rat poison. He stuffed it into his jacket pocket as he heard the guard coming.

'Huv ye finished they fuchsias?' asked the guard.

'Yeah . . . all done.' Nathan walked out of the shed.

'He, er, said to tell you that he loved you and everything was going to be all right.' Karl glanced from the window to Keighley's battered features, feeling stupid. It was as though they were playing a game in which they pretended not to know each other, but one look at her split lip and grazed, bruised head reminded him that this was far from make-believe.

'Huv ye goat a photie of hum?' she asked. 'Ah don't know whit he looks like.'

Karl shook his head. 'Sorry,' he said. 'I haven't.'

'If ah hud a photie ah might remember why he attacked me.' She looked puzzled, as though she was wondering why a guy who said he loved her would want to do such a thing.

'Keighley, he wasn't the one who attacked you. I know the police are saying that but they've got the wrong man. It was Josh.'

'Mah boayfriend?'

'Yeah, well, he used to be. He's in prison now. He won't be able to hurt you any more.'

They sat in silence for a minute, looking out of the open window into the gardens. The warm breeze wafted into the room, bringing with it the scent of the roses planted underneath her window and cut grass.

'It's nice here, isn't it?' she said.

He gazed at her as she stared out of the window. He felt sorry for her ending up like this. He'd been wrong about her. How could anyone think she was trouble? He felt like shit for having such a low opinion of her, and hoped no one would pass the same judgement on his girls when they grew up. He watched as she reached out for a jug of iced water and poured herself a glass. She held up the jug as though offering him some. He shook his head and smiled.

'Keighley, darlin, can't you remember *anything*?' he asked.

She faced him and shook her head.

Josh's soup and bread roll sat on a tray a foot away from Nathan, but Josh was too busy spouting about football to the guy in front of him to notice that Nathan had swapped places with Chick and was now standing right behind him. Nathan put down his tray, took the wrap of paper out of his pocket and opened it. He covered the rat poison with the palm of his hand and picked up his tray with the other.

Josh leaned forward to make himself heard in the debate and his tray swung out to the side. Nathan saw his chance and tipped the powder into the soup where it sat in the centre before slowly disappearing into the green broth. He scrunched up the paper and threw it under the counter.

Ten minutes later while eating his dinner he thought he'd been rumbled when Josh, still banging on about football, dipped his roll into the centre of the soup and swirled it around. When he raised it to his mouth Nathan could see the unmistakable blue grains among the vegetables that were stuck to the roll. Nobody noticed as Josh crammed it into his mouth and munched.

Nathan wondered what he'd done. What if Josh died? It would serve the bastard right – but Nathan knew he had no right to take a life. How could he sleep at night after that? He hoped he'd given Josh just enough to lay him up for a while, and secretly hoped he'd suffer as much pain as Keighley had. If things got serious he could always say he saw *someone else* put a blue substance into Josh's food. That way the doctors would know exactly what he'd taken and they'd be able to sort him out. Nathan watched Josh spoon the last of his soup into his mouth, then make a start on his sausage casserole. He hoped the bastard got everything he deserved.

Karl sat down in the staffroom and took a sausage roll out of a paper bag. He picked up the newspaper and turned to the TV guide. He hadn't been out since Nathan had been arrested, and he didn't miss it. He knew that if he went into the pub some of those narrow-minded locals would have him down as a rapist's accomplice and he didn't need any more grief. Besides, the last thing he felt like doing was socialising – he just wanted to get the job finished and get the hell out of there.

There was a knock on the door and it opened slowly. Karl glanced up from his paper and saw Stuart standing in the doorway, clutching the box of photos.

'Ye said later.' Stuart indicated the box and slowly walked forward.

'Let me guess.' Karl put down the paper and reached out for the box, which Stuart handed him. 'The moon, is it?' He took a bite of sausage roll then rested it on the paper bag.

'They're fir you.' Stuart backed off nervously.

'Hold on, mate, hold on.' Karl lifted the lid off the box. He took out the prints. 'That's very nice of you but what am I going to do with photos of . . .' He looked at the print in his hand and felt as though he'd been punched in the stomach. It was a photo of Josh and Keighley. He had her pinned down across a tree stump and his trousers were down by his ankles: it was clear from the expression on her face that he was raping her. Karl looked at another. Josh was pulling her along by her hair. In the next he was aiming a punch at her, and the one that followed was similar – taken a millisecond later. In another the blow was making contact and her head was tilted back with the force; the next showed her reeling from Josh's fist. He flicked through the others, which showed her lying unconscious and Josh walking off through the woods. There were about twenty in all.

Karl looked up at Stuart, amazed. A thousand questions sprang to mind.

'A present,' said Stuart, nodding to the prints.

'You're going to have to take these to the police,' said Karl. He was unable to grasp the magnitude of what he had in his hands. He noticed that the time and date from the databack camera had been superimposed into the bottom right-hand corner of each print, and realised that it would also be on the negative – clear evidence that they hadn't been tampered with. Stuart took the prints from Karl.

'What?' asked Karl, not understanding what the hell was going on.

'Ah cannae go the polis,' said Stuart, stuffing the photos back into the box.

'But you have to.' Karl watched as Stuart shook his head. Why had he shown them to him in the first place?

'*You* tek them . . . Tell the polis *you* took them.' Stuart put the lid back on the box and held it out to Karl.

'I would, mate, but they'll never believe it – I was in London at the time. You have to tell them what you saw, why you were in the woods . . .' He reached out for the box again, but Stuart pulled it tight to him and shook his head violently.

'Stuart, you've got to!'

'Nooo!' Stuart ran for the door. Karl leaped out of the seat and rushed across to him, jamming his foot against the door as Stuart pulled at the handle.

'Stuart, mate, listen a minute, will you? This could put Josh away for good—'

'I wanted you to do it!' said Stuart, trying desperately to get out of the room.

'I *can't* do it,' said Karl, impatiently. 'Don't you understand? The police will want to talk to you!'

'No! No police!' In a panic Stuart shoved Karl, sending him stumbling across the room. He flung open the door and ran off down the corridor.

Karl gave chase but he lost sight of him at the end of the corridor. When he got down there Stuart had gone – vanished into thin air. He walked to the end of the corridor but there was no sign of him. He made his way back to the psychiatric ward and popped his head round the door. Lianne was in there, talking to a patient. 'Lianne, can I have a minute?' he asked, out of breath.

'I'm busy.'

'Lianne, this is really, really important. You are not going to believe what just happened.'

'Ah'll no be a minute,' she said to the patient, then followed Karl out into the corridor. 'Try me.'

'Stuart has got photos of Josh attacking Keighley in the woods the other night.' He watched her jaw drop. 'It's got the time, date and everything on them. This could put Josh away and get Nathan out,' he said.

'Are you sure?'

'I've just seen them.'

'Where is he?'

'Don't know. He took off the minute I mentioned taking them to the police.' Lianne sighed, as though it was the last thing he should have done. 'Well, I didn't know, did I? What is all this police business anyway?'

She bit her lip. He could see she was trying to weigh up whether or not she could trust him. 'Ah'm gonnae show ye somehun,' she said, 'but ah don't want ye tae tell anyone. Yir no supposed tae see this . . . right?'

'Right,' he said. She looked down the corridor and indicated with a nod that he should follow her.

'Ye remember the miners' strike?' she asked.

'The nineteen eighties?' he said, 'Yeah, bits of it.'

'Well, yir lucky cos Stuart disnae remember much aboot it at aw . . . no since his *accident*.' She emphasised the word as though it was a far cry from what Stuart had actually had. She stopped at an office and pulled out her keys. 'Stuart's goat post-traumatic stress . . . *neurosis*. He's bin here longer than me.' She unlocked the door and went inside the office. Karl followed and she closed the door.

Karl looked about him. He remembered this office – it had been one of the first rooms they'd rewired. A large desk sat side-on to a window with a view of the dense trees at the back of the hospital. Lianne switched on the light and a fluorescent tube flickered into life. She pulled out the top drawer of the filing cabinet that sat next to the door and her fingers walked over the plastic file tabs with patients names on them. She located one labelled S. Wilkie, pulled it out and went over to the desk. Karl followed.

'Huv a seat.' They sat and she pored through the bulky file, searching for something specific. 'He wis referred tae this place in the eighties from a medical ward in Glasgow after he'd tried tae tek a couple ay overdoses . . . Ah, here it is.' She took out a bunch of seven-by-five black-and-white photos and handed them over. He looked through them, not understanding what he was supposed to be looking for among the shots of landscapes and people. They looked like the kind of photos he'd seen a million times in *The Times* supplement.

'Soarry, no those wans.' She turned up a shot of a

group of proud-looking miners. Karl glanced with interest at some shots of a riot where the police were dragging people along the ground. One policeman with a bloody face was being helped by two of his colleagues. 'He won an award fir that wan,' she said.

'I thought I'd seen it before somewhere,' said Karl. 'Stuart took this?' he asked, waving the print at her.

She nodded and took back the photos, searching for the one she wanted. 'He wis a press photographer before it happened. This wis the laist photo he took.' She pulled it from the pile and handed it to Karl. He stared at it and tried to take in just what Stuart had gone through in his quest for the perfect photo. A wild-eyed policeman with a raised baton was charging towards the camera. It looked distinctly like a young PC Gordon.

'Noo ye know why the polis frighten hum so much. The minute they're mentioned he's right back there as though it wis yesterday.' She indicated the print. 'The flashbacks are so vivid he believes they're real.'

Karl put down the print and sat back in the chair, dumbfounded. 'But he's *got* to go to the police – Nathan's in jail for something he didn't do.'

'Aye, think ay yir mate. Don't spare a thought fir whit mah pal went through, will ye? Or whit Stuart's goin through.'

'Look, I didn't mean that. I feel just as sorry for what happened to Keighley as you do, but the only way we can help the situation is by getting the police in on this.'

Lianne folded her arms. 'He'll no speak tae them,' she said.

'He'll fuckin have to,' said Karl

'Especially hum.' She pointed at the baton-wielding policeman in the photo. 'Ye know who he is, don't ye?'

'Sandy Gordon?'

'Aye . . . he's the wan who gave Stuart hus metal plate.'

'Did they do him for it?' Karl looked down at the photo again.

'Ah heard that when it went tae court Stuart wis too shaky tae gie evidence properly. There were no eye-witnesses at the time – it aw happened so fast. The case jist didnae ston up an Gordon goat aff wi it. That's when Stuart took his first overdose.'

'Poor bastard.' Karl tried to imagine what he must have gone through, and he could only hope that Stuart would have a change of heart about the prints of Keighley.

'The polis came in here once tae see Colin aboot somehun . . .' said Lianne. 'Stuart saw them an nearly put hissel through the wall tryin tae git away fae them. It put us back ages wi his treatment . . . Somehun like this could finish hum aff.'

'So what are we supposed to do? Wait till he gets better?' he asked, sarcastically.

'He might never git better. But ye cannae force hum – ye'll huv tae find another way.'

Karl couldn't remember ever having been in such a bizarre situation before. 'What's all this business with the moon anyway?' he asked.

Lianne picked up the print of Gordon and put it back in the file with the others. 'Ye mean why dis he tek photies ay it aw the time?' she asked, standing up and straightening the front of her tunic. Karl nodded. 'Well, the way ah see it, it's cos the moon cannae herm hum.'

Yet again his camera had got him into trouble. This would be the last time. He looked down at the dented Nikon with its smashed lens on the tiled floor of the corridor. He should have known better than to take photos of something that didn't concern him, but it had been instinct. Until that point he'd been quite happy taking shots of the moon for his records . . . that was, until he heard all the screaming and shouting. Then he saw him hit her – hold her hair and rain punches down on her head. When he recognised who it was he felt he had to help, but he knew he was in no fit state, either physically or mentally, to challenge Josh. Before he knew where he was, the situation had been taken care of: the photographer of old had resurfaced and taken over – snapping away as though on auto-pilot.

He should have known better than to try to get Karl to help him, but it was the only thing he could think of.

Stuart scrunched the last print into a ball and tossed it on to the small pile in front of him. He looked up the deserted corridor, lit only by the emergency lighting, knowing he would be safe here as people rarely ventured along this way. He struck a match and set fire to the pile, immediately feeling a sense of relief. He'd sailed close to the wind this time and vowed to be more careful in future.

The smoke rose as the photographs caught fire and the smoke alarm above his head started to beep. Cursing his stupidity, he got to his feet and jumped up to try to reach it but it was too high up. He picked up the broken camera by its strap and swung it at the alarm a couple of times, but it missed and bounced off the ceiling tiles. A third swing, and he hit it. The cover sprang open and the alarm went quiet.

'Stuart, whit are ye dein?'

He looked up the corridor as Lianne hurried towards him. She grabbed a fire extinguisher from a recess, pulled out the pin and hurried towards the fire. Stuart ran in front of her and tried to wrestle it from her hands.

'Let go, will ye?' She tried to tug it from him and point it at the blazing prints.

'Let them burn!' he shouted.

Lianne wrenched the fire extinguisher from him and pointed it threateningly at him. He covered his face with his arms. She levelled it at the small fire and gave a quick blast. The foam covered it like a blanket of whipped cream. Lianne put it down and watched as Stuart slowly removed his hands from his face and stared down at the foam-covered ashes.

'Are you gonnae tell me jist whit the hell yir playin at?' she said. 'Ye could huv set fire tae the whole place.'

He let out a gut-wrenching sob and started walking about the corridor as though he was a dog that had lost its bearings. 'I want Keighley!' he said.

'An ah want an answer!' she shouted.

He ignored her and continued to pace.

'Is it the photies?' she asked. 'Look, Ah know whit Josh did tae Keighley,' she said. He stopped pacing and stared at her. 'Karl telt me,' she explained.

'Ah'm no speakin tae the polis.' He shook his head. 'They'll kill me this time!' He let out another frightened sob. Then, as though it was all too much for him, he backed into a corner, slid down the wall and curled up into a ball. He rocked backwards and forwards and wailed in fear.

Lianne wondered how best to approach him. She imagined Lily, watching her to see if she was going to live up to her promise to be a more caring person. She decided to put it to the test. She sat down beside him and slid a comforting arm around his shoulder. She smelt the unmistakable whiff of warm piss and looked down. He was sitting in a puddle that was starting to gather around his shoes. She felt sorry for him. He was like a baby in a man's body.

'Stuart . . . no aw the polis are bad, ye know. The guy who hit you, well, he wis jist a bad man . . . like Josh.' She tried to imagine the fear he was feeling and for a moment she wished Keighley were here to deal with him. She held his head closer as she sat beside him, aware that the piss was trickling nearer to her shoes. It was all part of the job, she reminded herself. She should be immune to it by now.

'Josh . . .' he stammered. She felt him start to shake.

'He's in jail . . .' she replied. 'He's no gittin oot . . . no if the polis git they photies.' She glanced at the pile of ashes and realised it was pointless: that was the last they'd ever see of them. She sat and stroked his head until his breathing slowed. She ruffled his hair and stood up. 'Come oan,' she said, holding out her hand and helping him to his feet. 'Let's git you cleaned up an tae yir bed.'

Lying in the dark, in the peace and quiet, was what he needed. It was a chance to think straight, clear his head. It had all gone on for far too long and it was time now to exorcise his demons. He'd had enough of running away. He wanted his life back.

People like Keighley and Lianne had spent years helping him and caring for him. The least he could do was repay that kindness.

It was an awakening that he'd never dreamed would come. A sign – a message that showed him just how easy getting better could be. No medicine, no therapy, just love.

He'd sat beside Keighley's bed that morning and held

her hand and told her who she was. He couldn't get used to the fact that she was sitting here talking with him and couldn't remember him. It upset him having to tell her who he was. She apologised, explaining that she had retrograde amnesia. He looked into her eyes and could see that she genuinely didn't know him . . . but she wanted to. That was the main thing. She said that if he was a friend of hers he must be a nice person. She picked up his card and smiled at it again. 'The moon,' she said, thoughtfully.

'Ye used tae sing me songs,' he said. 'Frank Sinatra, Tony Bennett, Nina Simone.' She raised her eyes upwards, as though trying to pluck a memory from the air. He sat and stared across the room, remembering the bond they had had. How she'd dress him for the cold weather and walk him to the bus stop so he could go on day-release. It was Keighley who'd organised it for him. She was the only one who had shown an interest in what he was doing. Before he left he told her he missed her and wanted her back . . . the way she used to be. She smiled and asked if he would come and see her again. He said he'd visit her every day till she was better.

Billy lay in wait behind the door, sniggering to himself at the thought of Stuart's face when he walked through it. He pulled at the elastic behind his ear and tilted his plastic police hat straight on his head. Taking a deep breath, he tried to compose himself as he heard Stuart approach. He waited till Stuart was through the door before he slammed it shut and stood in front of it to block Stuart's escape.

'Nee-naw, nee-naw! It's the polis – the polis, Stuart!' He waved his chubby arms about wildly and fixed his gargoyle features in a mock-frightened grimace. Stuart was unfazed. What was wrong, thought Billy. Hadn't he heard him right? He tried again. 'Nee-naw—'

'Aye, ah heard ye – *the polis are comin.*' Stuart walked across to his bedside table and pulled it away from the wall. He turned to Billy, who was standing behind him, bewildered. 'Big fuckin deal!' said Stuart, reaching behind the unit and tearing off the carefully taped set of negatives from the back of it. He put them into his pocket, slid the unit back into place, walked past Billy and out of the door.

Karl had been lying under the floorboards, in a world of his own, pulling mains cable from one end of the office to the other. He nearly shat himself when he looked up and saw Stuart looming over him. He got to his feet, thinking he was here to give him an explanation for what had happened last night. Karl was ready to tell him it was all right, he wasn't going to pressure him. There would be no point telling him he knew all about his past brush with Gordon, though. The poor guy had enough on his plate without thinking everyone had access to his medical records.

Stuart pulled out a large manilla envelope from behind his back and offered it to him. 'What's this?' asked Karl.

'Open it.'

Karl took out a set of ten-by-eight prints identical to the ones Stuart had taken off him the day before.

'Stuart, does this mean what I think it means?' he asked.

Stuart nodded. 'Ah'm ready tae speak tae them if it'll git yir mate oot . . . It's no right whit they did tae hum.'

Karl grinned broadly and stuffed the prints back into the envelope. He grabbed Stuart by the sides of the head and planted a smacker on his forehead.

Gordon had been bemoaning the harshness of Josh's sentence since Harvey had nabbed him. He'd wished secretly that he had been in the car at the time of the arrest. That way he could have tripped Harvey up as he ran along the embankment to get him – anything to give Josh another chance. The way he saw it, the longer Josh could stay out of trouble and out of jail, the easier it would be for his laddie to get a job as his apprentice. The only hope Gordon had now was that the charges wouldn't stick. After all, a rapist with a grudge had made the statement. It wasn't worth the paper it was written on.

His boy's apprenticeship had still looked a vague possibility until that cocky London bastard came in and asked to see Harvey. When Gordon had asked, 'Whit's it aboot?' all he would say was, 'I'd rather speak to your colleague, no offence.'

If only he'd known what was in the envelope he could have been prepared for that as well. He couldn't hide his surprise when Harvey called him into the office and showed him the photos. 'So much fir huvin yir man,' said Harvey. 'We're lookin at a wrongful arrest here!'

'Haw, wait a minute—' protested Gordon.

'No, *you* wait a minute – you've goat some explainin tae dae. Karl Weston sais he's already bin in an telt ye that Strachan wis yir man an ye telt hum tae git tae fuck!'

'No in so many words.'

'How come ye didnae tell me aboot this?'

'He wis talkin shite.'

'Och, git oot mah fuckin sight.' Harvey grabbed the prints and stormed out of the room with them. Within a minute he was on the phone to their superintendent.

The cat was well and truly out of the bag and had no intention of getting back in again. Gordon sat on the edge of the desk and fumed. That fucking Strachan had some explaining to do.

It was as though he was shitting broken glass. His stomach was in knots and rivulets of sweat ran down his face. Josh grimaced in pain as he felt his bowels give way a second time. He looked between his open thighs to see the blood

305

running down the porcelain. He knew he'd have to see a doctor but he didn't have the strength. All he wanted to do was sit on the lavvy till the pains in his stomach eased off. It was a bleeding ulcer – had to be. With all the worry he had had lately it was hardly surprising. He groaned again as another wave of pain washed over him. He gripped his knees, braced himself and held his breath.

She was waking up, aware that someone was sitting beside her, humming and stroking her hair. It couldn't have been her mum because she was dead – she knew that much now. Whoever it was was humming along with that Frank Sinatra tune, 'Fly Me To The Moon', which was playing beside the bed. It made a nice change to hear the real thing, not just bits and pieces of it in her head. What was surprising was that she could even remember all of the words.

She wondered if she was in her flat and had fallen asleep with the CD player on. Then the fear hit her as she remembered who she shared the flat with. She hoped it wasn't Josh stroking her hair. She opened her eyes slowly and saw Stuart sitting on the edge of her hospital bed. She smiled at him and breathed a sigh of relief. He leaned across to the bedside unit and turned down the volume on the CD player.

'Stuart – thank God it's you. Ah wis huvin a horrible dream,' she said.

*　　*　　*

Karl didn't know what had made him happiest: getting Nathan out of prison or keeping Josh in; watching Colin the community manager sign his name on the job-release form, or calling Liz to tell her he was coming home. He drove the van to Kilmarnock Prison and watched as Nathan came through the gates beaming at him. He slung his belongings into the van and jumped in after them.

'I've already packed your stuff – police released it this morning,' said Karl, looking at his friend. He could swear he'd aged in the short time he'd been in there. Maybe he was just tired. He couldn't see how he could have had much sleep in a place like that. Still, he had the compensation to look forward to as soon as this thing had been dragged through the courts by these incompetent fucks. He hoped he'd take them to the cleaners.

'You all right, mate?' he asked, as he started the engine.

'Yeah,' said Nathan, staring through the windscreen as though he was in another world.

'You get your head down, if you want. I don't mind doin all the drivin.' Karl swung the van away from the prison gates and headed back through the town towards the motorway.

'I'm not goin home,' said Nathan.

'You what?' Karl glanced from Nathan to the road, wondering if he was hearing things. It was a joke, surely. Prison humour, perhaps?

'Drop me off at Glen Leven,' he said.

'You've got to be joking!' Karl said, then realised Nathan was deadly serious. 'Why the fuck would you want to go back there?'

'Why do you think?'

He was too upset to speak when he first saw her, blaming himself for what had happened to her. He knew that if he'd been upfront with her in the first place none of this would have happened. He'd understand if she wanted to tell him where to go, and that she never wanted to see him again, but he had to hear it from her – no one else. He wanted her to look him in the eyes and say she never wanted to see him again.

It never happened.

The minute he walked into the hospital room she beamed at him in a way that melted his heart. 'Hi, Nathan.' She stood up to greet him. He didn't know what to say.

'Are you all right?' he asked.

'Doctor says ah'm gonnae be fine. Jist as soon as the bruisin disappears.'

His eyes flicked over her injuries. She looked as if she'd been in a car accident, with her black eye and bruised face. Her short-sleeved nightgown revealed bruised and cut arms. 'Bit ay a mess, eh?' she shrugged.

'Oh, God, I'm sorry.' He took her in his arms and hugged her gently. 'Can you forgive me?' he asked.

'There's nuthin tae forgive.'

'Any chance we can start again?' he asked

'Ah thought ye'd never ask.'

He held her face in his hands and kissed her. It was as though she'd never been away.

Gordon trudged along the prison corridor. The old saying was true – it's not *what* you know but *who* you know. That was definitely the case here. If he hadn't gone to police training college, all those years ago, with his old pal Murdo Fitzgerald, there was no way he would have been granted access to this part of the prison. Keeping in touch with Murdo since he'd left the force to work as a prison officer had been the best thing Gordon had ever done. They hadn't seen much of each other lately, but with the promise of a family get-together in the near future he'd bought himself this ten minutes alone with Josh and, more importantly, the blind eye of a mate who knew only too well the meaning of the word 'justice'.

He walked along the ward and opened the door of the private room. The prostrate figure of a decidedly un-healthy-looking Josh Strachan lay on the hospital bed. His leg twitched and he grunted in pain. Gordon sneered at the sight of him, wondering how one man had managed to make him look so fucking stupid. He was now the village idiot of the force and was to be investigated owing to his relationship with this cunt. His son was talking of working away from home as there was nothing for him in Glen Leven, and this morning he had had to watch his wife crying over her breakfast, talking of how her family were all flying the coop. This bastard had a lot of explaining to do.

Gordon noticed the patch of dried blood on the back of Josh's hospital gown and smirked to himself at the idea of adding to it. He was glad of the perks of this job.

He let go of the door, reaching for his baton as he approached the bed. Josh turned his head as he heard the door creak shut. His white face peered up at Gordon through dark-ringed eyes.

'Hello, Josh,' said Gordon, slipping his baton from its holder.